"To inflict the demand of 'utility' on a novel is to succumb to just the sort of doomed tech logic that Dyroff skewers so nimbly and with so much intelligence in her debut novel. Nonetheless, if one use for literature is to make us feel less alone, then the author has succeeded brilliantly with *Loneliness & Company*. **This is a tender, visionary, wide-hearted book that offers itself as a course corrective to our hyper-quantified, algorithm-craven age.**" —Hermione Hoby, author of *Virtue*

"Dyroff's novel brilliantly uses a futuristic, slightly off-kilter world to highlight the absurdity and pain of our current reality. However, **Dyroff's sharp, electric prose and wry humor** keep *Loneliness & Company* from ever feeling weighed down by its circumstances. With her debut, Dyroff has pulled off a truly impressive feat—writing a story about loneliness that isn't so much a cautionary tale, but **a tender, heartfelt reminder to value your time on Earth and the people that make your days more than just a sunrise and a sunset. A new and talented writer to watch.**" —Jean Kyoung Frazier, author of *Pizza Girl*

"This book is **funny, tender, strange, and modern.** Dyroff has written a bildungsroman for the robot set, a **profound** look at human curiosity and longing in a finely wrought near-future New York. *Loneliness & Company* resonates and pops; it infiltrated my dreams." —**Kate Greene, author of** *Once Upon a Time I Lived on Mars*

"*Loneliness & Company* is a **stunning novel, full of lyricism, brilliance, and quiet integrity,** boldly tackling the most complex philosophical ideas. How do you define loneliness that plagues all of us, increasingly so? Is it a personal affliction or an existential condition? I'll be thinking about this novel for a long time." —**Lara Vapnyar, author of** *Divide Me By Zero*

"In Dyroff's **deeply original** novel, it is possible to see the future. *Loneliness & Company* invites us into a techno-laden world that is not so far from our own. **A riveting and unforgettable story of ambition that also reminds us how essential friendship is.**" —Wendy S. Walters, **author of** *Multiply/Divide*

Praise for *Loneliness & Company*

"Dyroff's near future-set book is a bewitching story about technology and isolation. It will grip readers with mesmerizing writing and a tautly-paced plot." —**Debutiful Most Anticipated Debuts of 2024**

"Charlee Dyroff's *Loneliness & Company* is a **sharply etched and strangely propulsive** story about artificial intelligence and authentic feeling: **a canny, tender exploration** of the stories we tell about our bonds with each other, and the realities we'd rather not face about our bonds with the technologies that shape our days." —**Leslie Jamison,** *New York Times* **bestselling author of** *The Empathy Exams* **and** *Make It Scream, Make It Burn*

"Naturally intelligent. An **inventive, timely, and perceptive** story about human connection and being alive." —**Emily Austin, author of** *Everyone in This Room Will Someday Be Dead*

"It's such a great premise: a future in which loneliness has allegedly been eradicated. **I was hooked from the start, and marveled at the poignancy of watching Lee relearn the basics of friendship for the sake of an AI program.** Honestly, it felt like where we might all end up if we continue to let social media dominate our lives. Dyroff's **brilliant** story will make you want to hold all your—real—friends closer." —**Jessica Francis Kane, author of** *Rules for Visiting*

"Charlee Dyroff's *Loneliness & Company* brings us into a world in which technology has solved almost all of our problems except that most universal yet alienating emotional condition of all—loneliness. **Tender and hopeful, Dyroff's story glimmers with humor, empathy, and profound insights into the inner workings of the human heart and psyche.** Her vision is utterly **singular, captivating, and full of heart,** reminding us of the incalculable intimacies of being alive. Reading this book felt like catching up with an old friend, or meeting a new one." —**Gina Chung, author of** *Sea Change* **and** *Green Frog*

LONELINESS & COMPANY

LONELINESS & COMPANY

■ A NOVEL

CHARLEE DYROFF

BLOOMSBURY PUBLISHING
NEW YORK • LONDON • OXFORD • NEW DELHI • SYDNEY

BLOOMSBURY PUBLISHING
Bloomsbury Publishing Inc.
1385 Broadway, New York, NY 10018, USA

BLOOMSBURY, BLOOMSBURY PUBLISHING, and the Diana logo
are trademarks of Bloomsbury Publishing Plc

First published in the United States 2024

Copyright © Charlee Dyroff, 2024

ISBN: HB: 978-1-63973-208-1; EBOOK: 978-1-63973-209-8

LIBRARY OF CONGRESS CATALOGING–IN–PUBLICATION DATA IS AVAILABLE

2 4 6 8 10 9 7 5 3 1

Typeset by Westchester Publishing Services
Printed and bound in the U.S.A.

To find out more about our authors and books visit www.bloomsbury.com and
sign up for our newsletters.

Bloomsbury books may be purchased for business or promotional use. For information
on bulk purchases please contact Macmillan Corporate and Premium Sales Department at
specialmarkets@macmillan.com.

For Brooks, my brother and best friend

Attention without feeling, I began to learn, is only a report.

—MARY OLIVER

Loneliness, longing, does not mean one has failed, but simply that one is alive.

—OLIVIA LAING

PROLOGUE

L ights flick on as I round the corner, picking up speed. My steps echo off the walls, and even though I've walked this route every day for the past six years, something about it feels different. The familiar hallway is a luminous tunnel. Simple. Sterile. Beautiful.

I hold my award carefully with both hands and keep moving away from the noise. Away from the conversation seeping out of the auditorium where graduation took place. From the laughter in the cafeteria where classmates are enjoying the one night a year liquor is served, and the hushed goodbyes in the dorms where others have begun to pack. In the morning, our Placements will arrive, sending us all over the world.

The glass doors at the end of the hall register my face and slide open, revealing the lab's lofty ceiling. I stride past rows of sparkling instruments and ergonomic test stations to my desk in the corner, where I set down the award, carefully lining it up with my Screen. Now that I'm finally alone, I let myself study it: a globe twirling one way and then another above a small plaque. When I bend down to face it, a glimmer glides across, highlighting the etching of my name.

No one was surprised earlier when they called me onstage. I've published the most research and scored the highest marks. But even though I knew I'd win, the applause that broke out when they announced it startled me. Seeing my professors' serious faces contort with smiles, shaking their papery hands under the hot stage lights, it was almost too much. I could hardly breathe, let alone look at the object they handed me.

But now, in the empty lab, in the comfort of the place I love most, I examine the award, and a wave of pride washes over me when I think about everyone cheering; about the knowing look, small but visible, my mentor Masha gave me when I finally met his eye.

Thinking of Masha reminds me there's still one more dataset left to analyze before I leave tomorrow. I could pass it off to the younger fellows, but I've been taught that how you do one thing is how you do everything, and I want to finish this Program the way I started: strong.

Besides, there's nowhere I'd rather be when the Placements arrive than here in the room that shaped me. I want to be here when I confirm what everyone else already suspects: I'll land one of the coveted spots at the Big Five, companies with the best research centers in the world.

Focus, I think, jabbing my Screen awake. I block out the lab, my thoughts, questions, hopes, and dive into the data while hours disappear outside my brain. It's not until I'm done that I notice the soft morning light splayed across the floor, telling me it's almost time.

After sending this final analysis to Masha, I check my project portal and see everything is done. There's nothing left to do but wait, so I begin pacing the expansive space, staring at the large, angular numbers marking time on the wall.

When I pass my desk, that lovely performative glimmer runs across my award and I pause for a second, walk a few steps away, then back, and it streams again. Of course, I think to myself. It's programmed to shine when I'm near, and discovering this makes me treasure it even more. It's designed just like everything about this place. Intentional. Intelligent. Exact.

I continue pacing, thinking about what's next. A role everyone dreams about. An opportunity, Masha said when he first started priming me for it in my second year. Small prongs of anticipation jab my stomach. Which one of the Big Five will it be? What team will I be on? What will be my first assignment be?

The award continues to glisten, and the numbers on the wall slowly switch places. I watch the clock, time dripping in front of my eyes, until finally my Screen collapses into darkness.

This is it! The Placement! I rush over and lean in close. So close, I feel the heat of it: my future. Flying through the ether on its way to me.

Two seconds pass, three. And then it arrives, words crashing through the dark, raining glitter across my Screen. I blink, trying to process the name sitting there. A company I don't recognize. And I know every company, or at least every good one.

The Placement disappears and bursts onto the Screen again. My throat swells as I stare at the impossible, watching those terrible sparkles rain.

Breathe, I tell myself as the lab begins to spin, becomes too bright, too hot.

This can't be happening. This can't be right.

PART ONE

CHAPTER I

I open my eyes to a strange room with blank beige walls and feel as if I've never slept, or as if maybe I've been asleep for my whole life and am finally waking up. The bed hasn't molded to my body yet. The air is muggy. Even the sheets feel off, starchy instead of smooth.

I study the paintbrush strokes on the wall. A hairline crack stems from the window, and I stare at it as I do my best to not think about anything. But it turns out that not thinking about something generally makes you think about it. So I struggle back and forth, thinking and not thinking, unsure what to do with myself.

When I can't lie in bed any longer, when my phone warns me I'm about to be late, I force myself up and pull on jeans, fumbling with the cold metal button between my still-sleeping, seminumb fingers. I throw on a white T-shirt from the top drawer, where I must have folded my clothes in a daze last night.

As I drag myself down the hall, hoping to find coffee, my new roommate, Veronika, pokes her head out from the bathroom, making me jump.

"Nope, uh-uh. Go change," she says, a pink towel on her floating head. Her skin puffs out, makeupless.

I was so concerned with getting my mind right that I forgot she existed. Forgot that last night, when I first arrived, she wrapped her arms around me as if we'd known each other for years. I forgot her dimpled smile, her perfectly curled blond hair, her large boobs. How overwhelming all of her—all of this—is.

"You can't wear that on the first day," she says, as if this were a simple fact.

I blink, trying to figure out if I should turn around or keep moving. Whether she's serious or attempting to make me laugh.

"Here, let me help. First impressions are important."

Veronika closes the door and emerges seconds later swaddled in a pink robe that matches the towel on her head. In my room, she pulls open the drawers and digs around, ruining the neatly organized piles. She plucks a pair of tan slacks and a blue sweater from the mess and lays them on the bed.

"This top will bring out your eyes," she declares, and walks back to the bathroom.

I look at the outline of a person on the bed. After spending the last six years in uniform, I'd forgotten I even owned these slacks, this sweater. At the Program, we wore all black. The only thing that differentiated us was our skills, our research, our talent. Not our appearance. Is it possible to miss a uniform's stiffness? To want the security of simplicity? Will Veronika be doing this all the time? Weighing in on my outfits, my habits, my life?

I've never had a roommate before, and it's strange to share a space with someone, to have two lives crash together in one apartment. I'm used to my small, neat dorm room. To quiet routine. Uninterrupted thought.

I know none of this is a dream. When I touch my arm, it's still warm, slightly hairy, real. When I put my finger in my eye, it waters, rejecting the poke. But everything feels blurred at the edges, as if time is moving faster than I can think. My classmate published a report on the moment after a decision is made and a person is suspended between what once was and what will be. *The Gray Area*, he called it.

Well—former classmate. Ex-classmate? How long can a person get stuck inside The Gray Area if the decision wasn't theirs to make?

I change quickly into the clothes on the bed. Technically, the decision was mine, I remind myself. I entered the Program understanding that after I received my degree, I would work one year wherever the Placement System assigned me. Usually, the System puts you somewhere that benefits your personal development and that of the Country. But being placed here seems to follow none of those criteria. In fact, it seems to follow no logic at all.

I feel strange in my own clothes, but when I exit my room for the second time, Veronika peeks her head out again, face much tanner than before, and nods in approval.

THE OFFICE IS near the water in Tribeca, just above where the old Financial District used to be, or so Maps tells me with its small, dotted outline commemorating land that doesn't exist anymore.

I squish into the subway with all the bodies, and no one takes their jacket off as the train speeds downtown, so I keep mine on, too, forearms growing damp in their sleeves. The ads spin and turn, targeting new people when they step on.

When I arrive at the address, I gaze up at a crumbling stone building. A fire escape dangles from the side like a barnacle and looks like it would blow away if rust weren't holding it in place. I walk up to the door and run right into the glass pane that I thought would slide open but remains stubbornly solid. Rubbing my forehead, I step back and try to pull on the door's handle. A small camera blinks in my face.

Levels too low. DENIED.

The door remains sealed. I wait in the cold for a few minutes and think about what to do, studying my breath as it escapes and lingers in the air. We received an Onboarding Packet, but I couldn't get through it. Normally, I would have read it three or four times. Normally, I over-prepare. But when I started swiping through this one, the first section was filled with stupid, empty buzzwords about how sometimes small, unknown things can change the world and blah, blah, blah. Besides, the less I know, the less real this seems.

I check my phone for the thousandth time this morning just in case. Any minute now they'll realize the glitch. A representative from the Placement System will call to correct it. I'll be understanding, of course. These things happen, I hear myself saying calmly, even though they don't. The System is nearly infallible, at least historically.

A throat clears behind me, and I step aside to watch as a large man looks up into the camera and smiles, his face transforming from tired to thrilled. The door clicks open and his smile vanishes as he steps inside and the door slides shut behind him.

Fascinating.

I can't tell if this is an antiquated system or a new one. The way things operate here is strange: noticeable. Back at the Program, everything ran seamlessly without calling attention to itself. The buildings simply scanned you without making such a fuss.

I step up to the door again, look into the camera, and copy the man, using muscles I haven't tapped into for a while. I force the biggest smile I can, the camera blinks, and the screen flashes green.

Work happiness levels 91%. Have a productive day!

The door slides open and I step inside, feeling victorious until it dawns on me what I've done. I've entered the office.

CHAPTER 2

A s Janet watches the familiar faces step off the elevator, she can't help but smile. From the glass conference room, she studies them, these people she'd recognize anywhere even though they've never met. It's thrilling, really, to see them here in the flesh. Janet loves watching her ideas come to life.

Toru types away next to her, sending a message to their Tech Team located across the globe. She nudges him softly, and he glances up at the small half circle forming in the middle of the office, nods, and returns to his phone. After years of working together—gosh, how many now, fifteen?—Janet knows this gesture is equivalent to a thumbs-up. She knows that Toru's way of showing emotion, especially good ones, is to bury himself in business.

Janet shuffles things around on her Screen, stalling. She and Toru have founded multiple companies together and she knows how to build a successful team. She's learned that the first few minutes colleagues meet can be uncomfortable, but also provide a crucial opportunity for bonding.

Just a few days ago, Janet and Toru had sat in this very room, sifting through profiles in the Placement System. They'd jumped through countless regulative hoops to convince the Government that what they needed for this particular role was precision. Control. It wasn't that they didn't trust the System to give them quality candidates, but this was an entirely new kind of role. One it had never matched people to before.

When the Government reluctantly gave them the green light, Janet had their own developers reprogram the Placement System with very specific criteria. And then she and Toru used it to select their newest employees.

They projected the candidates on the wall, and Toru flipped through them as Janet watched patiently. The first four were easy. The System surfaced them right away. But the final one was more difficult to find. Toru stood at the front and flipped through a pool of people with a small flick of his wrist.

Flick, flick, flick. Faces flew through the night. Hundreds of people appeared and disappeared in an instant. Narrow jaw. Wide eyes. Large forehead. Bunchy bangs with hidden freckles. Red lips forming a very large, very sad smile. A blink, a smirk, a shrug, and when Janet or Toru saw a few red marks on the side indicating they fell short from the criteria, flick, they were gone.

Finally, after hours, they found their fifth and final match. As Janet filled out selection forms, Toru played around with the Placement System for the fun of it, scanning the pool of talent and commenting on how the more rigorous Programs become, the more monotonous minds they produce. Young people ground down to nubs.

Janet nodded along as she worked. She'd heard similar rants from him before, but each round has new nuggets of insight. That's one of her favorite things about Toru, the way he thinks. The way he approaches problem-solving: with intelligence and, sometimes, a necessary reck-lessness. He's not afraid to try things, to experiment.

And neither is Janet. It's one of the reasons they work so well together, why they've been so successful. They're both deeply competitive, deeply committed to approaching projects differently than everyone else. Freely. Which is why it was shocking when the Government invited them to work on this project. That's how Toru likes to phrase it, anyway, although they both know it wasn't really an invite but more of a demand.

Janet finished the forms just as Toru stopped speaking. Stopped flicking through faces. She looked up to see him staring at one that stared back. A plain face, no makeup, with hair pulled in a low bun. The girl spoke about the Program she was about to graduate from, her research and awards. She spoke with an irritating confidence and a naïve devotion.

Janet thought Toru would use her as an example of how these Programs were just making everyone the same. But he didn't. Instead, they listened as she finished her introduction by saying, simply, that she was the best. She said it without blinking, without smiling, while looking straight through the Screen.

"We're done," Janet said, closing her Screen. "We don't need any more."

Toru grunted, showing he'd heard her. But something had sparked his curiosity, and he tapped into the candidate's profile anyway. Intellect, work ethic, dedication: her qualitative scores were high. Research methods, data analysis, critical thinking: her skill scores even higher. Technically, she *was* better than everyone they'd seen so far.

"Interesting," Toru said, flipping through her publications, references, and behavioral mapping.

"She's not a match," Janet pointed out. Relieved to see that the Placement System showed the candidate lacked one crucial criterion. It highlighted the deficiency in red.

"True," he said, eyes still glued to her files. "But she outscores everyone in the other categories. And she seems . . . bored. You can hear it in her voice. And people who are unsatisfied—"

"They're always open to more," Janet said.

"Exactly. And this role you came up with, J, it's brilliant. But not for the fainthearted," Toru said, still digging around on the Screen. "But your call. I'm just thinking out loud. I trust you on this stuff."

Toru's phone rang and he picked it up, nodded to her, and stepped out, leaving Janet with the candidate projected on the wall. Something about the girl repelled her. Maybe it was the way she didn't smile, not once, but didn't frown, either. Or maybe it was the way she acted so certain, as if her life were already set. But Toru was right: she outscored almost everyone in the skill sets they needed. It couldn't hurt to have one more talented researcher, right?

Someone's nudging Janet's shoulder. She blinks to see the same wall where the faces had been projected, but this time it's blank. Toru taps his watch and points to the circle of people in the middle of the office. It's time.

Janet gets up slowly to open the door and let her new team into the conference room. In the last few seconds before it all begins, she watches them through the glass, shifting from foot to foot, laughing too loudly or not at all. And as she does, she feels a strange attachment to them. A desire to protect them, though she isn't sure from what.

CHAPTER 3

Welcome to your new home!"

A tall white woman standing at the front of a large glass conference room gestures around. I think about what I just walked through to get to this room: mismatched chairs, idea boards, abandoned Screens, and headphones strewn about haphazardly. The office is a mess.

I lean back in my chair to study her and the others, assessing who does what and how important they are. It's clear the people at the front of the long table all know each other. I can tell by the way they chat or sit in silence with such ease.

The other five in the room are new, like me. Their eyes dart around, they shift in their chairs. Across from me, a man in a suit nods at every word. Next to him is a woman with big wire-frame glasses. Long, beautiful black braids fall down around her, and she keeps her arms crossed over her chest.

There's a lanky boy with acne, a loud girl who laughs shrilly when nothing is funny, and one with green eyes that remind me of a cat's. She stares at me and I stare back, neither of us wanting to break eye contact first.

"We're thrilled to have you all here!" the woman at the front continues. She's strange, birdlike. Smiling without showing any teeth.

"I'm Janet, and this is Toru."

Small gold bracelets slide down her wrists as she gestures to the Asian man sitting next to her, who gives a quick nod without looking up. His black hair shoots up in different directions, like a porcupine on top of his head. He types furiously on his Screen, as if he doesn't have time for this orientation bullshit. I like him better than the rest already.

"We have a lot of work to do. Toru and I are excited to dive into the project a little bit more now that you've all signed the Agreement."

Agreement? What Agreement? I sift through the files in my brain to try and remember when I signed something, and if so, what it was.

Everything from the last seventy-two hours is hazy. There I am under the bright lights of the freezing-cold lab, analyzing just one more dataset. There I am pacing in circles, waiting for the Placement. There I am as it bursts onto my Screen.

From then on, the memory becomes a mess of precise objects and gaps. The zipper of my suitcase. The single cloud in the sky above the dorm as I leave without saying goodbye. My parents, Greg and Cindy, sitting sockless at the wooden kitchen table in my childhood house while I collect my belongings. Eating a hamburger on the airplane and not tasting a thing.

But among the mess of memory, I find it, deep in the recesses of my brain. My stomach grows heavy as the scene clicks into place. I'm in the lab trying to make it stop. Those ridiculous shiny words placing me at a company I'd never heard of in a city where no one wants to be. A company with no prestige, no brand recognition, no track record of success.

All I wanted was to get the Placement out of my sight, to get it away from me, to stop those terrible joyless sparkles from raining down over and over again.

The scene becomes clearer. There I am in shock, placing my pointer finger on the Screen, signing an Agreement just to get it away from me.

What choice did I really have, anyway?

THE WOMAN NAMED Janet is somehow still talking. According to her monologue, we're supposed to be developing an artificial intelligence that will operate as a friend. She says this slowly, as if selecting each word with care, as if she's telling us a secret. The goal is to build something so humanlike, so natural, that people won't know it's not real.

"But then again, what is real and what is fake anymore?" Janet laughs. "See, these are the kinds of questions we need you to be asking."

As her mouth moves, questions pop into my mind, pushing through the fog.

Who are these people? Did they come from other Programs? Why is the headquarters in a ghost city? Do we have funding? What strategies are they utilizing to teach the technology? Why create an AI when there are so many already? Even in this hopeless Placement there's still some primal part of me that, at my very core, wants to understand, solve, and help.

Questions used to be one of my strengths at the Program. Masha always encouraged them. One query could lead to years of investigation, discovery. It could open minds and instigate other ideas, he said. But where have they landed me now?

"We have a prototype," Janet beams from the front, with that same lippy smile. "But it needs a lot of work. We're counting on all of you, our Humanity Consultants, to guide and develop the cognition and humanization of our product."

Humanity Consultants? There are thousands of things I'd rather be called, thousands of roles I'd rather do. Janet keeps talking, repeating the same limited information in different ways. I'm convinced she wants to say more but can't. Something about her is suspicious. Something about her charm or cheer is fake. Practiced and hollow.

"Her name is Vicky," Toru interjects. His voice is loud, excited, more energetic than I expected. He's been silent the whole time, seemingly preoccupied with other things.

"Right, Vicky." Janet smiles, looking at us as if she's letting us in on a secret. "At least that's our nickname for it."

Vicky. What a strange name. I gather what I know about it: Female, low on the name popularity chart. Meaning victory or some sort of triumph.

Images flutter around inside my head from past studies I've done. A woman with purple glasses. Someone with red hair. A crazy aunt.

A roommate who wears socks with frogs on them. She could be a high school chemistry teacher. A professional who records sound effects for pizza commercials.

Her name is Vicky, they say proudly, as if it were the most extraordinary thing to name artificial intelligence after someone I may know but have never met.

I WAS RIGHT. The two employees who were sitting nearest Toru and Janet at the front of the room have been here for a few months already. They're in charge of showing us around the office, and they introduce themselves as Ted and Nikita, the Co-Heads of Relationships, whatever that means.

I repeat their names a few times so I can look them up later to see where they came from and what their accolades are. Ted is large and boyish, with a goofy smile and bright blue eyes. Nikita is tiny next to him, with long frail arms and long red nails. They show us the kitchen, the bathroom, the storage closet, the dartboard, and the fridge packed with craft beer.

"Seriously?!" the giggling girl says in her shrill voice. And then she laughs in the same octave. She also can't believe there's a water dispenser for dogs. Or that the mugs change colors depending on your mood. Or that there are charging stations at all of our desks. In fact, she's shocked we even have desks. Seriously?!

Ted and Nikita explain that the empty ones belong to the totally awesome Tech Team, who occasionally rotate in but mostly work remote. We can also work from home whenever we want. Most of the team does on Monday, Tuesday, and Friday. Everyone marks this in their phones, so I do, too.

With their morning orientation duties complete, Ted and Nikita hop on calls. They'll be on them for the rest of the day building connections, they say. What kind of connections? With whom? Why is everyone speaking so vaguely? I want to ask, but don't want to draw attention to myself. I need to blend in until I can figure out an escape.

I follow the other Humanity Consultants to a row of six desks with stacks of new products and watch everyone out of the corner of my eye, thankful to be on the end. The tall, lanky boy sweats and sweats. The woman with the wire-frame glasses doesn't touch a thing and keeps her arms crossed over her chest. Finance Guy and Shrill Laugh Girl flirt on their way to grab coffee in the kitchen.

"See those chips?" he says, nodding to a huge wall of them. "At my old job, I put together a portfolio for the salt-to-sale ratio."

"Seriously!?" she says, and then laughs in that almost admirably high pitch.

I fiddle with the stuff on the desk. A new Screen. An adapter. Some sort of energy bar. A heat-resistant, flower-scented T-shirt. When I spot the shirt, I can't help but think of Greg. His wardrobe is covered with company logos printed on pockets, on backs, down sleeves. When I was younger, I thought he wore them because he was proud, as if they were souvenirs from jobs he loved.

But as I grew older, I asked Greg more questions about work, and he shrugged it off as just that: work. It was confusing. Why leave me to order dinner by myself just to stay in the office upstairs and push email around? Why spend so much time doing something that makes you feel useless? That ultimately *is* useless?

Cindy was the same way. They both worked as project coordinators and were always being pinged or called into meetings or finishing tasks last minute for bosses they despised. They jumped around between companies and roles, looking for something better, or at least that's how I saw it. They worked so hard to make money, but even when they had it, even when we had a good house, good clothes, they didn't seem to enjoy it. Instead, they seemed comfortable oscillating between stress and boredom, pouring time into the abyss instead of something they cared about.

I pick up the T-shirt from the desk, a flowery smell emanating around me. The woman with the Cat Eyes is watching me, so I fake a yawn and tuck the shirt into my bag just in case I can find a way out tonight. Then I busy myself with the theatrics of pretending I'll be staying, opening my new work Screen, peeling it out of the box carefully, so as not to shake the machine.

AS SOON AS it's acceptable to leave, I do. I walk out, hide in the shadow of a doorway a few avenues down, and think through my options. Now that I'm here, now that I've seen the office, met the people, I understand the Placement is real. There's no mistake. No glitch. I'm thousands of miles away from where I should be and need to do something about it.

I crack my neck and try to think. I could go straight to the airport. I could board the next flight back to Minneapolis, go to the Program, and explain the mistake. But leaving without permission would mean breaking the Placement, wouldn't it?

I've heard stories about people who defect before their year is up, stories passed only in whispers. They're banned from the Placement System entirely and have a hard time finding work. Worse, they lose all credibility.

I crack my knuckles and beg myself to think. I can't break the Placement. I've never broken a rule in my life. Besides, I like the programs and systems the Government provides. They've never led me astray.

Except now, a small thought interjects. A small, useless little thought. I push it away. There has to be something I can do to get out of here, to get back on track. I didn't work this hard to disappear in the underbelly of a city at a company no one cares about.

A car roars past, then another. What if I call Masha? Surely he's seen the Placement results by now and is just as confused as I am. He'll know how to handle this.

I pull out my phone, begin typing his name, and then backspace quickly, heat rising to my cheeks. What am I doing? I graduated top of class. I taught Critical Thinking Methods to First Years the past few semesters, and yet here I am: dumbfounded. Panicking without all the information. I can't just call Masha and ask for help without doing my due diligence. I need to know everything I can about this company.

Determined, I open Search and get to work finding the holes in this operation. I type the company name, but all it leads to are pages and pages of generic tea brands and cycling tours and mustache salons. I type the company name and add "Toru" and "Janet": nothing. Is the company really so insignificant it doesn't surface in Search?

The air is chilly, thick with the earthy smell of rain. I lean against the cold, cracked cement of the doorway and run search after search. I need to know what I've gotten into. What is this place? I dig deeper, searching Ted and Nikita, uploading photos I took when they weren't looking for more specific results. It spins for a second and then shows people who kind of look like Ted but aren't. People kind of like Nikita, but who are in Norway at Beauty School.

I try uploading the Onboarding Packet, the office address, and still nothing. What is going on? I've found better results with worse. The more I dig, the more pathetic I feel. This company seems to be as small and negligible as a fly. Even a top performer could get lost at a place like this, forgotten, buried.

The truth? This was always a possibility: to be placed somewhere terrible. But the chances were so low. There are patterns. Precedents. Expectations! Students like me are placed in specific roles. We're trained for them. Told exactly what to do so the Placement System lands us at the best companies. It's not necessarily cheating, just knowing how the System operates and planning accordingly.

I did everything I was told. I had the highest test scores, took more classes than anyone, and did all the extra trainings. Everyone else before me with similar track records was placed at a Big Five, established places with resources and impact. Teams of the smartest people who shape the world we live in. I was supposed to lead one someday. My professors told me I would, if only I worked hard enough. Did I work hard enough? Could I have worked harder?

I scrunch my eyes tight, and when I open them again, I notice the arm of my jacket is wet. It's begun to rain. Small drops dripping from the sky, sliding off the cement and hitting half of me while I stand in the doorway of some random apartment complex. I open Maps to see where I am, and it loads a path back to the apartment building, leading me north through a small park. I didn't realize it was close enough to walk. I could use some fresh air anyway, some movement to let my brain breathe.

As I walk, I notice for the first time how eerie the city is. Buildings hide in the mist. Bodies pass, wading across the sidewalk like ghosts. It's embarrassing to be here, really. I heard most people left New York years ago when the flooding started. I try not to think about it and instead veer toward a pigeon that doesn't move until my foot is a centimeter in front of it. Cold drops fall harder, hitting my cheeks, the tops of my hands.

A small thought, tiny, really, slips into my mind and grows heavy: What if there's no way out because this is where I'm supposed to be?

A chill skips down my spine.

What if I'm not as skilled as I've always thought I was? What if Masha and the rest of the professors have known all along that I was a lost cause? Did they pity me? Was I an experiment to them? A joke?

No. It couldn't be. They wouldn't have accepted me into the Program. All of this is just messing with my head. The grungy office, the orientation, the strange way the others seemed *excited* to be here. It's all throwing me off. I just need to breathe. To keep moving.

Concentrating on the sidewalk to clear my head, I notice it's wet. Near the curb, someone dragged a finger while the cement was moist. It says: *I was here.*

Here. The only thing I know about this city is that it's not where I want to be.

"Tell me about New York," I ask my phone over the static sound of rain dying against the pavement. From inside my pocket, it spouts information:

> New York is a city composed of five boroughs. It's situated where the Hudson River meets the Atlantic.
>
> Manhattan is where small talk goes to die, street food reigns, and strangers are kind but not nice.

This city, man, people say all kinds of shit about it but they don't know a thing. I'll tell you the truth, and the truth is there's a damn good chocolate chip scone on Waverly if you know where to look.

New York has everything you could ever want right next to everything you hate.

An ever-changing mecca with the mood of a goddess.

New York is the place to kiss strangers in dark corners and trip and watch others trip and catch your reflection in a discarded mirror on the sidewalk and decide for yourself: this is the life.

My new apartment building looms ahead, dark gray, like the sky behind and the street below. Is an ancient city sidewalk harder than others because of millions of footsteps pressing it down over time? Is it possible that drinking too much coffee on an empty stomach can facilitate a person's propensity for doubt? Why does rain fall unevenly but still feel like it hits you all at once?

My socks are soaked and rub uncomfortably against my skin. I run up the stoop and press my finger to the keypad. The door pops open, and in the hallway, the balls of my feet throb from walking farther than I have in months. When I check Maps, the little blue dot has arrived safely to its programmed destination.

CHAPTER 4

I was thirteen when I discovered the Program. We'd just moved to Minneapolis for reasons I didn't understand. Cindy and Greg were always doing that when I was younger, picking new places, hoping to inject some excitement into the monotony of their days.

But Minneapolis seemed to work for them. They were drawn to the Midwest's endless opportunity, to the promise that you could make something of yourself, though I never saw them take advantage of it. I think they liked knowing that if they wanted to, they could be the kind of people who went to fancy dinners, who strolled the promenade after a drink, who went to museums just for the fun of it. I wished they were those people, too, instead of just the kind of people who wished they were those people.

When I realized we were going to be staying for a while, I joined the track team. I liked to see how far I could run after school before my lungs couldn't take it anymore. There was something stoic about it, I felt. Something interesting about a body on the verge of collapse, in the way a mind could be so commanding, so harsh. We'd run around the track after school and then everyone would go home, but I'd keep going.

One day I ran farther than I ever had before and ended up on a bridge near an expansive campus with tall, silver buildings. As I caught my breath, I watched groups of people in all black stride in and out. They moved with a purpose, shoulders back and chin up. They walked quickly, deep in conversation. I don't know how to explain it, but I could feel a difference even watching from afar. I could feel the energy from where I stood.

I sprinted back to the house and looked up the place. Despite my limbs being numb with exhaustion, I stood there and read as much as I could. It was a world-class Research Program. I pored over the mission, the classes, the professors, the projects they'd won awards for. I watched videos about the individuals studying there who were doing ground-breaking research, who were creating the reality that everyone else merely moved through.

Students and professors spoke with a passion I hadn't seen in many adults. It was as if they were allowed to be curious and encouraged to ask questions. Pushed to be creative. It was exactly what I was looking for without ever knowing I was looking for something.

I didn't want to go to any other Program after I discovered that one. The more I read, the more I knew I would do anything in my power to be accepted.

That's it!

I jump up from the bed in my strange new room. Blood rushes to my head, and the walls spin. I've stood up too fast, but all this thinking about my younger self reminds me where I've come from, which reminds me I have a past, which reminds me that, if I search my own name, there has to be some sort of news, even a release from the Program about where our cohort has landed and what we're doing.

From there I'll be able to trace myself to the company and the company to the other employees. Once I find a way in, I'll have more context, more answers. I'll know what we're really doing, who Janet and Toru are.

When I type in my name—expecting to see the studies I coauthored, the contests won, my profile photos, my terrible track pictures I've been meaning to request to have taken down, the Placement announcement— nothing comes up. I type my name in and try again and again. But according to Search, I've never existed.

★　★　★

THE NEXT DAY, my calendar reminds me to work from home, though I'm still not sure what I should be doing. When Veronika clank-clank-clanks down the hall and out the door, I migrate safely to the small kitchen–living room and busy myself setting up a little workspace. This mostly consists of flicking a crumb off the wobbly, white kitchen table and placing my Screen in the center of it. As a finishing touch, I set my phone down next to it, making sure the edges line up perfectly.

Now what? I walk the full length of the apartment a few times. I'm not used to idleness. Could a person get stuck this way? Doing nothing forever? What's the difference between something and nothing? Is it just a matter of opinion?

Before I fall any deeper into the black hole of existential thought, a message pops onto my Screen from someone named Chris. When I hover over his name, it says he's the Head of Data. He must be my boss.

Chris's message is confusing. I scan it quickly, get up, open all the cupboards in the kitchen, and survey the mess of cups and bowls and utensils. I don't *want* to be interested in this strange message from this strange person. But if I'm curious, it's mostly out of duty, right? Every quality researcher has a core curiosity, right? I close the cupboards, sit back down, and lean in closer to read Chris's message again.

If you think about it, a human being is a collection of experiences. We are shaped each day by who we encounter, what we see, what we hear, the decisions we make, etc.

Because our goal is to make Vicky a "friend," the AI must understand and relate to all kinds of human experiences. Essentially, it must become humanlike itself.

This is where you come in. I'll give you assignments to collect information and experiences within specific categories. You'll input your research in the Data Program, which will then convert it into a format for Vicky to process.

Please note that for the duration of this project, your personal information has been archived. As soon as we complete the task it will be restored in perfect condition.

No wonder my searches were coming up blank. I guess it makes sense to try and eliminate bias, to avoid meshing the wires between our data and the data we collect. I gain an ounce of respect for whoever this Chris person is, even if he needs to learn the art of concision.

When I'm done reading, I exit the message and the Data Program automatically loads, dropping me into a page with black boxes. We used a similar program at the lab, so the interface is familiar. It looks like I can add links, tag comments, highlight and flag important aspects. I can upload images, videos, and recordings, and it shows my phone is automatically synced.

But when I type in one of the boxes, my letters are purple instead of white. The deep, beautiful color of amethyst.

I play around with the Data Program for a while, and just when I think I've mastered it, I tap a button that sets off a security alarm, and my Screen begins yelling I'm an alarm! I'm an alarm! Alarm rhymes with farm! Never eat bad parm! I don't have an arm because I'm an alarm!

A bird flies off the windowsill. I exit the Data Program quickly, making a note of that button for when I open it again.

*   *   *

TREAT EVERY PROJECT *like a person,* Masha said to me once while we were staring into the Observation Room watching a child speak to a robotic mouse.

The room was brilliant, my favorite at the lab. It could be programmed to mirror all kinds of environments, and the best part was that we could observe everything through the walls.

For this study, I'd programmed the Observation Room to be a pleasant, familiar nursery setting so kids felt at ease. We were studying the effects of play on childhood development, and some mice were designed to engage more or less with the subject depending on the test group.

I remember the project well because it was the first one Masha let me lead, but also because it was when he taught me a crucial lesson of being a researcher. I'd been busy taking notes when he appeared beside me and began surveying the child in the room. He looked at the boy and the mouse, then at my notes. The boy, my notes, the mouse, my notes.

"What's the point of this study?" he asked, and I rattled off verbatim what we'd written in the proposal. "No," he said, shaking his head. "Think bigger, Lee. What is the reason for this study? Why does it matter?"

I remember wanting so badly to have the right answer but being at a loss for words. After a long pause, he turned back to the room with the child.

"When you look at the boy, you don't just see his arm, or his nose," he said. "You see him as a boy who wants to play. Each study is larger than its parts. Each project has a different reason for existing, just like him. Just like you and me."

He spoke slowly and I clung to every word, staring at his profile, watching his icy blue eyes follow the child's every movement. "When you look in this room, don't just search for statistics you need to publish. Don't just take notes for the sake of taking notes. Learn to treat each project like a person. Learn what each project wants, the *why* behind it, the real underlying reasons it exists, and then you'll be able to find the best way to solve for it."

Now, I look around at the clunky, eclectic apartment. The worn green couch. The chunky cupboards. Despite it all, I do my best to focus. If I can treat this Vicky project like a person, maybe I'll be able to come to terms with the Placement. If I can figure out the *why* behind the quest for an artificial friend, maybe I can solve it faster and get out of here.

The thing is, I can't believe an AI like Vicky doesn't exist already. There has to be something like it; I swear I've interacted with one before. But as I run searches and find hundreds of AIs in specific industries, roles, and services, not a single one has been able to operate successfully as a true friend. I feel like I'm getting close to understanding something. To uncovering the reason we're here, the *why*.

What the Vicky project wants is to work, of course, but there has to be a deeper motivation than that. I know it, I can feel it, but it's just out of reach.

I take my headphones off and crack my back, interrupting the silence, reminding me it's there. Above the refrigerator, a small black dot hangs on the wall. Veronika brought a Sound Collector home yesterday. I guess she has to test out new products before she can pitch them.

No larger than my palm, it sucks the external noise out of a room so we don't have to hear horns and trucks and conversations from outside the apartment while we're inside it. She says it's perfect because the world gets too loud when she's watching TV. Plus, ambulances make me nervous, she said, her forearm flexing as she pressed the device on the wall.

I used to enjoy silence, but in this apartment it feels heavier. With that thing on the wall, all I hear is absence. The ringing emptiness of me and the air.

When I turn back to my Screen to do more research on why a company might want to create an AI friend, a message slides across my Screen.

chris [10:00 A.M.]
good morning, lee
how was ur weekend?

lee [10:00 A.M.]
good
yours?

chris [10:01 A.M.]
awesome awesome
went to this concert at The Bodega
new underground venue below the bodega on Linden
good stuff
makes ur ears bleed but in a good way, u know?

lee [10:02 A.M.]
that's cool

chris [10:03 A.M.]
do u like punk rock?

lee [10:03 A.M.]
sure

chris [10:04 A.M.]
listen to this then
let me know what u think
[Spritzy.m43]

lee [10:04 A.M.]
kk

The link wiggles impatiently on the page and when I tap it, noise pours out of my Screen. Someone screaming, pots and pans, drums. It echoes through the small apartment, and I shut it off quickly, sit for a second, then turn it on again in case this is some kind of test and Chris can see whether or not the whole song has been played. A cacophony blares in my face. Is this how we have to earn assignments?

When the song finally fades with an angry whisper, I message Chris back.

lee [10:06 A.M.]
pretty good

chris [10:06 A.M.]
u like??
u should come with us next time then

lee [10:07 A.M.]
sounds good

chris [10:08 A.M.]
okay cool cool
so the first category for collection is Communication
data not just on how people talk

but where, why, when . . .
all of it
any questions?

lee [10:08 A.M.]
no
sounds good

In the Data Program, a new section labeled "Communication" is assigned to me. I see Chris's white cursor blinking for a few moments and then it disappears, leaving me alone with the blank black box waiting to be filled.

I expand my Screen, sliding it up and pulling out the wings so it surrounds me. Then I dig in, opening various databases I've used before. In each one, I type: how do humans communicate. Thousands of entries load instantly: How grunts turned into words. How to become someone people want to tell their secrets to. How to comfort others. How to give and receive advice.

Each search leads to another. Throwing myself into archives and databases and portals is comforting, like being able to exhale again after holding my breath for days. I've been trained for this, and it feels like the only thing that makes sense. I parse as much as I can. I forget lunch. Forget where I am. Hours pass, and outside the apartment, night arrives, cloaking the city in dark velvet light.

EVEN THOUGH IT's late, I'm not tired in the slightest. After researching for hours, I feel energized. But I feel something else, too, a familiar restlessness.

In my room, I grab my running shoes and lace them up. At the Program, we had scheduled fitness activity and a nice room full of machines. It's been years since I've run outside, not since I lived with Cindy and Greg.

Once I start, it's as if I could go forever. I feel good, free. It turns out I've missed the feeling of cardboard rubbing my throat when my body can't get enough oxygen, the dull throb of the earth pounding against my joints. I forgot how refreshing it is to crave air.

I breeze through parts of the city I've never seen before, and when I'm miles away from the apartment I notice the buildings are all different. Some are made of rusted metal, others of a shiny aluminum or eroding stone. Some are tall and skinny, others are squished and wide. One even has a decrepit winged angel statue resting on its pointed roof. After being in the same place for years, every detail in this city feels new. Singing out for me to look.

A light flicks on in an apartment across the street, highlighting a figure striding back and forth. It reminds me of the first time I saw Masha in the flesh. I was walking through the buildings on campus to familiarize myself with them during the first week at the Program when I turned a corner in a seemingly empty wing and saw a figure moving behind glass doors at the end. A body standing in front of a Screen, excitedly moving things around on it, working late into the night.

That was Masha. A man with so many ideas and not enough time to pursue them all. He was a renowned behavioral scientist and one of the main reasons people wanted to attend the Program. His lab was a place to learn, but it was also a fully operating research center. Masha's work didn't just sit in archives; it could be traced through the movements of human life.

I remember reading how one of his earliest studies about "cuteness" led to a reworking of education for young children. All because he discovered a child's ability to focus was amplified by the release of brain chemicals after they viewed a small dog or a cat in a tuxedo.

I remember reading about his research on serotonin and norepinephrine, and how movement at specific intervals throughout hormonal cycles can decrease sadness and loss. It was utilized by Fitness to shape workout routines for those diagnosed with depression. It helped millions of people.

Of course, I knew all about Masha's work before I applied to the Program. I also knew that only some students were chosen to work with him as fellows in the lab, mostly advanced ones. But three weeks after

I arrived, the professors released their lists, and Masha's included four Sixth Years, one Fifth Year, and me. The only First Year to receive a fellowship in the history of the Program.

My feet tap the pavement as I run, creating a rhythm for my thoughts. I turn a corner and breeze past a row of shadowy shops, their grates pulled down and locked. A few neon signs blink sleepily in windows.

Do I miss Masha?

Of course not.

I knew it would be different after graduation. He has new fellows to look out for and experiments I'm not involved in. And I have my own Placement to worry about.

I have started to see glimpses of him everywhere, though. His wiry arms on the dim, humid subway platform in the morning, his long torso rushing down a crowded street after work.

One day, I heard a bumpy laugh that could only really be his, and I turned quickly, heart skipping a beat, to see a short, round man laughing into his headphones. He looked nothing like Masha, whose silver hair and chiseled Nordic features gave him a youthful look even late into his sixties. My mind is betraying me.

The problem, I think, while hopping over a crack in the pavement, is that I'm in an adjustment period. The frontal cortex is firing on overdrive, yearning for the familiar rather than these foreign, crumbling sidewalks.

I'm just used to the lab—to having Masha around to bounce ideas off, especially when I feel stuck on a project. He was the first person who made me feel that my questions were valid, my curiosity worth taking seriously. He was so different from Cindy and Greg, who seemed jaded by everything.

The streetlamps flicker, illuminating potholes in the road, weeds in the sidewalk, a soda can leaking its insides, and a greasy pizza box lying half open with two slices left.

No, I don't miss Masha. If anything, I miss who I was at the Program. I miss knowing exactly what to do, where to go. We spent a lot of time together, but the whole point of a mentor is for them to prepare you to perform well without them.

But I'm not performing well, am I? I'm not approaching this work the way I was taught. I've been sitting around waiting for something to change. But Masha always said that you can choose how you approach the world.

The balls of my feet smack the pavement faster, faster, faster. I ask Maps to help lead me back to the apartment and it dictates when to turn left or right as I race the time it projects I'll need to get there. Bricks, planters, broken glass shining in the moonlight fly by in cinematic sequences.

I have a choice.

And—if what I read is true, that no one, including any of the Big Five, has been able to create an AI to serve as a friend—I could do something groundbreaking. Can you imagine what they'd say about me if I pulled it off with this strange, hopeless little company?

Heat rips through my lungs and I pump my arms, sprinting the last little bit. I finally get it. I finally know what to do. If I'm really stuck in this Placement, then I'll make it work for me. I'll make this year worth it. And by the end of it, the Big Five will have no choice but to accept me.

My feet propel me forward. Faster, faster, faster. As I struggle for air, I can see Masha smiling, nodding in encouragement.

*　*　*

I QUICKLY LEARN Veronika is the kind of person who doesn't know how to be in a room without making noise. Even if no one else is around. Sometimes, from my room, I hear her in the kitchen dropping lip gloss and letting it roll, throwing her purse on the counter, turning on the faucet full throttle so water shoots into the sink, all of it amplified in the loud silence caused by the Sound Collector. It's as if she's afraid of being by herself, so she just makes noise all the time.

When we run into each other in the kitchen or bathroom, she asks me about my day and I don't quite know what to say, so I tell her it was good and try to squeeze past. But then she ends up telling me detailed stories about hers. I learn that Veronika was placed here by the System a few weeks before me. That she graduated from a Program in Charleston focused on sales and seems happy with her Placement. I try to keep our conversations courteous and to be respectful of her time, but she seems to have the opposite goal.

Today, when Veronika gets back to the apartment, I'm working at the wobbly white table in the kitchen–living space, but she doesn't notice. She starts talking as soon as she steps through the door, telling me that Jared, or "cute guy from the accounting team," as most of her friends know him, walked by her desk twice today even though he could have gone a different direction.

"And, get this," she says, throwing her bag and coat and shoes everywhere. "Yesterday, my friend from middle school came out as a lesbian, and her dad, who's like this extremely Catholic dude, won't talk to her."

It's a little shocking, to go from being fully immersed in research to having someone talking loudly at you. This never happened at the lab. Productivity and focus were sacred there, respected.

"I mean, I feel terrible about it," she says, leaning against the counter, her forehead scrunched in concern. "Everyone should be able to love whoever they want, you know? And do whatever they want. But I also feel bad for him because he's been brainwashed, like her dad has these whack ideas programmed in his head. I don't know. I don't really know what I'm saying."

I look at my Screen and then at Veronika and back. There's no way I'll be able to find my way back into the research with her gabbing away, but I also don't know what to say in response to her predicament. I sort through what I've researched in the past about Catholicism, and gender, and relationships, to figure out what might be useful. Nothing seems right.

"It's just a weird situation and it sucks for everyone," Veronika continues, doing some curious thing with her cheeks, blowing air into them and then letting it out. "Especially for her, though. I can't imagine if my dad didn't like me because of who I dated. I mean, my dad and I aren't even close. It's not like I call him and tell him everything. He helps me when I'm interviewing, and that's our relationship, and it's a good relationship, but it's not like he's my best friend, you know? And I also don't like girls, so who am I to really say what that might be like. Well, I like girls, but you know what I'm trying to say. I don't *like* like them."

I really don't know why she's telling me all this. It seems like a personal matter. I wish she didn't bombard me and expect me to have the answers. Any good researcher knows that answers take time; they take digging and finessing.

Maybe if I get some fresh air, I'll be able to think better and give her an adequate solution. I get up slowly and grab a coat off the back of the chair, slipping one arm into it and then the other.

"Like, what am I supposed to do?" she says, throwing her hands up in the air. "Like, her life's a shitshow and I'm just sitting here, about to watch some TV."

My armpits are heating up, and I realize I didn't put on deodorant. If I don't get outside into cold air in less than two minutes, I will break into a full sweat. I inch toward the door, seeking any sort of escape, when all of a sudden it appears. Something I read this morning while researching Communication. **People text people to show support when things are hard.**

"Maybe just text her," I blurt out. Veronika seems to consider what I said for a moment.

"And say what? 'Hey, I heard you like women and now your dad hates you, hope you're doing well'?"

She takes a cup out of the cupboard and slams it on the counter with a thoughtless roughness. I stare at her. A headache is forming, clouds behind the skull. That's not what I meant at all. This feels like an ambush. I reach for the door handle just as she breathes out a huge, audible sigh and smiles, one dimple showing.

"No, no, you're totally right. God, I'm just so stressed with work and stuff. I'll text her and just be normal. Like, I'll ask her how she's doing. That's good, right? That's not weird?"

"No, yeah, perfect," I say.

Veronika uses her butt to push off the counter and comes toward me with her arms out.

"Thanks for your help, Lee. I'm really glad you moved in. This is going to be so much fun!"

She wraps her arms around me, and I stand there in my jacket, unsure of what to do. It's nice for a second before it's too much, before it becomes suffocating.

"Okay, see you," I say pulling away, slipping out the door and rushing down the stairs into the night, letting the air cool my face like a wet cloth.

DAYS FLY BY in a content haze. I love the experience of discovering something new, as if the world is full of Easter eggs if you look close enough. Tiny zips of awe run through me when I learn things. Like how this lady calls her gaming partner "Zug" or "Zuggie" because she's so exact in her style of play that she's constantly forcing others to be on the defensive, and how, if you go even further, Zug is a piece of Zugzwang, the German word for exactly that: forced commotion or movement. And there's something so beautiful about a secret nickname being made from a word so singular. So specific. As if the two gamers have their own language made of language.

It all loops back to language and communication. And how nicknames can be endearing or annoying, depending on how they come to be and what they mean and who uses them. These are the subtleties Vicky may need to know about how to make someone feel comfortable, seen, supported when befriending them.

I keep busy, but sometimes, in the early hours when I first wake, my thoughts wander on their own. I study the wall, the small crack near the window, and think about what I wanted. What I still want.

At the lab, I created studies that examined the way a brain takes in information. The way humans behave depending on their situation, their surroundings. How outside stimuli affect fluctuation on the Emotional Index. How humans interact with technology and vice versa. I was fascinated by it all. Still am.

There's something amazing about how much there still is in the world that we don't know. That we *could* know. I always thought my research could be like a flashlight, a small stream through ignorance. That maybe it could help people somehow.

Lying in my bare, creaky-floored bedroom, disappointment still lingers behind my sternum that this is where I was placed. I don't know if I'll ever be able to recover, if I'll ever be able to get back on track for my goals. If my work will ever matter.

I let myself feel pity for a moment, and then I remember Masha's advice about accepting challenges, embracing them. I jump out of bed, make my first coffee of the day, and dive into research freshly determined to do anything and everything to make sure I come out of this terrible Placement on top.

★ ★ ★

A FAMILIAR LOGO spins, flips, morphs colors, moonwalks, cartwheels, explodes into pieces, then reappears in the center of my Screen again.

Go Ahead, Log In to Your Life.

I've been avoiding Home. Dreading it. I know as soon as I log in, I'll be able to see where everyone else has been placed and how wonderful their lives are while I'm out in the boonies attempting to complete this impossible task.

But I know I have to sign in. It is, after all, where most communication in the world takes place. I've never felt completely myself there, but you can't get away from it. Home is everywhere; it has been for as long as I can remember.

I crack my knuckles and press my finger to the Screen to log in.

Account not found. Please sign up.

Strange, sweet relief. I forgot I've been completely archived. It occurs to me that my new account can be simply for research purposes. It doesn't have to be me, really. I can just use it to see what others are doing, pluck the particulars, and get out.

I create an account, providing as little detail as possible. I skip uploading a photo, and a message pops up warning me that without a well-lit image, I will have 30% fewer friends. I accept, and it logs me in to a waterfall of colorful tiles. Faces, words, noises, videos, articles. An entire world populates my Screen, swallowing me whole.

Home suggests a new friend: Amanda Turnel. I hesitate, studying the bright-blue doorways from her honeymoon in Greece and videos of her thirtieth birthday where someone dropped a homemade strawberry cake on the floor.

> sooooo pretty
> love u
> cute
> there in spirit
> U guys, I'm dead
> Hair . . . !

Normally I wouldn't waste my time, but what if this random "friend" can help me? If I'm making this profile to observe the way people communicate for Vicky, I should be open to everyone, right?

I tap to accept.

Home suggests fifty more. There are people who maintain the same jaw-clenching smile across every photo. People who wear dark sunglasses in cafés. People with overhead shots lying on grass so green it hurts my eyes. Some post endless montages of champagne: zoomed out on bottles squirting in the air, zoomed in on bubbles floating frozen.

★ ★ ★

ON FRIDAY, I'M filling a glass of water in the kitchen when an email from Chris pops up on my phone. I set the glass down in the sink and open Mail immediately, hoping it's a progress update for this first category.

Congratulations on completing your first assignment! As a team, we gathered 64% of the expected data Vicky will need in order to learn more complex human Communication. Not bad for our first collection round.

Not bad? Even if he's setting stretch goals, 64 percent is objectively low.

"Ew, what's that noise?" Veronika stomps down the hall and appears in the kitchen. My glass has begun to gurgle and spit as if it's being drowned by the faucet.

"Oh, shit." I reach over and turn the water off. The glass makes one last sputtering noise and then quiets.

"Trying to kill the poor thing?"

"I was reading something."

"I'm kidding. I didn't even know they did that. Probably programmed that way so people don't waste water or something."

"Yeah," I say and think about telling her how the sinks in Minneapolis just turn off instead of the glasses acting so dramatically. But I'm not done parsing Chris's email.

"I'm going to dinner with some friends, wanna come?" she asks, opening her purse and digging around inside.

"Didn't you go to dinner last night?" I say.

Veronika's laugh is a high-pitched hyena noise that shakes her whole frame. I can't figure out what's so funny.

"Yeah, but people have to eat every day, Lee," she says as she applies lipstick haphazardly. The smudges around her mouth evaporate, leaving her lips dyed a deep strawberry. "It's not like we're robots."

She's right, we do need to eat. But there are drinks with full meals in them, and vitamins that can keep hunger away for at least five hours. Plus, every kind of food can be delivered almost instantly.

"So is that a yes?" Veronika asks. "It would be so fun. Everyone will love you."

"I can't. I have to work."

"Okay, next time," she says. Her phone rings with a video call. She picks it up and starts gabbing, waves goodbye, and slams the door shut.

I wonder where she's going, and with whom. But then I remember that concerning oneself with others can hold you back. I learned that early on at the Program. Some of the students would spend their free periods together, but the faculty discouraged anything that broke too much from the schedule, which was designed for us to be high performers.

I return to the email, rereading it from the start. Chris explains how Vicky will take what we give her and continue to learn from it. There can never be enough data for each category, he writes, but we have to move on to keep up with the overall timeline.

At the end is a link to a section in the Data Program called MASTER. When I open it, a rainbow wall of text and links and voice notes and videos floats on the Screen. My purple research is mixed with neon pink, sky blue, synthetic orange, cherry red, and lime green. It must be all of the Humanity Consultants' data combined.

I gloss through it, studying the information to see how mine lines up. I seem to have done the most thorough job, which is not surprising, but something catches my eye in the pink sections.

Whoever it was went to a class on how brands can utilize consumer preferences to communicate with them. They uploaded hundreds of interviews with speech therapy experts, observed the way people communicate with one another in an office setting and on a date, and included transcripts from teenagers talking about French fries, geometry, and their least favorite thing about their faces.

It looks like whoever it is has been collecting experiences from databases and portals online, but also from outside them. Extracting experiences from the physical world itself.

I crack my knuckles, the space increasing between my finger joints causing gas bubbles and fluid to burst, making that k-k-k sound. Where did Pink's strategy come from? Is it a strategy—or some kind of mistake?

All human experiences are documented online. It's efficient and accurate to collect research there, especially if you know how to do it right. Or there are Observation Rooms for close studies. But observational research can be time-consuming. It's extremely useful for some projects but seems unnecessary for this one because AIs need so much data. Hopefully Janet or Toru or Chris will correct whoever this pink-data person is. And soon, too, because we're clearly not doing well. I've never received a score as low as 64 percent.

Chris hasn't given us the next category yet, so I close the Screen and lie down in bed fully clothed. My muscles are heavy, but sleep never comes. On the back of my eyelids, the data darts around: orange and pink, purple and red, green and blue. Thousands of bits of information are being converted for Vicky. Thousands of experiences being sliced, chopped, and whittled down to zeros and ones, zeros and ones, zero, zero, one, one.

CHAPTER 5

Three weeks pass as we cruise through categories: Belief Systems, Emotions, Money, Childhood. Focus, I tell myself, adding research about how money affects human language. People don't respond to "How are you?" with "Good" anymore, but rather "Busy" or "Tired," and this is connected to the idea of value associated with time.

Focus. Information on data literacy. How seeing numbers inspires trust.

Focus. Data on the evolution of sadness.

I add as much as I can and then, now that I know it exists, I check The MASTER link. There's something satisfying about the way data looks when it's all combined in one place. About how when it's organized, extensive, and dedicated to a goal, the information itself becomes a sort of art. At least to me.

This morning, I punch a button on the coffee machine and set up my spot at the table while I wait for our next category. I pull up The MASTER link and can't help but notice the neon-pink research is still going rogue, adding way less than the rest of us because they're still collecting from the physical world. Shouldn't Chris have said something? It bothers me that he hasn't, especially because we've been performing poorly, averaging about 71 percent Efficiency score.

As I sip my coffee, the thick comfort of it like drinking the sun, it occurs to me that maybe the low scores, the gap in research, are actually a good thing because now I have a chance to prove myself. To pick up the slack.

I imagine myself in the future: a small figure working late, limbs thin from stress, eyes iced over with focus. There I am: the physical, glorious proof of determination. Pushing myself to a limit most people don't know how to push themselves to.

I see myself being picked up out of New York by one of the shiny Minneapolis transporters, my clothes baggy, maybe even some dirt on my face. The visible remnants of being committed to something etched into the loose skin under my eyes. News cameras begging to interview me on how I did it: How did you pull off such a complex research project? How did you create a friend for everyone using such limited resources? How did you —

Ping.

My daydream fizzles. A message from Chris floats on my Screen. Ten A.M. on the dot. At least he's consistent.

I want to ask him about how to improve our work, about the other Consultants' data, but I'm not sure how to approach him yet, and besides, he's already on a tangent about how scrambled eggs reflect a Type B personality. Before I can respond, he wishes me luck and sends me a link to the Data Program. I open it to see a new category, Food, and dive right back into the portals again, eager to improve our Efficiency score.

Online, I find thousands of photos of people eating. Biting, chewing, slurping. Smiling with their arm around a bowl of spaghetti as if posing with a friend. On Home, a woman holds up sushi with chopsticks and describes herself as a 'sushi queen'. People go crazy in the comments.

> Omg, you *are* such a sushi queen!
> So you!
> Love it, love you.

> **You are what you eat**, she responds with a winky face.

I'm not sure what using sushi as an adjective to describe oneself means, and I debate whether or not it would count as quality data for

Vicky. At first, it seems an irrelevant piece of information: to label oneself queen of a specific type of Asian cuisine. But on second thought, maybe this reveals something crucial about the woman. Claiming royalty over sushi may reveal a desire for power. Or maybe it's impressive to associate one's identity with a small bit of rice and a chunk of raw fish? I move the post and all the comments into the Data Program.

I add studies about nutrition among elementary school students from various neighborhoods and chat room debates landing on a shared truth about how **chocolate syrup is life**. I wade through cyber tacos. Swim through pixelated ginger garlic soup. I'm so deep in food content, I forget to eat lunch again. Only when Veronika comes home at the end of the day, throwing her things everywhere, do I realize my stomach is grumbling politely as if clearing its throat.

I FINALLY FEEL like I'm in a good rhythm. I either put on real clothes and take the subway to the office or keep my pajamas on and shuffle into the kitchen to make coffee. Where I am doesn't matter; I slip into research like a second skin.

Sometimes it happens to me at the office. I'll be lost in my work when Janet and Toru come in, swirling in like the wind, asking us questions, giving us updates, and calling impromptu meetings.

They show presentations about the "vision" of the company, and Janet talks and talks but never gets to the point. It's so strange. Not just the lack of structure in comparison to the Program, where we knew what was expected of us each hour and nothing was "impromptu"—but it's like I'm waiting for something, the center of the spiral of her long speeches, and it never comes.

Today, after one of these long meetings, I walk into the kitchen to refill my coffee and am shocked to see Finance Guy and Shrill Laugh Girl holding hands. They immediately let go and begin opening cupboards. I don't say anything, refill my coffee, and walk back to the desk, as the mug blushes a smoky red color.

* * *

THE PINK DATA in The MASTER link has begun to haunt me. I open it to look at our information, expecting to be comforted by how much I've added, but all I can focus on is the persistent pink. It's surprisingly detailed, and today as I scroll through, a pesky thought surfaces in the back of my mind: What if it's good?

Masha said learning is an infinite endeavor. Even though he was a stickler for order and systemization, he also said we should be able to adapt. That we shouldn't let commitment to a process ruin our capability to think outside of it.

I stand up and begin pacing the small kitchen–living room, mulling things over. I think I finally understand what Masha meant by this. Even if my collection method is good, I should still try this strange new tactic to learn how it works. Or prove it doesn't. Taking one more peek at The MASTER link, I throw on a coat and rush outside.

Confronted with the instant rush of cold air, I realize I haven't thought about where to go, what to do, or how to even begin collecting experiences from the real world. I stand paralyzed on the sidewalk, a staccato panic running through my veins.

Has the other Consultant been trained in this, or are they making it up? What was the pink person's plan? How did they know where to go?

This is good, I tell myself. I can apply my skills to a new scenario, which means I'm in a position for growth. Besides, I've run plenty of studies in the Observation Room. This will be like that, except in the world. It will be an uncontrolled environment, but I can still use the skills I've learned. I can still go, observe, take notes, leave. Now all I need to do is find people.

Maps directs me to a street a few blocks away where cars speed past—tossing air into my face—and fluorescent boxy stores with kiosks blink in the daylight. This street looks similar to the ones back home. It has the same clean storefronts, the same large shops with clothes rotating behind large panels of glass. I watch as a man with a black scarf is drawn in by the display of two mannequins salsa dancing. He presses his finger to the glass to purchase one item, two items, three.

Something about his beady eyes, cushioned in his face, or how aggressively he presses his finger to the glass, seems a bit off. But I'm looking for data for the Food category, so I keep going. Best-case scenario, I find someone who's actually eating. There are tons of restaurants, but each time I peer inside, all I see are drones packing biodegradable boxes and slingshotting them through the air, humming to themselves.

After what feels like forever, I pass a place on a side street that surprises me. It's so rusted and faded into the background that I almost miss it. One of these still exists? I've only ever read about them.

I do a walk-by, studying the window and mostly just seeing my reflection peering back at me—mousy and concerned. I'd forgotten that underneath my coat I'm still wearing pajamas.

My fourth time circling, I go in.

Warm air streams from the ceiling and I look for a Screen to order from, but all I see are rickety tables with groups of people. Where did they all come from? A small plaque on the wall says this diner has been around for more than 175 years.

"Welcome, welcome." A plump woman appears, making me jump. I look around but it seems she's talking to me. Her accent is thick and I try to place it in my mind. Eastern European, it seems? Russian, maybe.

"Look at you. Skin and bones. You came to the right place."

I stare at the woman, confused about why she's commented on my anatomy. And if so, why do it so vaguely?

"Come," she says. I follow her to a booth with worn maroon cushions near the window.

"Sit," she instructs. I'm not sure what else to do, so I slide into the booth.

"Just you?" she asks.

"Yes. Just you. I mean me. Just me."

I try to breathe. I wasn't expecting to have to talk to anyone; I was just hoping to observe.

"No problem, baby," she says and leaves me with some large plastic rectangular thing that folds up and around me.

Baby? Why would someone call a twenty-seven-year-old a baby? I look at the floppy plastic thing she put in my hand and slowly realize it lists items of food, and that they seem to be separated by category. Why

42

did she give it to me to hold on to? Would it be rude to set it down? My eyes jump around until I realize that what I'm looking at is a real old-school menu. I've only ever seen photographs of these artifacts online. How fascinating. How limiting, to have food sorted on one laminated sheet. I set it down and the woman appears again.

"What would you like?"

I should probably order something for my bones, since they were so noticeable today, but I'm not sure what that would be. I just assumed she'd suggest things I might like, the way Food does on my phone.

"Eggs?" she prompts.

"No, thanks."

"Waffle?"

"No, thanks."

"Peanut butter toast?"

We can't go on like this, so I agree.

"Yes," I say, but she doesn't move. I begin to doubt my order. Maybe I should have read the options. I think back to the research I've been doing for Vicky and remember `chocolate syrup is life`.

"Can I have chocolate syrup, too?"

She nods with a concerned look on her face and walks away. I haven't had someone judge my order before. It seems an intimate thing, to know what someone eats. When I look around the room, I notice a group of women in their seventies crowded around someone's phone, giggling uncontrollably. At another table, two teenagers argue over who gets the last pancake.

Finally, a whole six minutes later, the woman returns with a slice of toasted bread, a clump of peanut butter on the side, and a small ceramic bowl filled with glistening chocolate syrup. As I stare at the array of items my mouth begins to water. I spread them on the hot bread and gaze up at the ceiling, blinded by my first bite. As the flavors crash into one another, I begin to understand, even if just momentarily, why someone would claim food as an identifying characteristic, why there are thousands and thousands of entries about what people crave.

When I finish the first slice, the woman brings me another, and another. Mellow jazz plays from a speaker in the corner. Knives scrape lightly against ceramic plates, a chair squeals as someone pushes back from the table. The smell of omelet lingers. Salt, butter, the slight wisp of sweet syrup. Cups clink, something sizzles, and the Russian woman whizzes around the room throwing food down on the tables, calling everyone baby.

IT'S NOT UNTIL I step outside the diner that I realize how full I am. I never knew peanut butter could be so smooth, even though I've definitely had it before, haven't I? I never realized chocolate syrup dazzles in bland light. Or that listening to music while eating could be pleasant. My senses are firing with the smell, the noise, the people! So many of them in one place.

Even though my stomach is heavy, my steps are light. The last rays of sun linger, kissing the pavement. It's later than I thought. I spring up the stairs to the apartment and close the door behind me, still floating, until I see my Screen blinking at me from the wobbly kitchen table. A sinking feeling creeps in. I check the Data Program on my phone and realize there's nothing there from today, nothing at all.

I begin feeling too warm. Too full. When I look around, the apartment is too messy with all its mismatched items, and unbearably antiquated. I was so distracted today, I didn't collect a single item of data from the diner.

In the bathroom, I splash water on my face, and when I look up, I concentrate on the drops collecting on my chin, so I don't have to look myself in the eyes. Before I can think too much about any of it, I sit down at my Screen, pull it up around me, and dive back into the portals to make up for lost time.

CHAPTER 6

Toru shoots off the elevator wearing khakis and a hoodie. He looks like a kid on a mission as he marches through the maze of the office. Janet follows behind gracefully in navy jeans and a crisp white blouse. They call an impromptu meeting, so we grab our things and hustle into the glass conference room.

Instead of launching into a pointless lecture, as she usually does, Janet looks silently at us from the front, forcing a smile that makes the hairs on the back of my neck stand up.

"Welcome, welcome," she says, while Toru fiddles with something on his Screen. "We wanted to call you all together today because Toru and I thought it might be time for you to understand a bit more about this project. Why we're all here."

Toru finds what he's looking for and flings it onto the wall. The blinds drop, the lights flick off, and the room flashes dark except for what he's just projected: a series of graphs and charts pulsating blue. I sit up in my chair to get a closer look. I've seen hundreds of reports before, but never one like this.

Janet clears her throat.

"Now, what you're looking at might be a little bit shocking, and we're going to do our best to break it down," she says, her voice reaching out through the dark. "Have any of you heard of loneliness before?"

Loneliness?

I distinctly remember the word because it was the only time Masha ever made me feel dumb for asking a question. One day I stumbled upon a line in an archived study that mentioned a strange term I'd never heard of before, "loneliness," and I tried to ask him about it. His face drained of color for a split second before he recovered, forced a laugh, and took the study from me, immediately destroying the digital file.

"Be careful what you allow inside your mind," he said, tapping his temple. "There's a lot of nonsense floating around in the world, a lot of information you can't trust. Don't bring that term up ever again. It doesn't exist."

He said it quietly, but in a way that made me feel naïve. I remember returning to my lab station stunned, embarrassed. I'd never been dismissed so quickly.

"Loneliness," Janet says, pulling me back into the conference room— even the word itself sets me on edge—"is an emotion, a state of being, really, that was removed from the Emotional Index completely a few decades ago. After many attempted cures, the scientific and medical community decided the only way to solve it was to eradicate it completely. While the strategy seemed to work for a while, this report demonstrates the opposite. That even without knowledge of what loneliness is, even without a name for it, people can still feel it."

I tug at a piece of skin near my nail. Is this why Masha was so strict about it? Is this why he didn't want me to know? We sit in silence for a few minutes and study the strange report. Blue dots pepper it. As it shifts, zooming in on different parts of the world, they continue to pop up, speckling the wall like freckles.

"Loneliness . . . well, you see, it's difficult to explain because it appears so differently in everyone. But essentially, it's when a person feels little meaningful connection to the world, to others," Janet explains, "to anything, really."

My brain whirs on overdrive. Is this some sort of test? Are Janet and Toru measuring what we know, how susceptible we are? I stay quiet, my lips glued shut. Masha said never to say the term again. I completely erased that moment from my mind, blacked it out, and now the memory, the word, Masha's disgust, his usually patient voice cut sharp, comes rushing back in full force.

I sit stiffly. Should I have asked Masha more? Should I have insisted he explain it to me? Why did he react so strongly? If it is a real thing, if it does exist or did exist at one point, was he part of the group that advocated its removal?

I continue to tug on the skin around my nail, pulling it back and forth. I bite my cheek. Keep my eyes on the table. I don't know what to think, what to believe. I try to tell myself that Janet is making all of this up, but for the first time in a long time it feels like she's finally speaking freely. Like she's finally allowed to say what she's been dying to say.

"Excuse me, Janet, but I'm having a hard time following. Can you really remove an emotion from the Index?" Finance Guy says next to me, speaking in a forcibly polite voice. But something else shines in his eyes. Fear masked as disbelief masked as frustration. I'd forgotten the others were in the room. They've likely never heard of loneliness at all.

"Yeah, I don't understand," Shrill Laugh Girl agrees in her high-pitched voice, just the tip of her pointed nose visible in the glare of the report. "What is this report, and why wouldn't we have seen it before?"

For the first time I begin to feel a little more respect for the other Consultants, who seem to have the same questions as I do.

"These are good questions," Janet says patiently. "You see, this is the first time anyone has ever tried something like removing an emotion from the Index. And as I mentioned, it seemed to work well for decades. But recently, they've discovered that there are still thousands of cases. People may not know what they're feeling, they may not have a name for it, or the name they give it isn't 'loneliness,' but they still suffer from it just the same."

No one moves. No one breathes. Blood beats in my ears as the report continues to flip through various charts. It's an interesting theory, really. If you don't name something, can you identify it? If you never learn an emotion, can you feel it?

"I know this is a bit hard to follow," Janet says, "but once a few scientists realized loneliness never really went away, they began monitoring it in secret. That's essentially what we're looking at now, a manifestation of their work: The Loneliness Report.

"When cases hit a high enough threshold again, the Government got involved. They selected a small cohort of inventors and entrepreneurs to try and find a new solution," she continues. "Which is why we're here. It's still all highly classified, which is why everything—all the details about the company, Toru and me, all of you—is hidden for now. And while we don't know who the other companies are, or what they're working on, we're confident Vicky is the best solution."

The Government? They only get involved in prestigious, worthwhile companies and projects. I study Janet closer than I ever have before. Then I look to Toru typing furiously in the back while walking back and forth. Who are these people? And why would the Government seek them out?

If it really were such a high-profile project, they would have called Masha or some of the other professors from the Program. He's worked with the Government before. Tons of the faculty have. *Were* Janet and Toru faculty of a Program like mine at some point? A fog begins to form behind my forehead, making it hard to think.

"Anyway, as we progress with building Vicky together, we thought it only fair for you all to learn a bit more about what's happening. We need you to understand the gravity of what we're working on." Janet peers at us across the dim room. "Why we're building the AI, and why it's crucial it operates like a true friend that can connect with people meaningfully."

It's difficult to follow what Janet is saying. A thousand questions pop around inside my skull like carbonation. I finally pull hard enough that the skin around my nail bed rips clean, revealing a strip of raw red.

When I look around the table, everyone is shifting in their seats. Finally, Cat Eyes breaks the silence, and then a chorus erupts. Confused, angry, shocked.

"Why wouldn't we have heard of this before?"

"People can just remove—"

"Where is this information coming from?"

"—an emotion?"

"I've never even heard of it."

"What is—"

"—loneliness?"

"Is this a test?"

"Will someone please tell me what's going on?"

"Enough!" Toru's voice cuts through from the back, where he's been pacing. "Janet, did you have Chris compile the materials for them?"

Janet nods.

"We understand this is a lot to take in," Toru says gruffly. "So here's what we're going to do. You're going to go home for the day. By the time you arrive there, materials on loneliness will be waiting in your inbox. Go through the research and familiarize yourself with the emotional concept, and then we'll answer any of your questions."

Silence. This feels like some sort of absurd dream, and I'm not sure what to think, where to look.

"We need you to be fully invested in the success of Vicky," Toru says, a shocking intensity in his eyes. "We need to increase the efficacy of our data. And we need to move much faster. Should you read through everything and decide you're no longer aligned with our mission, you may leave the company. We'll agree to release you."

The Loneliness Report hovers on the wall. Tension is thick in the air. This must be what Janet has been talking circles around for months. The *why* behind the project; the reason it exists.

Toru says the meeting is over and strides out of the room, but no one else moves, stuck in the shock. I stare across the table at Cat Eyes, who stares back, her green irises glinting in the light from The Report.

"It's strange, isn't it?" Janet finally says, reaching out to touch the wall where The Report flips to a new location, blue dots raining down again indicating the cases in the area. "How you can go years, decades even, so sure of everything. And in just thirty seconds your whole understanding of the world is pulled out from underneath you."

She seems to be looking past us into another life for a moment, two, three, before she blinks, taps a button on the Screen, and The Report

49

is sucked away. Lights flick on, the blinds roll up, and the day rushes through the windows, blinding us.

"As Toru mentioned, classified materials on loneliness are waiting for you in your inbox. And of course, we can answer any questions after you take time to sit with everything," Janet says, packing up slowly.

"We know this is difficult, but we believe in you all," she says. A line that hangs there, suspended in space.

THE CONSULTANTS SCATTER. I walk back to the apartment, heartbeat still throbbing in my ears, pulsing in my palms. I feel the urge to laugh about all of this. My brain is on overdrive, but as I walk up the stairs to our apartment, something Toru said snaps into place. It looms large in my mind, playing to the rhythm of each step: "We'll release you."

This is it. The way out. The way back to Minneapolis. My Placement will be considered complete, and I'll be able to apply to the Big Five with Masha's help. I know they'll accept me after seeing my track record in the Program and my resilience here. This is it. All I have to do is tell Toru and Janet I don't believe in this project anymore. All I have to do is say it and be free. Right?

I push open the door to the apartment, throw my bag down. It's an easy decision. I should just call Toru and Janet right now. At the Big Five, my research will impact products that millions of people use. I'll collaborate with people like Masha who will recognize my work, who will understand me. Besides, everyone at the Program expects me to be there. I was trained for it. That's why I was chosen as a fellow, why I was given the award at graduation. I can't let everyone down. I need to get back on track.

But instead of picking up the phone, I begin to pace, looping the apartment. The truth is, I've never heard of something being removed from the Emotional Index. I've never heard of anything like this: A secret affliction? Loneliness? I can't picture it, can't hold it in my mind. Is it dangerous? Is that why Masha reacted so strongly when I found a mention of it years ago?

Instincts tell me to learn more about it. I've never met a concept I didn't want to understand. Never seen something new I didn't want to conquer. There's a control in knowing things, a control I don't feel anywhere else. Leaving before understanding what loneliness is, if it's real, would cement a trail of questions in me forever, wouldn't it?

In the kitchen, I open the drawers, see the unorganized rows of cutlery, and begin sorting through them while I think. If the term has been washed from public domains, the only information available is in the files that Chris sent. Files that could be filled with lies. What if they're making it up? What if I read what Chris and Janet and Toru want me to read and come to believe in something that doesn't exist? What if Masha was protecting me?

When the forks are in their own row, I move on to the spoons, the knives. Janet seemed off balance today, as if she were shocked by our shock. What if she's finally telling us the truth about the project? What if the Government is involved and this is a confidential, urgent task? That would explain why I was placed here in the first place, right? And it would be a serious mistake to leave something the Government is behind; even Masha would admit that.

But that's the part I'm having the hardest time wrapping my head around. Why wouldn't Masha or anyone at the Program have known about The Report they showed us today? If it's real, if this task is coming from the Government, then Masha would have known about it. He's an expert. The Government relies on him to advise on other projects all the time.

And if he did know about it, he would have told me, or contacted me before my Placement here. He would have at least given me some sort of indication that this was okay, that this was right.

I finish sorting and examine my work, the mismatched utensils lying neatly in their own rows. My thoughts are spinning, but I do believe there is an order to things. And none of what happened today, none of what's happened so far this year, seems to follow any logic. As I examine the newly organized silverware, I think about how much better it is to have everything where it should be.

I close the drawer, head to my room, and pull my suitcase out from under the bed. I'd be a fool to lean into chaos. To believe such a dramatic story about an emotion being removed from all society. I'd be a fool for passing up this chance to get back on track. A fool for doubting Masha. I need to trust who I was before, that my dreams are still my dreams, that the life I imagined at the Big Five is still the life I want. One of power, prestige, purpose.

Ping.

chris [1:31 P.M.]
hey lee
how r u doing
lot to process today

lee [1:33 P.M.]
hi

I type out an explanation, delete it. Type a question, delete it. I wonder if I should tell Chris I'm going to leave. I want to ask him about everything from today. I want to ask about loneliness. What is it really? I want to ask about The Report, about the Government's involvement. I type and delete. Type and delete.

I throw stuff in my suitcase faster, not even bothering to fold it this time. I've got to get out of here. It's best not to get too tangled. It's best just to leave now while I can.

chris [1:39 P.M.]
have u seen the files I sent yet?

chris [1:40 P.M.]
read the first few
think it will help u

chris [1:41 P.M.]
and then ping me

im around
we can chat through it

Be careful what you allow inside your mind, Masha had said. I pull up Chris's email with the information on loneliness and delete it. I see that the next flight leaves tonight. I'll land and go straight to the lab.

I take my phone out of my pocket and search his name. A small red flag hovers next to it, warning me I'm not allowed to contact anyone from my past life.

I text him anyway before I can think about what I'm doing, about what this might set off. Before I can think about the pit of questions growing in my stomach.

Masha, my Placement went wrong. Terrible mistake. I'm sure you've seen.

I've found a way out. I'm coming back.

See you tomorrow

And then I go for a quick run to let the pain of being in a body overwhelm the confusion of being in a mind.

CHAPTER 7

Janet closes the door softly behind her and enters the room full of noise. Developers, Engineers, and Data Scientists are everywhere: sitting on the floor, lying stomach down on the ground, lounging in office chairs. At the front of the room, a colorful array of data is projected onto the wall. Orange, pink, purple, blue, green, red. She recognizes it immediately: the research from the Humanity Consultants, all of it being processed and flipped into code.

No wonder Toru hasn't been picking up the phone, Janet thinks to herself, slipping off her coat and draping it over a chair. No wonder he's been showing up to meetings with bags under his eyes. It would be easy to get lost in the energy of this room. To forget time. When was the last night he slept?

A few weeks ago, they flew the Tech Team in from around the world to work in New York for a while. It was Toru's idea. When he brought it up, he referenced ancient theories on knowledge transfer, on the uptick in efficiency when bodies sit next to each other. Theories Janet had taught him two companies ago. She agreed with him and went right to work finding the accommodations, filling out the endless forms documenting their every move for the Government.

She and Toru have always been a good team. He leads product and development. She runs operations and people. But they always make decisions together. And surveying the room—now that she's finally been able to peel herself away from work to see it firsthand—Janet is pleased.

She spots Toru at the front, switching between studying the colorful data, asking questions to the group around him, and writing notes. Something about the way he moves, jumpy and jittery, alive in the chaos, reminds Janet of when they first met.

It had been the worst week of her life. A period of time she's all but blacked out. She'd just been kicked out of her Program, and the shock, the shame that shouldn't have been hers, still surfaces even now.

Janet remembers showing up to a conference, one she was originally supposed to present at, determined to track down her professor and make a case for herself. To do anything to clear her name and get accepted back into the Program.

When she walked into the convention center, booths stretched as far as she could see. Janet wandered around searching for her professor, but instead found herself in the center of the maze watching a student touch wires together, creating delicate sparks. First, a blue one. Then red. Then green. She watched, mesmerized. They were so simple, so beautiful in the oppressive convention center light.

"What are you looking at?" the boy said without glancing up. He ripped another wire from a large machine of sorts and then used it to create an orange spark.

"Me?" Janet said.

"Yeah, you."

"Why have a booth if you don't want to be looked at?" Janet retorted, annoyed. She needed to keep moving. She needed to keep searching for her professor. She couldn't tell what his booth was for, anyway, if he was breaking it or building it.

"I didn't want one. The Programs just like parading their best."

Janet snorted. What a know-it-all. He was a curious person: His skin was pale enough that veins shadowed his arms. Dark hair and dark eyes stood in contrast. She started inching away.

"You look terrible," the boy said, causing another spark to fly.

"That's rude," she said.

"True. But at least now you know I don't lie."

Janet rubbed her eyes, a headache growing. She hadn't slept, hadn't wanted to go home, and was stuck in the same clothes she'd been thrown out in. She almost certainly did look terrible, and it was refreshing, after everything she'd just been through, for someone to tell her the truth.

"Are you hungry?" he said, untangling another, much longer red wire.

Janet nodded. She was starving. In fact, she couldn't remember the last meal she'd eaten.

"Okay, meet me outside in five," the boy said, his spiky hair jetting out in all directions.

"What?"

And then he gave her a small look, brief, as if to say "watch this," before touching the red wire to another, smaller one, causing a gigantic spark. One that resulted in a small flame. Janet couldn't believe it: the boy had lit his booth on fire.

She watched as he stepped on a chair and started a speech about electrical currents, plasma channels, electrons. Energy. The way it can change a room. A small crowd gravitated toward him, and he picked up speed, volume, gesturing to the growing flames and speaking about heat transfer. About the hidden power inside machines, inside all tech. If you don't pay attention to the way things are built, he explained, if you don't take time to understand systems, they can betray you.

People didn't know what to make of him. They still don't. But on that first day, Janet saw everyone drawn toward him. Intrigued. Fascinated until they realized the fire was not part of what he was approved to show. Until they realized it was not in his control.

Because what is it about control that we want so badly? What is it about control we crave? Toru had said, standing there on his chair. As the security guards dragged him out, he winked at Janet, making her smile for the first time in days. She'd never met someone who would willingly put on a show and destroy their own project for a burger and a conversation. Destroy it so intelligently, so beautifully.

Now, even though Toru is approaching fifty, Janet can still see the joy he derives from chaos as he works at the front of the room.

"Enjoying the view?" Toru yells. He's finally spotted her. She makes her way to him. If he's joking around, something must be going right.

"How's it looking?" she asks.

"Good. We're seeing an interesting pattern," he says, glancing up at the data and then hunching back down to note something. From what she can see, it looks like all his notes end with an absurd number of question marks.

"The data is doing something—" one of the engineers standing with them chimes in.

"—peculiar," another says, completing the sentence. Chelsea and Eric. Fraternal twins. Janet remembers hiring them. Chelsea's bright pink hair. Her nervous, tattooed hands. Eric sucking an e-cig, voice floating like air.

"We just need more information—" Eric begins.

"—and more time," Chelsea adds.

"To help us figure out if the pattern is—"

"—a blip or a trend."

"A blip or a trend?" Janet repeats.

"Exactly!" Toru says, jumping up from his notes. Eric nods and lets out a puff of mist. He and Chelsea put their headphones back on, wave goodbye to Janet, and pull their Screens up around them.

Toru turns to the large data array on the wall and begins to walk Janet through the different patterns they're seeing, explaining why one of them has begun to stand out among the rest. As she listens, she can't help but think about the Consultants. Seeing their information, even in code, causes a foreign heaviness to settle in the bottom of her stomach.

It was Janet's idea to bring them here. Even though Ted and Nikita are doing a splendid job of making deals and forging partnerships to secure large amounts of data, Janet always knew Vicky would need more intricate information as well. Because what could be more particular, more specific, than being someone's friend?

She thinks of the people generating this research. The ones whose faces contorted in shock earlier today. A voice in Janet's head tells her she's an idiot for introducing The Report so suddenly. Sure, it would always be overwhelming and complicated. But she could have prepared them a bit better. She knows people, knows how to handle them. There were myriad ways she could have—

"Stop," Toru says.

"What?" she asks, startled.

"Stop thinking about it," he says, swiping through different pages of notes on his Screen. "The meeting was fine. They'll be fine."

"I'm not," Janet says. "What were you saying about—"

"You are. I can see it in your eyes."

"You're not even looking in my eyes."

Toru stops working and stands to face her. He's a full head shorter. Wrinkles forming around his mouth from that incessant frown. She remembers the freezing-cold night in Moscow when he kissed her while they were drunk after an award ceremony. Years have passed and they've never spoken about it. Not once. The thought of them as a couple faded into a shameful one, into a laughable one, into nothing. As Janet looks at him now, she's thankful for what they have. Not the passion of lovers, but something better: A deep understanding. The same kind old couples share.

"Everyone's going to be fine," he says, turning back to the Screen. "Besides, it's better they have all the information now instead of working with blinders on. And we're not trapping them. We gave them the option to leave if they can't handle the role."

We're still not really telling them everything, though, Janet thinks. The way they altered the Placement System, the new criteria they'd set, surfaces in her brain. But she pushes it away, at least for now. It's not worth thinking about now, when they're so busy, when it's too late to change what was necessary in the first place.

"So, this pattern," Toru says, turning back to her. "I want to show it to you. I think it might be something worth paying attention to."

Janet nods and clears her head. She leans down to take a look at the charts he's studying when an alarm slices through the noise of the room, causing what feels like at least fifty heads to turn and look toward them.

Zing. Bling. Ding-a-ling. Zing, bling!

Toru's Screen vibrates dramatically, threatening to buzz itself off the edge of the table. He grabs it just in time and begins digging into the source.

"A broken Agreement," he says.

But as Toru lists off the particulars—who it is, how they broke it, who they tried to contact—Janet is already walking toward the door through a sea of faces, her instincts kicking in again. She scoops up her coat on the way out and walks quickly toward a problem she knows needs solving.

CHAPTER 8

When I get back to the apartment, muscles heavy with exhaustion, Veronika is on the couch chatting with a friend. Except the friend is sitting with her spine stick-straight, legs delicately crossed, and is not a friend at all.

"Lee!" Veronika squeals, twisting her neck to look at me. "You didn't tell me you have such a cool boss."

She turns back to Janet. "Lee's so elusive, you know? But, like, in a cool way."

Janet laughs quietly. Her brown bob doesn't sway an inch. Has she ever laughed before? I debate retracing my steps back down the hall, but my legs won't move.

"She's great," Janet agrees in her usual calm, controlled voice. What is she doing here? It's strange to see her outside the office. She looks so harsh against the pilled pillows, the faded green couch.

"Should we have some wine?" Veronika asks, filling the silence. "Wine always makes me feel good, you know? Like, it never fails. I mean, sometimes it makes me emotional, or whatever, but even then I don't think that's a bad thing. Actually, I've been trying to embrace those ups and downs more. People say you should try to stay balanced, but I kind of like the extremes, don't you?"

She jumps off the couch and prances to the kitchen.

"Did you go for a run?" she says to me as she passes me. "Okay, I have red. But could easily order a white or bubbly if that's what we're feeling."

"That's so kind of you," Janet says, standing up and brushing nonexistent wrinkles out of her pants. "But I'm afraid I can't stay. I was just in the area and thought I might stop by to say hi to Lee quickly."

Veronika pouts at us from the kitchen.

"Okay, fine," she says, "but can we plan something soon? I'll invite my work friends, too. It can be like a mega happy hour or something."

"That sounds wonderful," Janet says, smiling her lippy smile.

Veronika seems appeased at the prospect of planning something. Janet grabs her bag from the couch.

"Walk me out?" she says. It's not really a question, and I still haven't recovered from the shock of seeing her in our apartment, so I follow her into the hallway, down the stairs, and out into the cold.

"You didn't just happen to be in the neighborhood," I finally manage to say, pointing out the obvious.

"No, I wasn't," she agrees, and her honesty is infuriating.

We begin to walk toward nowhere, our feet in a rhythm. Left, right, left, right. My tennis shoes, her boots that leave a small click-clack noise in their trail. Stiffness haunts my joints, but I keep up. I want Janet to speak, to explain why she's here, but we just keep walking, wrapped in soft city sounds.

"I'm leaving," I blurt out when we're a few blocks away from the apartment.

"I know," she says quietly, staring down at the sidewalk.

"You do?"

"We get notified when someone breaks the Agreement," she says, looking at me almost apologetically. "When you attempted to contact that professor, the Agreement alerted us. I figured that probably meant you were thinking of going back to your old life."

I remember seeing the small flag next to Masha's name but sending the message anyway. Why would I do that? Why wouldn't I have just waited a few hours to get on the plane and get home? I'm more detail oriented than that. Smarter. Did I want someone to know I was leaving? No, of course not. It was just an error. It's just been a long day. A long couple of months.

And what does Janet mean, my "old life"? That *is* my life, not this. Time has passed, but surely nothing has changed. I can go back and it will be just as it was.

But even as I think it, I know it can't be true.

A block passes in silence. Then another. Janet seems much taller, much older when we're next to each other like this.

"You're not going to try and convince me to stay?" I ask, a little dumbfounded.

"No, no. That would be fruitless. If you'd like to quit, that's up to you. I just came to say goodbye." Janet chooses her words carefully, enunciating each one. The slower she speaks, the more frustrated I become.

"I'm not quitting."

I've never quit anything. Even when I didn't fully want to be here, I worked hard, didn't I? Hasn't she seen the research I've been submitting?

"Right," she says in a way that makes me feel like she doesn't actually agree.

"I just don't believe in it," I try to explain. "Masha said it wasn't worth focusing on, so I just—"

Janet stops walking abruptly. She pulls her phone out of her bag, types something, and drops it back in with a thud. And then she looks at me, her hazel eyes full of something I can't quite put my finger on.

"It's been an honor to have you on our team, Lee. We wish you the best."

She holds out her hand for me to shake. It's cold, clammy. A black car pulls up and she opens the door and slides inside.

"That's it?" I call after her. "That's all?"

"No one can make up your mind for you, Lee. No one can tell you what to think," she says, and then pauses. "Unless . . . you let them."

Janet closes the door and the car zips away, the taillights growing smaller and smaller until they're just two specks dotting the dark winter night.

★   ★   ★

IF I'VE EVER been angry before, I've never known it. Because this feels like a different kind of suffocating. Blood hot, shooting around my veins. The audacity of it all. To show up unannounced. To suggest I'm a quitter. That I can't think for myself. To let me go so easily—as if I'm disposable.

As they taught us in the Program, how you do one thing is how you do everything. Clearly, Janet knows nothing about me. Clearly, she doesn't realize I dedicate myself 110 percent to everything I do, but that I'm not going to stick around to bail her out of this ridiculous hole of a project she's dug herself into.

I walk around the block until my fingers go numb in the cold, then head back to the apartment, where Veronika has opened a bottle of wine for herself.

"Do you want a—"

"Not now," I say, brushing past her.

Can't think for myself, I mutter, can't make my own decisions. A quitter. Who does Janet think she is? In my room, I grab my Screen, resurrect the materials on loneliness from Trash, and begin to sort through them.

I'll show Janet. I'll go through everything, lay it all out on the table of my mind, and then *still* make the same decision to leave.

> Loneliness stems from a biological fight-or-flight response. Millions of years ago primates survived by moving in groups to hunt and gather. If, for some reason, a primate ended up isolated, a physiological reaction occurred: they needed to know they were in trouble, that they were at risk for their survival.

> Loneliness is a very conscious feeling of separation. People who are lonely cannot—or feel they cannot—connect meaningfully with others.

> Loneliness tends to be such a distinctly painful experience that people will, even subconsciously, do anything to avoid it. They will shun others who are lonely or show signs of it.

Once a person recovers from loneliness, they often forget the intense way it felt and are unable to relate to others who feel that way.

Loneliness is iridescent. It changes depending on the person feeling it.

Loneliness leads to more loneliness. People who are experiencing it become self-conscious. Terrified and embarrassed of what they are feeling, thinking something is wrong with them, they cut off ties from others, only making the state worse. They don't want anyone to know, which can lead to dropping out of society altogether, at least for periods of time.

As I progress, the materials show a shift. The ideas begin to fracture. Questions show up, then doubt, then differing opinions. Some studies prove people can experience a whole gamut of emotions that are measurable, that activate and release specific chemicals, and argue that loneliness is different.

Loneliness is a false emotional state. One that humans made up. It is an untraceable blur in the brain and should be taken down from the Emotional Index immediately before it can do more harm.

What comes first? The name or the illness? By providing people with the name of loneliness for something that is really just a mixture of emotions we already know—sadness, anger, stress—we are providing them with a delusional state they will then convince themselves to occupy. Therefore, we propose to eradicate loneliness from society in order to save people from it. They will be able to seek help for anxiety, depression, or one of the other well-known and highly treatable states instead.

There's a video. Hundreds of the best scientists, researchers, and doctors met at a conference to debate the different findings. I watch people argue that naming something gives it power, and that by letting loneliness exist as a concept in the world, people are more likely to claim it, to suffer from it.

> It is decided that loneliness is a false state. It is a trick of the mind, and not an actual reality.

And then the materials skip decades. The next ones are dated more recently. I read through secret studies tracing a strange feeling appearing in people. Underground scientific and medical communities begin to collaborate on a report to share what they find. The same report that's grown into what Janet showed us.

I go through all the classified materials from start to finish, twice.

And then, when I'm done, I dig into the sources. I trace each article, each video, each recording, and to my surprise, all of them are credible from what I can tell. Some even lead me back to the Program! I look through everything again and again until my eyelids rub like sandpaper and I can't possibly keep them open any longer.

Until suddenly, I'm not in my dimly lit bedroom anymore. Instead, I'm in the freezing-cold lab. I'm not taking notes or researching. I'm not at my station sorting through data. I'm at the Observation Room, but this time I'm inside it, on the other side of the glass.

It's programmed to be entirely, overwhelmingly empty. I'm surrounded by pure white, blank and endless. A thick white like milk. I know one of the walls is a one-way mirror, but I can't tell which one. I know Masha is on the other side looking at me. I can feel him there, just out of reach. When I open my mouth to call to him, nothing comes out. I try to scream, but the deafening sound of silence drowns my eardrums, clogs my throat, and when I bang my fists against the wall for help no one comes to save me.

★   ★   ★

THE NEXT MORNING, I sink into the maroon booth at the diner while the Russian woman chides me for being too skinny again. Then she heads to the kitchen to grab peanut butter toast and a small bowl of chocolate.

I needed air, needed to move. I needed space to think, and my feet led me back here, where the noise is loud and the smell is strong.

When the woman clangs the dishes down on the table, she points to the bags under my eyes and tells me I look bad, walks away, then returns with steaming-hot coffee that she pours into a mug and slides in front of me.

"On the house." She winks.

I force a smile when I say thank you so she knows I mean it—I've never needed coffee as much as I do now—and then I make a note to look up what "on the house" means later. Sipping, I savor the magical burnt flavor. Then I slowly spread the peanut butter on the toast, making sure to drag it all the way to the edges. I drizzle the chocolate syrup on top with a steady hand, creating a perfect spiral. I admire my work before taking a small bite and staring out the window. A faded reflection stares back, chewing.

She sees right through me.

She knows I'm stalling.

She knows there's a decision to be made and that instead of making it, I'm just sitting, watching myself eat toast. I swallow and look away.

The truth is, I can't shake the walk with Janet. Or the materials Chris sent. Or the dream. I can't shake the deep-rooted feeling that I'm making a mistake, though I'm not sure what it is: staying or leaving.

My whole life before this Placement has been black and white. Each decision easy. Whatever would take me furthest away from the mediocre life Cindy and Greg built, the infuriating way they just let things happen to them. I wanted something different. I had goals and ambitions. Control. Purpose.

But sitting in this muggy diner in this crumbling city, all of that feels far away. I can't remember if I wanted to work at a Big Five or if that's just what everyone said I should do. I can't remember if any of the projects we worked on were about things I wanted to study or if they were just what Masha said was most important. I can't figure out what to do, what I believe.

If I leave today, get placed at one of the Big Five, and eventually lead a division, will a part of me always wonder what would have happened if I'd stayed here to see the Vicky project through?

What if this loneliness concept is real? What if the Government really is involved and it's extremely important? What if the other Consultants fail without me? Or worse, what if they succeed?

I take another sip of coffee, and when I set the mug down the same girl from the window looks at me, distorted in the black liquid. A stranger. Someone I recognize but hardly know. I can't get away from myself.

If I go home, finish packing, and get on a plane, will I always be the kind of person who leaves when it's difficult? And isn't being someone who never commits to anything just as bad as being someone who settles for everything?

I study the rim of my mug where coffee residue clings. It would be easier if the information I scoured last night was ridden with errors or filled with broken logic. But there's no denying that the sources pouring into The Report are legitimate.

I still have so many questions about loneliness. About how it operates. About why it was removed, how it was removed. But even if I don't fully understand it yet, the sources for those materials Chris sent were all from reputable places. And if the Government is involved in this project, it could be very important.

"More coffee?" the Russian lady asks, making me jump. She fills my cup before I can answer.

"Why you don't eat your toast today?"

We both look at my beautifully crafted toast. One small bite out of it.

"Oh, sorry. I was thinking," I try to explain.

"Thinking?" the woman says, laughing. "People waste so much time thinking. Worried about this or that. But you know what I say?"

She pauses and I can't tell if she wants me to guess the answer.

"I say thinking is fine, but doing is better," she says, gesturing with the strange, large coffeepot. I'm afraid it's going to splash all over the place.

"Doing is better?" I ask tentatively. I'm not sure if I should look her in the eyes.

"Exactly. You could sit all day and think, but nothing will happen. You need to go do something instead. So what? You do something and it's a mistake. At least you tried." She bends down to eye level with me. Her eyes have flecks of gold in their watery brown. Deep, sitting in puffed and tired sockets.

"You just keep trying, okay? That's what I say to my sons, anyway, but they don't listen to me, all lazy, lazy, lazy. But you, maybe you are different. You have to take risks, you have to try things!"

"Okay," I say, and nod.

I think I get it. I think I know what to do.

"Good. Now, eat," she says, sliding my toast closer before stomping away to another table. I take a bite while typing furiously on my phone, adding details into the Data Program for Vicky about the lady and how casually she interacts with everyone. If Vicky's going to work, she should know how to have these tiny, meaningless conversations that hold so much weight.

PART TWO

CHAPTER 9

I n the kitchen, I sip my coffee, staring at the small group of bubbles
hugging the side, counting them. Notifications slide across my phone
from Home: Mario is playing guitar. Josephine created a new line of
art inspired by vegetables. Jane is married. Dom is just waking up. I can't
help but wonder if any of them feel lonely but don't know it, can't
explain it. If any of them feel that conscious separation that one of the
studies described.

I sip and sit at the wobbly kitchen table, waiting for instructions. I just
made a momentous decision, but it feels as if nothing happened. The
apartment looks the same, I look the same, the coffee tastes the same.

Finally, a message from Chris slides onto my Screen. He doesn't ask
me about the events of the last seventy-two hours, doesn't quiz me on
the classified material he sent or The Loneliness Report, or why I was
offline so long yesterday. Instead, he asks about snow.

Don't you think it's magical, he writes, the way it covers the city like
a million shards of glass? Like fairy dust? Cocaine? Powdered sugar? Like
minuscule drops of frozen drool? I look out the window and see flakes
blowing sideways, tapping the glass. How had I not noticed them before?

As we talk, the knot in my stomach dissolves bit by bit. In the
Program, I would have been questioned for disappearing. For disobeying.
For deviating from expectations. But Chris gives me space. Finally, after
chatting for a little, he assigns me our new category: Body. What does
it feel like to be in one? How do the body and mind affect each other?

chris [10:12 A.M.]
oh one more thing

lee [10:12 A.M.]
sure whats up

chris [10:13 A.M.]
we need to shift the strategy
we've been studying the data
and some is performing better

lee [10:13 A.M.]
oh ok great
what kind?

chris [10:13 A.M.]
we need more observational research
for example
the research you collected yesterday
that scored high

I study what I added yesterday. A photo of the diner, of the menu, of a woman dropping a plate across from me. With it, hastily recorded details:

9:59 Russian woman working in diner. Always in a hurry. Walks with a limp, but hardly noticeable. Sleeves pushed halfway up her arms. Calls everyone "baby." Nods her head to music occasionally. Laughs unexpectedly, explosively. Otherwise, permanent frown. She talks about random things with people: the clouds, syrup, taxes. She doesn't fake smile. She gives people advice: "Thinking is fine, doing is better."

chris [10:13 A.M.]
we're already giving Vicky a ton of general data
scraped from other systems

so your info needs to be specific
it's like a guide for the AI
indicators of what to notice
if that makes sense?

lee [10:14 A.M.]
ok
more observational data

chris [10:14 A.M.]
yep perfect

This is good, I think. We're seeing patterns, we're following them. And now we have more direction. It turns out whoever was adding the pink data was right to be mixing in observations from the world. How did they know to do that?

Looking at my notes from the diner, I know I can do it. I can build on what I know from the Observation Room. I can grow as a researcher: learn, adapt. And the Government is involved, so once we're successful I'll be able to work wherever I want.

I turn back to the portals feeling freshly determined. I'll start with my strengths and then venture out again. Pulling up my Screen, I watch fitness instructors live stream from their rooms. I attend a virtual conference where scientists show diagrams of skin cells, pointing at the different layers of **the dermis, epidermis, and hypodermis**. Skin has a strange omnipotent presence, holding every part of us together.

I dive into research, losing myself in facts, ideas, opinions about the body. Even though my thoughts are still spinning, and I'm still worried about the decision I just made, something else, a feeling deep in my core, tells me I'm finally doing what I'm meant to do, that, finally, I'm doing something right.

★　★　★

THOUSANDS OF PEOPLE post videos of themselves crying online. Brows contorted. Lips curled. Eyes scrunched so tight they almost disappear inside themselves. The videos are strange, popping up in Home in hordes, enabling anyone and everyone to pause, rewind, and watch again.

A small, freckled teen with puffy eyes is turning shades of red on my Screen when a message floats over her. Nikita is inviting me to a party? A housewarming for someone?

The message hovers briefly before fading. I'll bet Janet put her up to it after shocking us with The Report. I haven't seen everyone yet to know what they think, to see how they've reacted. What a bizarre thing, to be months into a project together and then finally find out why we're working on it.

I thank Nikita for the invite and tell her I won't be able to make it. I'm on a roll and I can feel my research for the Body category is the best so far. The teen on my Screen keeps crying, then she fades and another video loads of someone climbing a ladder, doing a dance on a roof, then climbing back down.

Nikita sends the address just in case, and I tap on it out of curiosity. The building is a new high-rise downtown designed specifically to enhance community. "Luxury," the website says, the word popping out, dissolving into bubbles, and then reloading again. While tapping through videos—old marble stairs, new high-speed elevator, dynamic pool with aquatic sound system, and daily events to facilitate friendship—it occurs to me that I might actually need to go.

I think about what Chris said, about how we need more observational data, how we don't have any systems set up to help me obtain that, which means I may need to figure out how to facilitate this kind of research on my own. And here's an opportunity presenting itself to me.

I tap through images of the building online, and while staring at the rooftop views, I decide I'll go for Vicky. I'll take notes on what it's like for bodies to be in one space together, what they do, how they perform.

★ ★ ★

THE ELEVATOR IS a glossy black, and I examine the shadow of my reflection as I float up to the eleventh floor, tucking a strand of lifeless brown hair behind my ear. With Veronika out, my clothes are plain, randomly selected from my drawers, and now I wonder if I should have put more thought into them. While researching the body, I've discovered that people wear things and do things to make theirs stand out. But at the same time, some people just want to stand out so they fit in. It's really confusing.

Ding. The elevator spits me out across from the door to 9D, which is propped open. I stand outside for a few seconds debating whether I should walk in or press the oval doorbell. As I'm thinking through what to do, how to act, someone opens the door and almost knocks right into me. We apologize as we switch places.

As soon as I enter, I begin taking notes on my phone. The apartment is an angular space with one group of people standing in the kitchen near mismatched trays of food and another group squished on a couch or sitting on the floor near it, staring at a large Screen in silence. Suddenly, a question floats onto it: Do you like sports? I watch as conversation erupts. Loud, cacophonous, disjointed.

A pale woman with a flowery dress appears from nowhere and introduces herself as the host. She says she's so glad I could make it; she's heard such great things about me. I immediately forget her name, and she never asks for mine. As abruptly as she arrived, she leaves, flittering off into the room's kaleidoscope of faces and colors and smells. I move to a corner so I can continue observing without being interrupted.

Conversation dwindles. Clumps of people who have nothing left to say about sports sit patiently or lean against the wall. I glance around for Nikita or Chris or Ted. Finance Guy. Shrill Laugh Girl. Lanky Boy. Anyone who might look vaguely familiar. The apartment becomes completely silent for a few beats, and then a new prompt appears: What's the last dream you remember having?

Chatter explodes again. Deafening, roaring, jubilant, intimidating. In the kitchen, a green bottle of champagne wrapped with a gold label sits on the counter. It's taller than a two-year-old, and people tip it, struggling with the weight as they pour some in champagne flutes.

"Oh, this silly thing?" I hear the host say, swishing around in her dress. "Mike's boss gave it to him for closing a big deal."

I make a note in the Data Program for Vicky:

5'4" female with pale brown hair and a flowing dress moves around the small room and welcomes people with a hug, even people she doesn't know. She throws her hands in the air often, but gracefully. She enjoys showing off her things. She touches her partner when near, indicating that he is hers.

Partner is male 5'9" with a straight-line mouth. He keeps his arms crossed and stands in the same spot all night with two other men. When his partner comes back and touches him on the chest, on the forearm, on the elbow, he does not move away but also does not give her small touches back.

"Are you having fun?" a man says with a voice like a car horn right in my ear. I flinch, dropping my phone, and hitting my hand hard on the wall while trying to catch it. My fingers sting for a second, the **meta-carpals** my brain feeds me automatically, grabbing at research. I pick up my phone and then stand to look at him suspiciously. He swallows, pulls at his green collared shirt, and points to the Screen, where a new prompt is floating: Are you having fun?

I turn back to look at him, his receding hairline, his red blotchy cheeks.

"Yes," I say, tentatively. I look around for something, anything. He follows my gaze to the green bottle.

"Do you want some?" he asks.

"Yes," I repeat. Why is he talking to me? This wasn't part of the plan. He goes to the kitchen, wrestles with the bottle, and brings me back a glass. Bubbles race to the surface and pop, spritzing my face. We look at each other, unsure of what to do now.

"These luxury apartments are a good idea," he says. "Studios but with the community experience."

"You live here?"

"Yeah, next door!"

"Cool."

No hair peeks out of his shirt, just bare skin. I take a note in my phone. I wonder if Vicky will need to know the correct moment to tell someone to button their shirt a bit higher. Or if she would be the kind of friend that lets their friend wear whatever they want.

"Yeah, the new designs are killer. Custom made for people who live by themselves but still want that homey vibe. They even have movie nights!"

"That's great!" I say, desperately racking my brain for information on how to react to this man. An image from Home pops into my head of people knocking glasses into each other—cheers!—so I clink mine into his.

"Cheers!"

I do it too quickly, causing some of the champagne to splash out. He laughs and sips, so I sip, too, and we look around at the others who have also become silent and are looking around at us. I finally spot Nikita leaning delicately against the railing on the balcony.

"Thank you," I mumble, and smile, backing away slowly to an area behind the couch near the balcony where Nikita is. Close enough so she can see me, but far enough away so I can do my job and observe how bodies behave in a room.

LATER THAT NIGHT, I'm so exhausted I can't sleep. Spaces filled with people are bursting with energy, but they also require it—even if I'm just there to research.

Observing others out in the world has a meditative quality to it, like blacking out and waking up with detailed data. It's not that I actually black out, of course, it's more that there's a rhythm to collection that allows me to disappear in the task without thinking about anything else. When I'm working, there's a fluidity, a synchronicity, and everything *feels* as if it's moving together. Everything *feels* smooth. Observe, assess, input, repeat. And the time passes beautifully, fluidly, as if gravity is lifted.

But now, back in my room staring at the paintbrush strokes of the wall, the information comes back in different forms, floating around me. Flashes of the thin-boned host prancing around in that dress. Have I ever owned a dress like that before? One made of silk? One with small flowers?

I open my drawers to see the same clothes I've always had, the same pants, the same shirts. And then I lie down on the bed and gaze at the ceiling.

Lips. The host's. Stuck in that half smile and just a touch of red. Nikita's were noticeable, too, shining like gathered light. What would mine be like with a little bit of gloss? A little bit of color?

Bubbles. And the man with the receding hairline. The unexpected octave of his car-horn voice. It was nice of him to get me a drink, wasn't it? I don't think I've ever brought someone a drink, not even a glass of water.

I fall asleep slowly as a collage of body parts rotates through my dreams: the angle of arms, the length of legs, shirts clinging to the curve of back muscles.

In the morning, a small bag sits outside our apartment. I check the name once, twice, and am shocked that it's for me. When I peel back the packaging, a small ChapStick rests inside, and I briefly recall tapping to order it from my phone while half-awake, half-asleep last night.

I spread it across my lips the way I've seen Veronika do before, the way I saw so many people do in videos online, and feel the surprise of waxy support, smell the shock of artificial fruit.

★ ★ ★

ON MY FIRST day back to the office after The Loneliness Report, Toru and Janet are nowhere to be found. It's unusually quiet, and no one mentions The Report or references the meeting. Instead, everyone works with their heads down. For once, I wish there was chatter in the kitchen. The silence seems off, dense, and the day moves by slowly.

When the office empties out again, I pack up and hop in the elevator. Just as the door is about to close, a hand shoots through, flinging it back open. Cat Eyes. She steps in and stands there looking at me as the door slides shut behind her. I never noticed how short she is, coming only to my shoulder. We stare at each other as the elevator drops so fast my ears pop.

"So what do you think?" she asks. The question is suspiciously open-ended.

"About what?" I hope she's asking about The Report, because I want to know what the others think, but I wasn't expecting to do it like this, one-on-one, face-to-face. At the Program, they had designated Forums to discuss topics anonymously.

We walk down the corridor to the front, where the security camera blinks at us. I smile widely and then she does, too, and when it registers we are content with our workday, the door unlocks, allowing us to leave.

"The Report. That erased emotion. All of it," she says when we're outside and far enough away from the office. I wonder if she's afraid to say it: loneliness. I roll the letters around in my mind, and each time I do it feels unfamiliar, scorched.

"I'm still processing," I say. Does she know I almost left? Did she almost leave, too? I turn and she follows, matching her steps to mine.

"Yeah, same."

We cross the street and join a trickle of people walking uptown. I move quickly, but she keeps up. I'm dying to know what she thinks, who she is, where she came from, but I'm not sure how to approach it. How to ask. I stop short and pull over. She does, too, and we stand with our backs against a smooth marble building, letting others pass, her green eyes boring into the side of my face.

"So you believe in it, though? Loneliness?" she asks suddenly, roughly, to hide the desperation, the bewilderment. She spits out the term out, letting it hang there in the air.

I gaze up at the marble leaning into the sky, looming over us like a shadow. It's difficult to say whether or not I believe in something I don't fully understand. Not that I would admit that. I've been trying to push The Report from my head and focus on what I can control: the research. But every time I close my eyes, it's still there: those curious blue dots, the materials Chris sent, the memory of Masha's face, dismissing me so quickly.

"Hello? Anyone home?" Cat Eyes says, still staring at me.

"Oh, sorry, yes."

"Yes, what?"

"I believe in The Report. The data," I say. "I traced it all and it's legitimate."

"I'm not asking about the data. I'm asking about the whole concept," she says. "But if you don't want to talk about it, it's fine. I feel like you never want to talk about anything. It's like you think you're better than us or something."

"What? No, I don't," I say, startled. Maybe I do think that, but I've never meant for it to be mean, or for others to realize it.

We stand there for a few seconds in silence. I think about how Cindy and Greg used to tell me that being smart can make others uncomfortable. *People are just intimidated by you, that's all. Try not to make others feel dumb. Try not to say such big words. Please, just for once, try to fit in.*

But I have been trying. At the Program, being extremely focused and driven was applauded. So I've been doing that here. I thought the others would see it as a sign of respect for them, for this project. But now I wonder what their Programs were like, if maybe there are other ways to work that I might not be aware of.

"Look, it doesn't matter. I'm just glad they finally told us what's going on," Cat Eyes says, sighing. "I knew they were hiding something, but I couldn't figure out what. I definitely wasn't expecting them to reveal a whole new emotional concept."

"Yeah, same," I say, relieved she's moved on.

"It makes sense, though, from what I read, that Vicky would be the ideal solution for loneliness," Cat Eyes continues. "At least from what I've been able to gather."

"Yeah, true," I say.

"Have you heard of it before?" she asks, staring at me so intently it feels like she's studying my pores.

"Of loneliness?" I ask, proving I can say it, too.

She nods.

"Yeah, but only once. Only in passing," I admit, and as soon as it slips out of my mouth I feel the faintest relief.

"Really? Where?"

"I found a mention in an archived study a long time ago, but that's it," I say. She nods and doesn't press me on it, which makes me realize that she gets it. That sometimes when you're deep in portals, you uncover strange stuff. I wonder if maybe I've been selling the others short. If maybe they have more training and experience than I thought. If maybe they, too, had other places they wanted to land. And we were all placed here instead for a reason.

"It's such a weird thing," Cat Eyes says. "But it must be serious if the Government is involved."

"Yeah, totally," I say, and then pause for a second. "Did Chris tell you to add more observational research?"

"Yeah, he did. Makes sense. Our information needs to be experiential, rooted in the world, since they're already scraping so much other data."

We stand side by side against the marble, letting the cold stone seep into us. I wonder what she's thinking, if she likes it here in this strange city, what she misses most about where she was before.

"You heard about Rob and Tanya, right?" Cat Eyes says.

"Who?" I really do need to get better at names. It's like there's so much information bopping around in my head, sometimes the most obvious things don't stick.

"Rob. Tanya. They're done."

"What do you mean?"

"Done. Gone. Left. Released. Apparently they told Janet and Toru that they didn't believe it."

I freeze. She must be talking about Finance Guy and Shrill Laugh Girl, because I don't remember seeing them in the office today. How had I not thought more about their absence? Why am I missing so many of these small, important things? I try not to let my surprise show on my face, but I'm sure she sees it.

"Why?" I ask, then, "Are they going to bring in replacements?"

"Beats me," she says, playing with a row of silver rings on her fingers, twisting one and then the other. "This project, like we said, seems important. So why leave? Do they know something we don't?"

It is strange, I have to admit. I think back to my own doubts and wonder if Janet went to see the two of them the way she came to talk to me. I debate telling Cat Eyes about this but don't want to admit that I ever questioned the project. That I almost made a decision without thinking it through. What kind of a researcher does that?

"Maybe they're not thinking straight," I say, sounding a little pathetic.

"Ha!" Cat Eyes yells, and a man walking past us jumps. But she doesn't laugh. She's serious in a way I both fear and admire.

"None of us are thinking straight. Not when so much new information is being tossed at us," she says. "But whatever. I don't know about you, but I need Vicky to work. So keep me posted if you hear anything, and I'll do the same."

I nod. Is she trying to build a career, too? What are her goals? Does she know someone who is lonely?

"See you tomorrow," she says, and backs away slowly. We stare at each other until she looks away first, turning to join the flow of people streaming downtown.

★ ★ ★

FROM MY DESK the next day, I watch the elevator, hoping to hear the high-pitched voice of Shrill Laugh Girl or see the confident shoulders-back posture of Finance Guy.

By ten A.M., I know they're not coming in. Their desks remain empty, leaving an awkward gap between me and Cat Eyes, Wire Frames, and Lanky Boy, who sit at the other end of Consultant Row.

Two contrasting thoughts orbit each other: This is bad. I hate to admit it, but with the strategy we're running right now, the more minds working on it the better. But I also can't help but think: This is good. Because now when Vicky works it will be easier for everyone to see that it's because of me.

When I get up to pour a second coffee, Cat Eyes's gaze burns into the back of my neck. Returning to my desk, I take a sip and peer over the mood mug as it turns a stormy black. When our eyes meet, she raises her eyebrows, as if to say, I told you so.

CHAPTER 10

Janet looks away from her Screen and blinks once, twice, three times to help her eyes adjust. Outside her window, the sky has turned to ink. She stands to pour herself another glass of wine, then looks out at the endless blotch of night. It must be late, she thinks, checking her watch to confirm that it is, in fact, two in the morning.

A few stray lights punch through windows across the way. Janet eyes them and decides to do a gratitude exercise, something to decrease stress levels. Even though Vicky is making progress, the last few weeks have been anything but smooth.

So, taking a sip of her wine, Janet thinks about what she's thankful for. Right now? In this very moment? She's thankful to be here, in this strange city of grit. One where you can look up from work at two A.M. and see that across the way others are still up, too.

When she and Toru first began this project, Janet had insisted the headquarters be in New York. Toru was thrilled. Not just because there were cheaper office spaces so they could allocate more budget to his team, but because it was an unexpected choice. Not necessarily as shiny as having a headquarters in one of the new-age cities like Columbus, Minneapolis, or Milwaukee.

But Janet had specific reasons for choosing this place. She's learned that for a company to have a chance at success, there needs to be the right combination of money, talent, resources, time, luck, and location. It's the last one people often forget: the importance of setting. Where you are affects who you become. What you look at, what you're surrounded by, whether digitally or physically, affects how you act and perform.

And even though this ancient city is portrayed online as dead, lost, decayed, empty, Janet knows better. She's done her research. She sees there's still energy here in the fabric of the sidewalks, in the wonky way new and old come together. She chose New York because it used to be the epicenter of narrative, of creation, and bubbling beneath the cold smileless faces that wander past, behind the millions of shut doors, people are still dreaming. There's a pulse here she hasn't felt anywhere else. Maybe not as lively and new as the Midwest, which marches along to the beat of the future. But the future is lonely.

Janet wanted the headquarters here, in this city, because anyone can collect data, but not everyone can shape it into a story. And that's essentially what the Humanity Consultants are doing: telling Vicky a story, through specifics and experiences, about what it means to be a person. This is the missing piece. This is why no one else has been able to do it before. They've forgotten humans are made of narratives.

So yes, for all of this, Janet is thankful, very much so.

Turning away from the window, Janet runs her hand along the worn brick wall of her apartment and across her sturdy wood desk. She's thankful for all this, too. It's the reason she rented this apartment: the desk. Large, refreshingly solid. The kind of piece she hasn't seen for a while.

Janet knows she should go to bed and get some rest. She should end the night now, while the vibrations of gratitude calm her. But instead, she tops off her glass of wine and sits back down at her bulky desk.

The truth is, sometimes Janet revels in stress. Bathes in it. Welcomes it. A certain level buzzing beneath the surface simply means the project is worthwhile, difficult enough to wake her vitals, excite her mind. And if Janet loves anything, it's to be challenged.

Besides, the chaos of the past few weeks signals that they've reached what Janet likes to call the tipping point, the crescendo. The place she and Toru have been many times before, and which they both secretly enjoy: a slice of time where everything falls either together or apart.

She knows this is why Toru moved the whole Tech Team here a month ago. It's the reason she finally demanded permission from the Government to share The Loneliness Report with the Consultants. They've both been gearing up for this place of no return where taking risks is not just an option, but a necessity. When your back is against the wall is when real innovation begins. Or, as she and Toru like to think, the real fun.

Janet drinks her wine and taps through the Consultants' profiles on her Screen, wondering if any of them will connect the dots. If, now that they've had time to digest The Report for a few weeks, any of them have started to realize that what they feel or have felt is the very thing they're trying to solve.

That's why she and Toru reprogrammed the Placement System. When they were selecting the Consultants, they looked for qualified researchers, but they also wanted people who've experienced loneliness, whatever it is, however it appears. People who've felt it climb through their insides. Who still feel it flitting around, a constant shadow.

And from her conversations with the scientists behind The Report, Janet learned one key thing: people will do anything to stop being lonely. So even if the Consultants don't recognize it in themselves, they'll feel the primal need to fix it. That's what Janet does best: find a way to build teams of people who will sacrifice everything for the company's vision. And these employees, they're set up to give them-selves to this project.

Everyone, that is, except the girl. Janet hovers over Lee's profile. It hadn't surprised her one bit when she tried to leave. She's the only one they selected who doesn't have it: loneliness. The Placement System warned them, highlighting the mismatch in red.

Janet always wondered if this would make Lee less committed. If it would be difficult for her to empathize with the emotion, as someone who hasn't experienced it.

Thank goodness Lee was naïve enough to break the Agreement. And all just to contact her old professor. Did she really think he'd want to hear from her? A shame. Janet thought she'd made it clear in the Onboarding Packet that those messages won't go through.

She skims through the girl's profile, unsure what to think about her. Unsure what it is about her that still bothers her. Maybe it's the fact that the research she's collecting is actually good. Useful. Toru says the Tech Team's noticed an uptick recently; it's become even higher quality. Janet thinks back to their conversation. Does she feel bad about it? About knowing exactly what would get under Lee's skin?

No. Not at all. It's her job to ensure the people and operations of this company run smoothly. To find what motivates her team and tap into it so they can make Vicky work.

It's certainly not Janet's job to lose employees. Not midproject. Not Lee. Not anyone. Definitely not two at once, Janet thinks as she exits Lee's profile and pulls up the two Consultants they had to release. The ones who surprised her.

Janet knows it's a waste to keep tabs on them, but she can't help it. It bothers her that she missed it; that she didn't see it coming. Looking at their profiles serves as sort of a punishment—a reminder—that anything can happen if she's not vigilant.

By the Agreement, she and Toru get to keep all their data until the termination of the Vicky project, so she can see they've landed at middle-grade companies in Ohio. That they're still together, at least for now. As Janet scans their profiles, she wonders, not cruelly, of course, but out of curiosity, who will be the first to hurt the other.

In their exit interview, they told her, hand in hand, that they simply didn't believe it. That they didn't want to be a part of something that was made up.

"And besides, if it is true," the woman had said, her shrill voice shaking, "which we know it's not, we just don't need that kind of energy in our lives, you know?"

The guy nodded and planted a kiss on her head, his lips landing in the soft center part of her hair. It was such a small gesture, yet it's this image hovering behind Janet's eyelids when she's trying to relax. Something so insignificantly tender replaying over and over in the depth of night.

Maybe it's the wine, or maybe it's the time, but looking at their profiles floating next to each other, Janet feels an unexpected pang of nostalgia for something she can't name. Grief, just a lick of it, for a path she didn't take. There had been lovers in her life, plenty, but she'd never given them a chance at something more than temporary. Love would have been distracting. It would have kept her from reaching this point, the height of her career, asked to work on a secret project that could affect the lives of millions of people. Surely, this is a better use of her time. A better use of her life.

Besides, she finds passion and sex quickly anywhere around the world using Dating. And she has Toru. They have each other to work with. To collaborate, to create. A person to think with is the most intimate thing someone can have. And she has it, this connection that outlasts the body's demise, the heart's tantrums.

Janet swirls the wine in her glass. One of the lights across the way blinks out. When she takes a swig, the flavor of dry plum floods her senses, thick on her tongue. For the millionth time, Janet analyzes everything from the past week. She should have known that the two lovers were a flight risk. She should have known Lee was still connected to the straight-edge dream she was trained on. She should have, at the very least, introduced The Loneliness Report more strategically. Even after a decade of this, there's more for her to learn and perfect.

But this is what's exciting about this particular project, right? How complicated it is. It's forcing her to rethink her methods. Pushing her. And she hasn't been pushed for a really long time. The fact that they could fail, that others are already failing, that Janet has made irreparable mistakes and now must deal with them: it's interesting. To feel stupid again? It's motivating.

Just as Janet's about to map out what she needs to keep a closer eye on, what to read more about, where her blind spots could be, an alert chimes. She recognizes the sound. Even before she opens it, she knows what it is: a Failure.

Draining her wine, she immediately calls Toru so they can go through the details together. He'll be up. He always is. And his commentary on the flaws of the others' solutions, his excitement about outlasting another company, his boyish happiness at seeing very respected names fall, will be exactly what she needs to pull her from the early-morning admonishments eating her from the inside.

PERFORMANCE SUMMARY—FAILURE

Company Name: Vital Neuron Nutrition

Company Founder(s): Juju Jenkins

Brief Synopsis of Project:
Lonely people tend to show cognitive decline, including low levels of activity in the medial prefrontal cortex. Activation of the dopaminergic neurons in the dorsal raphe nucleus is necessary for isolated individuals to drive social interaction.

We've identified SK channels that can alter serotonergic neurons when a person is lonely. Hence, if we block these channels, we can help treat the illness. Our team was developing a tablet that users can ingest to increase activity in these targeted areas.

Employee Count: 14

Detailed Explanation of Failure:
In tests, one out of every fifteen people who ingested the tablets experienced induced elation for periods of time, which eventually receded into a coma or long-term elevated delusion. The product has proven dangerous and needs more testing over years.

Did you discover anything about Loneliness or The Loneliness Report you think necessary to flag immediately?

Yes. Data on sleeping patterns, food intake, exercise, patterns of serotonin and neural behavior, and more. Please see attached information and distribute to other companies if useful.

Thank you for your collaboration. We greatly appreciate your service.

CHAPTER 11

Sun shines through the kitchen window, revealing streaks of grime. I contemplate Chris's circular avatar in Chat—a goat with a long beard—and wonder if it, in any way, represents Chris's physical appearance. Or perhaps his mental state. And what that would mean if it did indeed mirror either.

Last night, he sent an email ending the Body category. I was nervous to see the results now that we have shifted the strategy and lost two Consultants. I wondered if maybe we changed too many variables at once, but to my relief, we scored a whole percentage point higher than on any of the other categories, which feels like progress, no matter how small.

Staring at Chris's avatar, the beard of the goat blowing in an unseen virtual wind, I wait for what will be our eleventh category and think about that small percentage increase. I think about how good productivity feels, like moving in a world where everyone else is frozen.

I open the Data Program to pull up The MASTER link so I can reflect on the information we added, but it's gone. Did they move it?

Ping.

Ten A.M. Chris jumps right into the new category. He seems excited, energized, just like me. Is it because of our progress? Is it because of The Report and the new sense of urgency everyone seems to have?

He says he's been holding this category until Vicky was more developed. Until she had enough data to understand, communicate, and learn at a higher rate. A new page pops up in the Data Program, and when I open it, I see the category I knew was coming: Friendship.

★   ★   ★

MONTAGES OF PEOPLE jumping in pools at the same time, lying on the couch with their hair tangled together, pushing strollers in a row, throwing baseballs, wearing funny hats, laughing and laughing and smiling and smiling as if friendship is the most easy, lighthearted joke. As if it's a story told under the stars on a warm summer night.

But friendship is layered. The deeper I dig in the archives and webs, the more its simplicity unravels, twists, becomes a matted mess. Best friends who are no longer best friends after a rum-punch incident at a bachelorette party. People who pretend they feel different, look different, have different income, just to be liked.

This whole being-someone's-friend thing is complicated. Not a campfire story, but a meandering epic woven with the thread of time, trust. Everyone has different hopes and expectations and stresses and needs. One scientist explains that friends are like **plants that need water and sun, but not too much water, or too much sun.**

While watching a video of kids playing tag, I notice a small ticking coming from the kitchen. Pop! A rush of noise enters through the walls: a crying child, the wheels of a truck, a bird scream-singing. I look over and see a small wisp of smoke twirling out from the Sound Collector. I forgot it was there! I leave it dangling off the wall and welcome the noise, letting it wash over me.

★   ★   ★

VERONIKA HAS A routine with the same group of friends. Most weeks they video chat, heads bobbing around on the Screen, but sometimes she has them over after work. Tonight, they're drinking in our apartment when I get home from the office.

"Lee! Oh my gosh, perfect timing," Veronika says, and goes to pour me a glass. I think of all the research I have left to do. All the portals and archives waiting to be scoured.

"Everyone, this is Lee! Lee, this is everyone!" Veronika says, unde-terred by my silence. As the room turns to me, I have a split second to figure out what to do. My instinct is to go back to my bedroom, but it's also been over a week since this new category was introduced, and I haven't been able to get quality observational research on Friendship yet. Maybe this is the perfect opportunity. Maybe watching Veronika and her friends could be exactly what I need. What Vicky needs.

I take the glass from Veronika, and everyone introduces themselves at the same time. I recognize some of them from Veronika's photos, but I don't think I've met any of them before. They wear pastel-colored blouses and tight pants. One of them wears a green-polka-dot-patterned blouse I saw in an ad on the subway the other day.

The friends switch off talking about various dates they've been on recently and I take notes on my phone, adding them directly to the Data Program. One woman refuses to let men pay for her. Another waits to respond to texts until at least twice the time it took the other person to.

When everyone has shared a story or update, they turn expectantly to me.

"I don't have a profile on Dating," I tell them, surprised to be addressed. They launch into arguments about why it's fun yet delusion-inducing, monotonous labor like chewing gum.

"We'll make you one this weekend," Veronika says to the relief of the group, and everyone offers advice at once:

"No photos with your ex-boyfriends . . ."

". . . cropping people out is weird and it looks self-centered . . ."

". . . lighting is key . . ."

". . . smiling is good, but not in all of them unless you want to be mistaken for someone who is always happy . . ."

". . . no sunglasses . . ."

". . . no crop tops or boob shots unless you're just looking to get laid . . ."

". . . which is totally fine, too, because we're all feminists here . . ."

". . . mix up the photos so they know you're both beautiful and active . . ."

I write it all down for Vicky, but also because I don't know how else to keep up. There seem to be so many rules. I've studied humans and human behavior for years. Shouldn't I know this? Some of it rings a bell, surfacing files from weird parts of my brain.

"What are your hobbies, Lee?" the one in the green-polka-dot top asks.

"Hobbies?" I say.

"Yeah, what do you like to do."

"Oh, I work a lot."

"But outside of work?" another asks, and I think for a little bit.

"I like to go to a diner."

Everyone just stares at me.

"She's new to New York," Veronika cuts in, tossing her blond curls behind her shoulder. "She likes to read, she's an expert barista, and she's a runner." I understand now why Veronika works in sales. She's good at packaging things, even me.

"Oh! You should include a picture of you making coffee or training for your marathon," someone from the circle offers.

"I'm not training for a—"

"That's a great idea," Veronika says, and then everyone refills their glasses and moves on to a new topic.

I MESSAGE CHRIS while lying in bed that night, still floating on the liquor, the conversation, the pulse of being in a room full of live data.

lee [10:06 P.M.]
observational research
I think it will really work
it helps with digital collection too
they build off each other
its amazing

It's true. The more I observe, the better questions I have when I turn back to the Screen. It's like after a session with the Observation Room at the Program, but better. More authentic. More intense. I wonder why Masha never had us do stuff like this? It's risky, sure. Loaded with bias, probably.

But there's something raw and natural about it. I feel that Chris would get what I'm saying; he'd understand this feeling bubbling up in me. A jolt of something that leaves me wanting to do more, more, more. What would someone call it? Inspiration?

As I lie there, I think about how Veronika moved so easily through the group: sitting, laughing, telling a story about a date where she flipped a shrimp into the man's lap. She seemed so happy tonight, fluffing her blond curls. A dimpled smile spread across her face.

The conversations play over and over in my mind. I took as many notes as I could, recording it all, and now I feel drained, but in a way that reminds me of how I used to feel after track meets in high school. Energy depleted for a purpose.

This is good. Very good, I tell myself. The AI should be able to provide the same entertainment the friends gave each other tonight, right? The same banter, the same parade of stories and jokes and the occasional pointed questions designed to get under someone's skin.

I can hardly keep my eyes open, so I order an energy shake from Food, and when the drone drops it off, I chug it while pulling my Screen up around me. I want to keep going, to capture everything while it's fresh. To let what I saw spur questions, guide investigations.

I run search after search on Friendship based on the group tonight, and when Chris finally messages me back, the alcohol has left my system and I'm a bit embarrassed. I apologize for bothering him so late when he's probably hard at work on other things, but he brushes it off, says he's here to chat anytime, and asks me about what I observed.

I tell him how one of Veronika's friends sat cross-legged on the floor and took large gulps of her drink. She pulled at the rug and laughed loudly, randomly, but didn't say much. I tell him how another one kept putting on different songs all night, playing about twenty seconds of it, and then choosing a new one. About how someone finally said, "Stop it, okay?" Do you think Vicky would tell someone to stop changing the music? Would she be able to alter her friendship with each individual?

Chris asks questions. Makes jokes. Dissects the observations with me. It's nice to have someone to debrief with. Someone who, just by listening, validates that what I'm thinking and seeing and wondering is worthwhile.

★   ★   ★

ON SATURDAY MORNING, Veronika knocks with three loud taps, and when I don't answer right away, wondering if it was a mistake, she knocks again, banging her palms against the wood.

"Get up! We're making a Dating profile."

She remembered? I'm both flattered and frazzled. I guess having one could be good for Vicky, just to see what it requires from start to finish. Besides, as a researcher, I should understand these things myself, shouldn't I?

I throw on a sweatshirt and brush my hair, pulling it back into a loose ponytail. When I emerge from my room, she's sitting at the table completely made up, already typing notes on her phone. She asks me what photos I've been thinking about. I haven't.

"You're telling me you don't have any photos of yourself? None?"

I shake my head. I don't think I'm allowed to tell her that all my details are archived.

"Okay, well, don't worry. We probably would want to take new ones today anyway so we can get them all right," she says.

"The most important thing to remember is we're making a more beautiful and fun but completely laid-back version of you."

She begins typing again.

"So we'll take one of you running to show you're driven and then we can do a coffee shop one to show you like trying new things in the city. Then we'll take a photo of you in a black dress in the hallway. It shows you can be sexy, too, so you'll look really interesting and well rounded."

"Okay," I say, even though it all sounds absurd.

IT'S CHILLY, A springtime fake-out where the sun is in the sky but the air still bites. Even so, Veronika says I can't wear a sweatshirt for the running photo. We're outside on our block after she's had me try on one of her old athletic tops that's too small for her. A T-shirt isn't form fitting enough, she says, even though that's what I run in all the time. You'll look like a fish, she says, or worse, a blob.

I walk to the end of our street, goose bumps dotting my arms, and then run toward Veronika as she squats in different stances and snaps away.

"You have to keep going past me," she instructs. "And relax your face a little. It looks like you're in pain."

I walk back to the corner and try again.

"Can you put your hair in a higher ponytail?" She's looking at the screen. "It looks like you're bald."

I walk back and try again.

And again.

And one last time, until Veronika captures a picture she likes.

For the coffee photo, Veronika picks out a purple scoop-neck shirt. She says it will accent my collarbones. We walk to a spot a few blocks away with baby-pink tables and a white tile floor that projects a different design every hour. Plants fill the crevices, and I recognize it from photos of others I've seen on Home. Veronika makes me order a latte instead of a black coffee.

When it's ready, we sit at a table in the window and I try to follow her instructions closely: cross my legs, look to the left, look back at the camera, smile, not that much, don't look angry, relax your eyebrows.

Veronika crawls around for the best angle, her boobs dangling as she bends over in her low-cut V-neck. Her long limbs flare out as she leans awkwardly from side to side and even considers standing on a chair for a minute. I've been trying to be a good participant because she seems so eager. But my skin has begun to feel as if the cells are moving away, crawling off me, leaving me bare. With each photo she takes, the heat in my cheeks, the stiffness in my jaw, the desire to scream increases. All I can focus on is her focusing on me, and it's not until she announces we're done that I feel like I can breathe normally again.

Back at the apartment, Veronika edits the images and creates a profile for me. She says the pictures have to appear in a certain order, otherwise the whole project is ruined. If the photo of me running is first, I will get no dates. If the photo of me in the black dress is first, I'll only attract fuckboys.

"Fuckboys?" I ask, but Veronika is concentrating and doesn't hear me.

"Do you like tacos?" she asks. "We just have to answer a bunch of questions about your preferences so it can pair you with the perfect match. Do you enjoy swimming?"

"No."

Veronika asks me more questions, and each one elicits thoughts from experiments or observations or studies about other people and I can't tell if I'm saying anything right. I'm usually so good with answers, but it appears that's not the case when they're about me. I watch Veronika's reactions and try to answer in a way she seems happy with. After what feels like hours, Veronika says we're almost done. Just one more section.

"Do you have any ideas for a bio?" she asks, splayed out on the green couch. "Something fun and pithy but not totally annoying."

"Hm. I'm not sure."

"No worries, let's ask the group."

The group? My phone flashes a message from Veronika and six other numbers I don't recognize. One of them immediately changes the name to: BABES.

> Hey guys
> almost done with Lees dating profile
> Need a bio . . .
> ideas?

Different messages arrive at once. One is a haiku about me being new to New York. Another suggests I use only emojis. Veronika likes this idea best and asks the group to each send one they think is a good representation of me. We end up with this:

{cocktail} {panda bear} {woman behind Screen} {flame} {Grecian urn}

Before bed, I look at my profile, unsure what to expect. I study my smile. My running posture. My hands hugging a cup. This woman looks just the right amount of beautiful, just the right amount of fun.

★   ★   ★

THE NEXT DAY, I decide to go for a run because I've been researching for hours and coming up short. Or at least it feels like it, as if I started strong in the morning and slowly became less and less productive. It occurs to me that because there are no strict schedules or programmed breaks, I have to figure out when to exercise in order to increase my output.

Jogging through the quiet early-morning streets, I pass graffiti that seems targeted just for me: "You Go Girl," "Baby," and that strange message I saw when I first arrived, "I was here." What does it mean? Why do people keep putting it out there? I keep running, but as I lose sight of the words, I can't help but think it means something obvious I can't grasp.

Maps bosses me around, telling me where to go, letting me operate on autopilot so I can sift through thoughts as my feet pound the ground, as my breath punches the air. Sometimes running helps me clear my mind, but today it just stirs things up in there. How did Veronika meet the BABES? What do they do for work? What do they think of me? Are people seeing my Dating profile? Why would Veronika help me with it?

I let Maps direct me toward the edge of the island, where I run along the water and through the morning mist, fueled by the excitement of the past two weeks. But as my body sinks into a rhythm, a memory I'd buried drips into my thoughts.

The Program's sterile lights, a quiet hallway, starchy uniforms. A girl named Jane. She was an incredibly smart Sixth Year, and the only other fellow who attempted to chat with me while we worked in the lab. I didn't blame them. I was, after all, just a First Year. No one knew what to do with me.

But Jane was quirky, funny, loud. She wore bright earrings, and I liked the way she spoke out loud while thinking through problems. It was like being able to see into someone's mind for a second.

When we were walking out of the lab one day, she gave me a friendly nudge with her elbow and invited me to her dorm that night. "A couple of classmates will be there," she said. "It's not really a party, we just drink some wine and talk, listen to music."

"Sounds like a party to me," I remember blurting out without thinking. She'd laughed kindly, as if I'd said just the right thing.

I don't remember who was there, what music was playing, or what the drinks tasted like. I can't remember the specific discussions, only the awe I felt while listening to them. Students talked about their research, debated theories, and occasionally gossiped about others in the Program. But all of it felt important.

That night I couldn't sleep, too excited, my synapses cracking off like fireworks. I couldn't believe my luck. I'd finally found a group I fit in with. People who liked the same things I liked, who understood me.

The next day, I burst into the lab and told Masha all about it. But as I spoke, he continued staring at his large Screen, dragging bits of information from one column to the next. When I realized he wasn't mirroring my enthusiasm, when I realized that maybe I shouldn't be talking so loudly, so much, I stopped, apologized, and began to walk away.

"You know, Lee, some people don't have what you have," he said when I was a few steps away, his voice matter of fact, as if we were discussing the temperature. He didn't stop what he was doing. "And if they do, they throw it all away."

"What do you mean?" I'd asked.

"Have you ever heard the saying 'good is the enemy of great'?" Masha said, running his finger across his Screen, looking for something.

"No." Lights blared down from the ceiling.

"It just means that those who settle for being good at something will never be great at it." Finally, he turned to face me. His blue eyes bored into mine, cold and warm at the same time.

"Jane, the others. They are good. Very, very good. That's why I selected them, of course. But you, Lee, you have unlimited potential. You could be great. But only if you don't get distracted. Do you understand?"

I nodded, feeling small in my uniform. Small surrounded by the instruments and Screens and tables.

"Okay, good," Masha said, turning back to his Screen.

From then on, I avoided Jane. She tried to catch my eye or talk to me in the hall a few times, and even though I felt a pang of guilt when I looked away, walked away, ignored her, I was used to being on my own and settled into it.

Instead, I immersed myself in my work. I'd never had anyone tell me I had potential before. That I could be great. I would have sacrificed anything to be seen the way Masha and the other professors in the Program saw me. It's an addicting feeling: belief.

Besides, the desire to be the best at something is deep rooted, and for me it snuffed out the desire for anything else. It made the feeling I'd had after the party seem small, insignificant, the mere longing for something like that, something so surface level, almost shameful.

Maps is beeping, telling me I've gone off route. It snaps me back to the street where I've been running. Alerts climb over each other on my phone, waiting to be seen. A rat scrambles across the sidewalk in front of me.

I thought I was doing well. But what if I've been spending too much time with Veronika? What if I've been getting distracted by the wrong things? What if I've been settling for good?

Just the thought of it makes me sick.

CHAPTER 12

C hris says it's windy outside his apartment. He records it and sends me a voice message, and in my headphones I can hear the air flying around, swooshing and shushing and whistling.

chris [10:03 A.M.]
also
knock knock

lee [10:03 A.M.]
who's there?

chris [10:03 A.M.]
little old lady
(u have to say this out loud or it won't work)

lee [10:03 A.M.]
little old lady who?

I type it and whisper it into the Screen.

chris [10:03 A.M.]
i didn't know u could yodel, lee!

lee [10:04 A.M.]
{laughing face}

chris [10:04 A.M.]
been reading knock knock jokes all morning

lee [10:05 A.M.]
why?

chris [10:06 A.M.]
dunno
just got sucked into them
what did u do this weekend?

lee [10:07 A.M.]
my roommate made me a dating profile

chris [10:07 A.M.]
!!!
do u like it?

lee [10:08 A.M.]
idk
its interesting
she seems very good at this stuff

chris [10:08 A.M.]
dating is funny
it's like everyone has to pretend what they want most in the
world
doesn't matter at all

lee [10:09 A.M.]
what do you mean?

chris [10:09 A.M.]
ppl pretend they don't care
when the whole reason they make one is because they do
care
they want to find connection
sex, companionship
maybe even love

lee [10:10 A.M.]
oh

chris [10:10 A.M.]
speaking of
guess what the new category is

lee [10:11 A.M.]
dating?

chris [10:11 A.M.]
lol lee
no!!!
love

Sure enough, an email ending the Friendship category arrives at the same time an alert from the Data Program pings letting me know I've been assigned a new one. I open the email first and read through Chris's note, desperately searching for a sign that I'm doing something right or wrong. Have I been selfish? Distracted?

Our Efficiency score blinks at me from the bottom of the email. It's the highest ever: 83 percent! I let out a sigh of relief and read through it again, staring at the 83 percent until my vision blurs. It's working. The observational research is working!

Masha said if I want to be the best in my field, if I really want to be talented enough to run a Research Division, I have to be open to continuing to grow even after I graduate. The way we're gathering the data is different from anything I've ever done, but the fact that we're scoring higher confirms I'm not making selfish decisions. I'm making calculated ones.

When I open the Data Program and see the new category waiting, I almost laugh, because even though the page is blank, I know it will soon be filled. I'm relieved. I knew I'd be involved in groundbreaking research after graduation, but who could have ever predicted this? That I'd be sitting here, tasked and ready to collect experiences for an AI about the category blinking on the page before me: Love, Love, Love.

★   ★   ★

Six months down, forever to go. So many people on Home seem to be counting down their love as if shooting toward death together. I've been sifting through millions of posts that lovers put up, and now my eyes are tired, dry and heavy, rubbing against their sockets.

I walk toward the diner for a quick lunch in the hopes that there will be a real, live couple there in the flesh for me to observe. On the way, I pass the main street with bright storefronts. More people are standing in front of them than before: perusing purses, selecting shoes, ogling overcoats. Everyone is silent, but music blares from each shop, and I watch as the people press their palms against the glass to purchase something, and then rush home quickly to meet it on their doorstep.

Why are there so many more shoppers than before? I read some-where that **people shop because they need things. But some-times people shop because they need to feel things**.

I think of The Loneliness Report, the blue dots. Each time Toru shows them, there are more cases. Maybe these people feel a bit "strange" right now. Maybe they think a new scarf, or hat, or toaster will help.

When I get to the diner, the Russian woman ushers me to the maroon booth and brings my toast. She rushes around the room, even though there are fewer people today. I look for couples but don't see any; it's just a few people eating by themselves.

When I'm almost done with my toast, the door flings open and the Russian woman jumps over to welcome a man and his teenage son.

They both order the same thing—blueberry pancakes—and enter into a discussion I can't hear. The father's forehead scrunches up in annoyance and he takes out his phone to draw something on the screen with his finger. The son nods, soaking in what the father says.

I stay until they leave, recording as much as I can. The man puts his arm around the boy for a second, patting his back as they walk out.

Maybe the peanut butter and chocolate have gone to my head. Maybe the sugar is causing hallucinations. But the way the father patted the son's back, as if to say, I'm proud of you, imprints in my brain. It was clearly an act of love, one I caught and put directly into the Data Program.

I think about it the whole way home, past the window shoppers and the planters beginning to bloom. Greg never did anything like that. I see him exactly where I saw him last, sitting in his office with a bored look on his face, eyes glazed over, doing monotonous tasks.

He and Cindy are proud of me, I know that. They told me they were when I got accepted to the Program. They both came out of their offices to look over the acceptance letter with me. But neither of them had helped me apply. They never talked through strategies with me or asked me why I even wanted to go. They never patted me on the back like that.

By the time I get home, I'm annoyed with Cindy and Greg. I open the bottom drawer of my dresser to take out the T-shirt that was sitting on my desk the first day and debate throwing it out.

But then I wonder if maybe things have changed. It's been a long time since I saw them or spent quality time with them. Maybe they've landed jobs they enjoy. Or found something else to care about, like a new show or hobby. Maybe I can try to explain this job more, this secret mission, and maybe they'll have questions about it.

I fold the shirt and place it carefully back in the drawer. A small twinge of something hits me, maybe sadness, because I know Greg will love it. He'll wear it all the time, even if nothing has changed. Even if he and Cindy will never understand what I do or why I do it.

★   ★   ★

THE BABES CHAT is always going off. The girls send favorite lines from shows and respond with lines from other shows. They send pictures of lipstick colors and food truck splurges. They share videos of pretty leaves that have fallen on the sidewalk in the shape of hearts. Buildings with doors painted blue. Articles about the history of music in Las Vegas and the science behind microdosing. I get used to my phone buzzing. To waking up to messages, to falling asleep with them. It's an unexpectedly good sensation, being included, surrounded.

I open Dating and examine the woman who is supposed to be me. Or maybe I'm supposed to be her. She's smiling at me, but I can't tell if it's a real smile.

I keep getting alerts about matches, and I wonder what it would be like to go on an actual date. For Vicky, of course. I've read about them and watched Veronika get ready for hers. But it seems that I'm missing crucial data for the Love category about actually being on one. I take a deep breath, remind myself that curiosity is not a bad thing, that, in fact, curiosity leads the greatest researchers of our time. And then I begin.

Once I start, it's easy to keep going. I swipe and like and tap profiles in bed at night, when going to the bathroom, while waiting for the subway. I see face after face. Shirtless body after shirtless body. I watch videos of people belly flopping into the ocean. It doesn't even feel like I'm handling real people sometimes; it's more like a virtual card game with an infinite deck of faces.

When I look up, sixteen minutes have passed. Twenty-three. Fifty-one.

Hazel eyes, okay. Jagged nose, no thanks. Cute nerd glasses, sure. Holding a pigeon, nope. Today, I match with a man who has pictures of himself rock climbing. His name is Corbin and he says: **Hey;)**

Dating autoloads recommended responses. It gives me three options:

Hi! If you had 72 hours to live, what would you do?
Hi there ☺ what's your favorite food?
Oh hey sexy, what's the first thing we'd do together?

I go to tap the second option but my thumb fumbles, hitting the third instead. My cheeks immediately grow hot, but before I can delete the message, Corbin responds.

i want to use my tongue

Dating suggests:

Cow tongues are sold in markets in Spain. Have you ever been?
I'm so wet. Tell me more.
Tongues are great. Do you ever stick yours out at strangers for fun?

I choose the first one, knowing it to be true from a video I watched while down a research rabbit hole. We message for a bit about tongues, Popsicles, and names for a baby ostrich. Eventually, our prompts guide us to meet for a date on Saturday. It highly recommends a video date, but Corbin insists on meeting for bagels in person.

At first it, seemed fine with me because I could count it as observational research, but now as I wait outside the place, I realize this means I can't just watch, that I'll have to actually do and say things even when I don't know what to do or say.

I debate leaving, but before I can a man shows up wearing a canary-yellow beanie pulled low over his forehead. He shakes my hand and I slowly levitate above my body, watching as the woman in the profile who looks like me but is someone else goes on a date.

We buy coffee and bagels, and when I go to the bathroom to read through some quick research on how to act on a first date, I return to a bite missing from my poppyseed with cream cheese. Did he do that? Did I do that? Who did that?

After the date, the BABES text me to see how it went, and I'm surprised they remembered.

He ate some of my bagel while I was in the bathroom.

It's the only detail that I think might be worth sharing, and my phone buzzes as I walk home:

What??

Wtf

Ur kidding—what did you do?

I think about how I ignored the small nibble and ate the rest of my bagel while we talked about the best dog parks in New York City even though neither of us own dogs. But then I also think about what one of them would have done. What I've read about. There are so many people in the world who do so many exciting things.

I took his bagel out of his hands and took a bite.

I type it. Delete it. Type it again and press send. I don't know why, maybe just to see what happens.

Omfg

Did you really??
You're such a badass

hahahha ur wild!

I fucking love youuuu lol
Wish I had the balls to do something like that

When I get home, I try to add as many details for Vicky as I can. The man. His mannerisms, the way he touched his nose when he was thinking. The blink, beep, bop of messages from the BABES that are almost more fulfilling than the date itself. I try to capture how strange it is to meet someone in real life like that, how strange it is that others want to hear a story about it after.

CHAPTER 13

A blue curtain falls over my Screen, surprising me while I'm in the archives. It floats there, calmly: please change locations to increase productivity. Is this a new feature?

I decide to try it and ask Maps to guide me to a café on the Lower East Side with stickers and graffiti lining the walls of the bathroom. The new productivity tool tells me my levels are high there, so I go back the next day and the next, and each time there's something new on the bathroom wall. It transforms like a communal art project.

Today, I snap a photo of one line an inch from the floor. It says: *this sentence is false.* I surprise myself by sending it to BABES.

Woah Lee you should post that on Home

Srsly . . .
ur super artsy

{Smiley} agree
I wish I took photos like that

Yeah it's really cool

It's interesting to see who I'm becoming in their eyes, how I can shape who I am by sending or saying or doing certain things. I never thought about taking an art class; at the Program it wouldn't have fit in the strict schedule. I don't think they offered art classes outside of The Art of Information, which I took and aced. But now, seeing the BABES' reactions, I wonder if maybe I do have an eye for art, if maybe I've just never given it a chance.

I read somewhere: **Hearts are designed for many things, not just to give away to others**. If people claim to want to marry places, make love to pizza, and be in a relationship with the Oxford comma, then it seems maybe doing what you love is something Vicky should know about, too. In the café, I open more portals, more archives, and dive into this new thread of Love, burying myself in research, in the magical feeling of forward progress, of chasing a goal.

* * *

chris [10:03 A.M.]
u should take an art class

lee [10:03 A.M.]
nah not right now
we don't have time

chris [10:03 A.M.]
theres never time for anything
unless u make it

lee [10:03 A.M.]
yeah maybe
idk
I'll think about it
do u think this picture is good?

I send him the photo from the bathroom. Are the BABES telling me the truth or just being nice? Is it artsy? I do kind of like it. I think it's meant to be sort of hidden, a secret message to the world, even though I'm not quite sure what it means.

chris [10:03 A.M.]
hahahahah
I love that

lee [10:03 A.M.]
why are you laughing then

chris [10:03 A.M.]
ya bc whoever wrote that is clever
also why r u taking photos of a bathroom

lee [10:03 A.M.]
it was cool!

chris [10:03 A.M.]
k fine
it's pretty good
I like it
u do have a good eye for noticing things
Which is why ur a good researcher
But go to a real art class!
seriously

lee [10:03 A.M.]
ill think about it ha
ok back to research
What happened to The MASTER link?

chris [10:03 A.M.]
had to move it, our team is doing a closer analysis
u don't need it do u?

lee [10:03 A.M.]
no but it was nice to see . . .

chris [10:03 A.M.]
lol lee
just focus on ur own stuff ok?

lee [10:03 A.M.]
fine fine

★　★　★

Our Efficiency scores get higher and higher, each one inching closer to a 90 percent. Chris told me they're running tests with Vicky as we speak, and I can't wait to see the results. With the dazzling effect of progress, I work long hours, but I still have the energy to work more. I answer the BABES texts, I write comments on Home, I check my matches on Dating, I ping-pong chats with Chris, and we keep moving. We keep going.

This week the category is Empathy, and I sit a few spaces away from Cat Eyes, Lanky Boy, and Wire Frames in Consultant Row as we tap and search and sort through information. Empathy: **the ability to connect with or understand someone different from you**.

Someone slams a beer down on my desk. When I look up I see Cat Eyes standing there with Lanky Boy and Wire Frames behind her. It occurs to me that this is the second time in the past few months someone has offered me a drink and how nice it is to be offered one, even when I'm not necessarily thirsty. Would this be considered an empathetic gesture?

I take the beer, and we nurse them in silence until Cat Eyes asks everyone how research is going. Fifteen minutes later, we're sitting cross-legged in a circle on the floor with Ted and Nikita.

"I can't tell you guys how glad we are you're on this team," Ted is saying. He looks at us with his big blue eyes and handsome face.

"Yeah," Nikita agrees. Her long hair is pulled back into a braid today and it moves each time she nods her head. "Sometimes, even after long days like this, I just feel so thankful to be doing a job that actually matters, you know?"

We talk about the people we know who are just clocking in and passing the time. I think about Greg and Cindy but don't bring them up. I don't want to admit that my parents are like that.

Then we all lament the constraints of sleep and how we can't work more. Lanky Boy nods but looks nervous. Wire Frames keeps her arms crossed but agrees.

"It's just so important," Ted says. "This company. This project. I mean, if Vicky works—"

"—you mean when she works," Cat Eyes corrects. Ted nods vigorously. His brown hair flops up and down.

"You're right, yeah, exactly. When she works, it will change everything. I really believe that."

Ted tells us about his First Year in his Program—one I've heard of—and how he almost dropped out because of anxiety. In hindsight, after reading through all the materials, he wonders now if maybe he was actually just lonely and didn't know it. Didn't have the word for it. He tells us about how he played on his Program's football team but then he got a concussion. After that, he felt as if no one understood him, or as if every interaction he had fell short of what he wanted it to be.

"If Vicky existed then . . ." He trails off.

Nikita pats his leg with her hand. Ted puts his large arms around all of us and pulls us into an awkward group hug. I can feel exhaustion in the weight of his biceps. It's nice to feel a part of something.

Ted lets go and gets up to grab another beer, and everything that was frozen around our conversation thaws. Nikita pulls out her phone and begins reading us an article about a rainbow that lasted for three days straight.

★ ★ ★

THE NEXT DAY, I ride the subway in a quiet panic, thinking about where it's taking me. I'm on my way to a running date, which according to Veronika is "crazy" and "just so you," whatever that means. She made me wear her running top, the same one I wore for the photo shoot, and helped me put my hair in a high ponytail.

On the train, I check my pocket to make sure I have everything. I did a little research before the date and some Forum on Home said real runners carry fuel with them, so I ordered energy chews to bring. Plus, my ChapStick.

As a lady and her small son get on the train, I pull it out and glide it across my lips. The ads rotate into a roller coaster that dips and dives across the car. It looks like it's promoting some sort of video game, and the son watches with big eyes.

When I get off the train and walk down toward the water, a boy from Dating is waiting nervously on the corner wearing yellow neon shoes. He's tall, all legs and arms. He reminds me of Lanky Boy except with a buzzed head and less sweat. When he sees me, he waves tentatively, and when I wave back, also tentatively, he smiles. *Just be fun,* Veronika said on my way out, but I don't find that advice very specific or helpful.

We run for a while and he talks and talks, which is good because my mind is racing, desperately sorting for the right things to say. I like his stories and try to pay attention, but Veronika's top has zero support and with each step my boobs rise, float, and pause before slingshotting down. I don't think the boy notices, but they grow tender and it's difficult to think about anything else.

After a while, we stop at a viewpoint on the water, my chest throbbing, and I pull the energy gummies out of my pocket and offer him one. He laughs, says his dad tried to make him eat things like this before his races in school. We both pop one in our mouths and it tastes like cinnamon glue. I'm about to pretend I like it, but the boy spits his into his hand and flings it into the water. Something about the gesture feels so free, as if he doesn't care what people think. As if he's just simply being himself. I spit mine in my hand and fling it, too, and we look at each other and laugh. A real laugh that unties the knot in my rib cage.

Across the water, the skyscrapers in Manhattan shine like crystals, the sky a perfect, cloudless blue behind them. He asks me about my job, and for some reason I tell him about Veronika's as if it's my own. It seems easier than trying to explain what I'm doing.

I tell him the very little I know about sales, about the products she brings home to test out. He seems genuinely interested and keeps asking questions, but I find each one traps me more in my own lie. We talk about our families and New York. And I can't seem to tell him one true thing about myself. I tell him I'm from here, that I'm really close with my mom, that I've run four marathons. The boy is excited by this and tells me about his marathon times, and I make up some he seems really impressed with. The truth is, I have wanted to run one, but the training would have taken up too much time at the Program.

We begin running again and I can't seem to answer a single question accurately, not because I don't want to but because I don't know what to say. To avoid falling even deeper into his questions, I stop to fake a charley horse, but then my calf really does begin to twitch and crumple. I can't put any pressure on it, and the boy is concerned, asks me if I've ever had one before. I admit to him that I run a lot but I've never experienced anything like this.

As the pain crawls through and strangles my calf, I admit to him that I've never run a marathon. That I'm not from New York. That my mom and I hardly speak; in fact, I've never even called her "mom," can't even remember why or how it became that way.

He seems bummed but not shocked, as if maybe this kind of thing happens to him all the time. I wonder how many people have lied to him, how many times he's shown up and been completely honest, completely open, only to be deceived and disappointed.

I don't usually lie, why would I now? The thing is, it didn't even feel like lying. It felt like choosing. I was just sifting, sorting, selecting information and spitting it out based on who I thought he would want me to be. It's as if I can see what I should be in this moment, see what I should say, what people online recommend that I say, but then when I actually do it, everything feels disjointed.

"I'm sorry," I say. "I just don't know how to do this."

"Neither do I," he says. "Neither does anyone. But at least you could try."

I am, I want to say, but all I can do is wince in pain. I think he may leave me there, but instead he picks me up and carries me on his bony back to the train, where he drops me off on a bench and, without saying goodbye, walks away with his buzzed alienlike head facing down, shoulders curved in. I follow his figure all the way down the platform and up the stairs, but he doesn't look back. When the BABES text asking how it went, I don't answer right away this time.

CHAPTER 14

S ame clunky desk. Same worn wood pushed against old brick. Same half-empty wineglass. Except this time, the apartment is full of sun.

It's morning and Janet's getting dressed when she hears the alert she would know anywhere. One she's been hearing more frequently now. She rushes to the Screen, one arm in and one arm out of a T-shirt, to see another Failure.

Janet feels no remorse taking what these companies leave behind— their hard work, their findings, their data—and using whatever they can for the Vicky project. But she has to admit it's strange to receive them so quickly. Down to four from fifteen, way faster than she'd projected.

Janet drags her arm through the shirt and pulls it over her head, patting her bob into place. This is good news, really. With each project that fails, Vicky is closer to success. They'll get more resources, more support. The only problem is that the Government keeps tightening its grip, asking for increased documentation and evidence that the project will work. Janet can hardly do anything without having to note it. She and Toru don't like to work on such a short leash.

Janet opens the Failure summary, watching it expand across her Screen. She grabs the phone to call Toru, but just as it begins to ring, she sees it. A name she wasn't expecting to encounter. Not here. Not ever. One she hasn't thought about in a long time.

Janet hangs up and sets the phone down. She rubs her eyes and opens them again to see it there still. Staring back at her.

Tina McCallister.

Her former professor. The one she'd been searching for the day she met Toru. The one she'd looked up to most, who had inspired her to study leadership and operations in the first place. The same one who got her removed from the Program all those years ago.

Janet remembers walking down the hall to their lab late at night. She wanted to put some final touches on her booth for the conference, but when the door slid open she was shocked to find people inside. Two figures tangled together.

Sprinting back to her dorm, Janet splashed cold water on her face over and over again, took a sleeping drink, and woke up the next morning ready to pretend nothing happened.

But after her first class, she was called to the Dean's office and expelled for falsifying information. It was just days before the most important conference of her career. Weeks before graduation. The Dean showed her the accusation, the proof, and as soon Janet saw it, she knew she'd been framed. Professor McCallister had too much to lose. An affair? With a student? It seemed so cliché. It seemed so beneath the person Janet respected most. The person who told her she could be great. But as soon as Janet saw something she shouldn't have seen, Tina couldn't risk it, could she? She made Janet disappear.

Janet stares at the name on the Screen and laughs. What a silly thing. What a silly, little, insignificant thing that happened so long ago. Is she glad to see that Tina's team has failed while hers is still going? No, Janet couldn't care less about what that woman is doing. It was so long ago. And besides, she's accomplished so much without Tina's help. Without that stupid Program's support.

Janet stands to straighten a painting on the brick wall in front of her. It was off by just the slightest, but now it's perfect. She looks out the window and takes a deep breath. Even though she's here, looking out at this city, she can still feel what it was like to be back at the Program. She can still feel the numbing shock of it all, of realizing how disposable she was. Not just to her mentor, but to friends who never even reached out.

Memory can be so powerful, arriving in the body even when the mind rejects it. It's why Janet likes to know the background of everyone she hires, the best way to know the core of a person. Because even though she's here, touching this brick, this windowsill, the pain of feeling insignificant and helpless still faintly punches her in the chest.

Janet's phone lights up with a call from Toru. A photo she took years ago when they were in Singapore for business floats on the Screen. It's one of her favorites because even though his mouth is full of street food, his eyes are smiling.

She picks it up and can immediately hear the energy of the Tech Hub through the line. Toru begins talking right away. She can picture him pacing back and forth, and welcomes his voice, letting it pull her back to this project, this reality. Janet tells him another Failure came through and sends it over so they can go over it together.

She wonders how long it will take for him to notice her old professor's name. Toru's the only one who knows what really happened, the only one who was there for her, and she's sure that when he sees it, he'll ask if she's okay. He'll ask to grab a drink.

A small part of Janet wants him to insist on it, even though she knows she'll brush it off. It really was so long ago, she'll say. And look at us now! Everyone else, her old friends, they're on normal, traditional, low-ceiling trajectories. And Tina McCallister? Her company failed!

But as Toru reads through the Failure, he doesn't notice. He doesn't ask her how she feels or remind her how stupid the Programs are. Instead, he dives into the data that Tina's company left behind. He talks strategy. For him, it's business as usual, and when they hang up, Janet knows she should feel thankful that she can just let it all go again. Bury it. But as she pulls on her boots to head to the office, where Ted, Nikita, the others will be today, something doesn't sit right. The past still hovers in her calves, behind her eyes.

Toru should have said something, right? Did he forget? He couldn't have. Maybe he'd seen Tina's name and didn't want to stir up painful memories for Janet. Maybe he was being respectful and giving her space.

That's probably it. Besides, he gets this way when they're in the middle of a project, singularly focused. She knows this about him, she loves this about him. It's nothing personal.

When Janet gets to their small, wonderfully chaotic office, she says hello to everyone and then shuts herself in the glass conference room. Her to-do list is long, but she has a hard time concentrating.

Instead, she paces back and forth the way Toru usually does. She paces and thinks, something bubbling up inside her. She'd all but blocked that period out of her life, but it still feels unfair. It reminds her of why she thinks Programs are inflated with false promises, preying on the vulnerability of young people. Even now, decades later, she can remember what it felt like to have a path so solid ripped out from underneath her. Not that she would want it anymore.

That's what rattles her now, this very moment: even though she wouldn't go back and change anything, she still feels the sadness that lingers long after a person's first sting of betrayal.

Janet glances out of the room and sees the Consultants, the four left, anyway, working in their row, all of them doing their best to make this project work. She vows to pay closer attention to her team. It's strange to know something about them that they may not even know about themselves.

She thinks back to when she and Toru first saw The Loneliness Report. The concept was shocking, of course. Had she heard of it? No. She'd read about the creation of the Emotional Index in school and hadn't thought much about it since. When they saw the report, heard of the secret assignment, they thought of it as a challenge to be conquered. A problem to be solved.

But now, studying these people in front of her who've been affected by it in one way or another, Janet can't help but feel like she needs to do something to care for them. The way she wasn't cared for.

She should at least do more team bonding, or one-on-ones. She can learn more about the affliction to help guide and nudge their work. She can't tell them that they're lonely, that could ruin the project altogether, but maybe she can find a way to support them more, even the one on the end.

Janet's eyes land on Lee and linger. The tug of annoyance she felt before is stronger, a repulsion that brings acid to her throat. She remembers sitting in this very room with Toru listening to the strange, mousy girl talk about her studies, how she's ready to help make a difference, how she's dedicated, how good her training has been, how perfect her Program is, how lucky she is to have such a mentor who supports her curiosity.

It hits her suddenly, sharply, why she dislikes the girl so much. As she watches Lee deep in the zone on the other side of the glass, fingers flying across the Screen, Janet's reminded of someone she used to know. Someone she used to be.

PERFORMANCE SUMMARY—FAILURE

Company Name: Central Construction JJM

Company Founder(s): Mann John, Bijou Johnson, Tina McCallister

Brief Synopsis of Project:
> We took 25 apartment buildings in 15 different locations across the country and fully redesigned them to become engaging community spaces wherein people who live by themselves can also connect with others.

Employee Count: 104

Detailed Explanation of Failure:
> 0/10 of our buildings crossed the minimum threshold of a 1.5 connection score that signifies interaction needed to create community. Less than 30% of events were attended and only 15% of tenants surveyed said they "felt connected to neighbors." One out of every four individuals who lived in our buildings for an extended period of time (3–4 months) with signs of loneliness remained lonely, despite our modern designs.

Did you discover anything about Loneliness or The Loneliness Report you think necessary to flag immediately?

> We are surprised at the inability of those to connect, even when put in an environment ripe with opportunity to do so. Please use our information however you need and let us know if we can assist any other companies. All of our employees are very concerned and have offered to work pro bono should any other company need our skill sets.

Do you believe any of your findings could help another company? If so, please expand.

> Yes. We collected significant data on the patterns of communication, connection, or lack thereof between neighbors and those in close quarters. There may be other useful material about living habits, areas for potential engagement, and the correlation between time spent at home and time spent outside.

Thank you for your collaboration. We greatly appreciate your service.

CHAPTER 15

The productivity curtain keeps falling on me at random times, and while it used to be nice, now it's becoming counterproductive. I find I'm rushing to new working spaces at odd intervals, and today I'm sitting in a new café, hoping I'll be able to collect some observational research.

People come in and out, hide behind privacy sliders, or shush each other, but there's no empathy in any of that, is there?

I'm getting antsy and consider messaging Chris to see how the Vicky tests are going when I notice a man in a navy suit chatting on the phone outside, gesturing with his hands. The way he carries himself, shoulders back yet relaxed: He looks happy. Like the world is his. Have I ever felt like that? Stood like that? Spoken on the phone so casually?

He hangs up and opens the door, and an idea crosses from my mind to my limbs, making me slide off the stool and tap him on the shoulder before I've fully thought it through.

"Hi, excuse me, sorry to bother you—"

"Sorry, I don't have time to sign up or donate right now."

"Oh, no, I'm not—I just—I just want to get you a drink. I've heard that's a nice thing to do."

He looks up from his phone, his eyes a glossy brown, and I try to explain.

"You see, you look different from me, and for work, I need to learn how to understand someone different," I continue quickly, thinking of what I read about Empathy. I try to smile my friendliest smile, a smile I've seen plastered all over Home.

"Different from you?" He raises his eyebrows at me, and then I realize how that sounds. How he's Black and I'm white.

"Oh, no, I'm sorry, I was more thinking about how serious you look in a suit. I've never worn one in my life. And you make serious phone calls. You look confident, like you could easily run a meeting or something in front of a room full of people."

I scrunch the bottom of my T-shirt in my hands.

"And you couldn't?" he says, and, finally, he smiles. Is he teasing me? "Also, don't let suits fool you, because anyone can put one on."

His watch lights up and he reads a message on it quickly. I open my mouth and then close it. It's harder than I thought to get someone a drink. How did the guy at the party do it so easily? And Cat Eyes? What am I doing that's making it so complicated?

"Were you watching me outside?" he says, turning back to me. A man working behind us clears his throat to let us know we're being too loud.

"No!"

He raises his eyebrows at me again.

"Well, kind of. But I was just sitting here and the stool faces the window and you were outside."

"Okay, so wait, tell me why you want to get me coffee again?" His eyes betray his amusement with this whole thing. I'd like to grab my backpack and leave, but instead I remember the yoga instructors from the Body category and take a breath.

"I'm studying empathy and have observed that getting someone a drink is a nice thing to do and could foster connection. So I want to test it out."

He thinks about it for a moment. His watch lights up again. He glances at it.

"That sounds kind of contrived, no?"

I shrug. The tile has a faded arc in it where the door swings open and closed. My sneakers are worn, yellowing. I study them while I feel his eyes studying me.

"Okay, let's do it," he says, surprising me, and when I look up he's smiling playfully. He steps toward the counter. "What do you like?"

"Black coffee."

He taps the Screen and orders two.

"But wait, what are you—"

"My treat." His voice is low, professional, and I watch helplessly as he scans his finger to pay.

"Wait, I was supposed to get you a drink."

"Yeah, and I got you one instead," he says. "So, what do you need to know about me for this . . . study? What do you want to understand? I have until the coffee is ready, then I've got to catch a train."

He doesn't seem much older than me, maybe early thirties. Smooth skin, short hair. Strong shoulders filling a blue button-down like the ones I've seen on the models on the subway ads. I open my mouth and hesitate. How do you tell someone you want to know everything? Behind him, I see a machine spit out the first cup and shoot liquid into it.

"Um, well, do you . . ."

The machine finishes the first cup and starts filling the second.

"Do you like who you are?" I blurt out as two coffees slide over the counter.

"Whoa, is that how you get to know someone?" He laughs and hands me one; the tips of his fingers brush mine, sending a small shock through me.

"Sometimes I do, sometimes I don't," he says, taking a sip. "But I've got to run. If you want to talk more . . ."

He reaches in his pocket, takes out a brown leather wallet, worn at the corners, and pulls out a small white card, handing it to me.

"Is this—"

"—a business card? Yes. They do exist."

I flip it over in my hand. I've never seen one in real life, only in archives.

"Yeah, we're very different. Worlds apart," I say, and he laughs.

"I know. Vintage, right? I like the feel of them."

He nods at me in a way that is somehow cool and steps out the door. I watch his tall frame move down the street and out of sight. As soon as he's gone, I exit the shop casually, look both ways, chug my coffee, toss the cup in a trash bin, and speed-walk home.

At the wobbly white kitchen table, I slip my Screen out of my backpack and jab it a few times to wake it up. Pulling the business card out of my pocket, I run my finger across the small letters. It's strange to hold another person's name in my hands. I try to breathe, to slow down, so I can record the experience for Vicky, but it's fading quickly, everything that felt so true, so important about it: lost in the tingling of my brain.

> *Man buys coffee.*
> *Man hangs up phone. Comes inside and buys coffee.*
> *Tall man with eyes. Coffee.*
> *Man in suit tells me I could wear a suit.*
> *Man in suit laughs at me.*

Nothing is right. Nothing captures it the way it was. I should have recorded it on the spot. I should have paid more attention to the important parts, but what were the important parts?

Footsteps sound down the hall. Veronika bursts into the apartment and immediately begins to speak. An undercover operation is taking place at her office, and she's convinced her work frenemy is behind it. Someone is programming notes onto the to-do list on the communal fridge with personal details about others in the office. No one knows if the scribbled secrets are true or not. Last week a note said: *Someone is wearing a polka dot thong they stole.* Today the note said: *Someone on this floor cheated on their fiancé with someone else on this floor.* Things are escalating, and Veronika is afraid she'll be targeted next.

"What secrets do you have?" I ask.

"That's the problem!" she says, throwing her hands up, knocking an empty cup over. "I don't even know what I'm hiding, and I probably won't know what the secrets are until they're revealed!"

Veronika pulls off her sweater and throws it on the counter. She spots the business card on the table next to me and picks it up, flipping it over in her hands.

"What's this?" she says, glad to be distracted.

I try to explain that I'm studying empathy, but she only hears the part about the man in the suit.

"Was he cute?" she asks.

"I don't know," I say.

"What do you mean you don't know? He gave you his card!" she says. "Are you going to email him?"

"No!"

"So he wasn't cute?"

"No! I mean, yes. He had beautiful hands."

"What?" she says, cornering me.

"I don't know. I'm not interested in him or anything."

Veronika laughs, a half chuckle, half snort.

"Beautiful hands? Are you kidding me?"

I refuse to respond.

"Some random, good-looking man who happens to have a rare, fancy business card buys you coffee and you're . . . not interested?"

"He was just being nice," I say, taking the card back and sliding it into the front pocket of my backpack so she'll stop thinking about it.

"No one is ever just nice," she says. "Email him."

★ ★ ★

ST. PATRICK'S DAY LANDS on a Thursday this year, and the BABES slowly trickle into our apartment to get ready for a night out. "What's going on?" I ask Veronika, and she drags me to the bathroom, where I sit dutifully on the toilet while she curls my hair, a faint smell of burning in the air. She nods along to a story one of the others is telling.

"Sounds like he's an ass!" she yells. I find myself nodding in agreement even though I can't hear a thing over the music. Veronika finishes and sends me to the kitchen to grab Zuri, who wants to borrow some green glitter. All of us have it sprinkled on our cheeks.

I look around the kitchen and try and repeat everyone's name in my head. Karen is setting up gold plastic shot glasses on the table. She's short, with platinum-blond highlights, and everything she does is tinged with intensity, even drinking. She looks up, scanning the room to count the heads, then turns back to the shot glasses and adds a few more.

There are two Olivias. One goes by Liv and the other by Olivia, so in the chat it's easy to know who's who, but here, seeing them in person again, I can't remember if Liv is the frail bookish one with freckles and Olivia is the friendly one who keeps turning up the music or vice versa.

"So, Lee, have you been working on your photography lately?" one of them asks as she hands me a green cup.

"What?"

"You know, those cool photos of the bathroom art you sent that chat. You're like a real photographer!"

"Oh, no. Those are just for fun."

"Just for fun! You're so modest." Liv or Olivia laughs, and returns to scrolling through her phone. She's liking pictures and responding to videos from others getting ready for St. Patrick's Day, too. People from her office bought tiny green hats to wear, and she's bummed we didn't think of buying some.

"But we have sparkles?" I offer. She doesn't seem to hear.

"Okay, time for shots!" Karen yells. She's finished lining up the mini glasses and poured tequila into each one. Everyone starts chanting, "Shots! Shots! Shots!" Veronika and Zuri come running from the bathroom, making a show of sliding in on their socks and almost falling.

"Karen, you poured an extra," Veronika points out.

Karen frowns.

"Well, someone can take two."

"Lee should. She's the wild one!" Zuri says, and Veronika agrees. What are they talking about? Are they thinking about the bagel-bite incident? The picture I took in the bathroom? I feel like I'm the opposite of wild, the opposite of interesting. What have I been doing that makes them think otherwise?

I shake my head, but a hand is already sliding the shots in my direction. We hold them up, and I swallow the first and then the second as fast as I can. It feels like fire scraping my esophagus.

Then we take turns posing for pictures together. When we finally arrive at an old Irish bar, we have to wait in line. Through the window, I can see people carrying pints of beer across the hay-covered floor.

"See, I told you this place is authentic," Veronika says to us.

While we wait, everyone checks their phones. I look at mine and see most of the girls have posted a photo or video from tonight on Home. Sifting through them all a few times, I notice that not a single post has me in it.

I suddenly feel stupid in my sparkles, embarrassed by the small specks of them in the reflection of the window.

As everyone chats and giggles around me, I stand in the back wondering what's funny, wondering what I'm really doing here. But before I can turn around and head home to the comfort of my Screen, to the place where I belong, the line moves, and we're pushed inside where I can't hear a thing. People wobble drunk through the wet hay in the thick, stubborn air, eyes wide and unfocused.

Veronika shoves her way through the crowd to a space near the bar in the back, where none of us can talk to each other because we're standing right beneath a speaker blaring Irish folk songs.

CHAPTER 16

T he glass conference room reminds me of a terrarium. Or a fish tank. Bright lights shine down from above, and inside time slows. Meetings morph from one hour to half a day, sometimes full days, especially now that our research is trending upward and we're getting Vicky what it needs. When we're in the glass conference room, nothing matters except our discussions, our research, and the daunting blue graphs rotating on the wall.

Today, two people I've never seen before sit inside of it. A man who sucks on a small e-cigarette every few minutes and a woman with bright pink hair. Small tattoos cover her hands and neck.

I study them through the glass, peering over Cat Eyes and Wire Frames at the other end of Consultant Row.

"I think they're from the Tech Team," Ted whispers from behind us. We all turn to look at him.

"Why are they here?" I ask.

"No clue." He shrugs, then answers a phone call and begins looping around the office.

I try to focus on my research, but every few minutes I look up to see the strangers in the conference room, exchange a look with Cat Eyes, then glance at the elevator across the office. Are Toru and Janet meeting with them? If some of the Tech Team is here, does that mean Chris will be coming in, too? I wonder if he'll be taller than me, if he'll wear a T-shirt or a button-up, if he'll smile more than he frowns.

In my peripheral, I see the man in the glass room get up. I turn back to my Screen and pretend I'm busy.

"Morning," he says as he passes our row of desks.

"Morning," we mumble back. I spot something red on his shirt as he makes his way to the kitchen.

Who is he? Has he been helping Chris run tests with Vicky? Are they working? They have to be working. We've been scoring so high. We've been in a rhythm. When he walks past us again, I swivel my chair and try to think of how to talk to him.

"What's on your shirt?" I blurt out, but the question seems silly, because now that I'm facing him it's obvious the red spot is a small heart cut out of felt and pinned to his pocket.

"Oh, this?" he says, looking down as if he's forgotten it's there. "It's a heart."

In one of our random chats, Chris told me about someone on the Tech Team who's an artist when they aren't coding. I think he was trying to convince me to have more hobbies. Is this the artist? Is this what they do? Make you look twice at things to see if they matter?

"Oh, cool," I say as nonchalantly as I can. "I like it."

He smiles and sucks on an e-cig.

"Thanks, me, too."

The man walks back to the room, leaving a vague smell of cucumber in his wake. I watch as he brings coffee to the woman with pink hair.

"Is that a heart shaped like a heart? Wow, I love shapes!" Cat Eyes says in a high-pitched voice when he's gone. Wire Frames and Lanky Boy stifle laughs next to her. I put my headphones on and ignore them.

Half an hour later, the elevator dings and Toru dashes through the office maze wearing a disheveled button-up. Janet strides gracefully behind him in a crisp black jumpsuit. They look out of place weaving through the apocalyptic collection of desks and chairs in the office.

"Good morning, team," Janet says, breezing past us. "Can we snag you for a quick meeting?"

We grab our things and hustle into the room behind them, unsure where to sit now that the strangers are in some of our regular spots.

Janet slides her Screen out of her purse and Toru paces in the back. Everyone is silent, assessing the energy in the room. Is it good, bad, somewhere in between?

"You may have noticed we weren't in the office yesterday," she says, and I try to remember what day it was. I don't think any of us were in the office yesterday.

"We were reviewing tests of Vicky."

"With Chris and the Tech Team," Toru interjects.

"Yes," Janet confirms. "Which is why we asked some of them to come in today and walk us through their findings. Chelsea, Eric, thanks for coming in."

Finally! Chris mentioned they were running some tests. I'm excited to see the results, to see how we're doing.

"Okay, so let's hop right in," Janet continues. I'm shocked she doesn't talk in circles, or make us do some sort of team bonding exercise. She smiles with that same lippy smile, and I can't help but feel she's hiding something still.

"First of all, we wanted to congratulate you all for your hard work. The tests are performing extremely well," she says.

A swell of pride warms me from inside. I knew our research was good. It had to be. I've been working so hard. I exchange knowing looks with Cat Eyes and Lanky Boy and Wire Frames. I think about when we all drank beers in a circle. Was that a week ago or two? Time keeps changing shape.

"Eric, Chelsea, can you walk everyone through what you found?"

We all turn to look at the strangers sitting there so casually.

"So, as J said, we've been monitoring Vicky closely—" Eric begins slowly.

"—how it learns, what it's missing, where the gaps are," Chelsea chimes in. They speak in a rhythm, finishing each other's thoughts, and I wonder how long they've worked together. If they chose to be here or if they're still finishing their Placement requirement like me.

"When we started testing a few months ago—"

"—Vicky was performing pretty poorly. It was learning, but just regurgitating answers. It had so much information, but none of it meant anything. The algorithm was simply a hodgepodge of data points," Eric explains.

"Hodgepodge, nice word," Chelsea says. They fist-pound, and I wish they'd just get to the point. They seem so relaxed, as if this were an ordinary meeting on an ordinary day about ordinary matters, when really it's the opposite. My career, my reputation, and everything that comes with it is relying on this company.

I watch Janet at the front, her foot rotating slowly, ankle cracking every third turn. Toru moves in and out of my peripheral vision.

"But recently, as J mentioned, Vicky has taken a turn," Eric says, and I sit up in my seat. They explain how over the past few months, the AI has started to gain traction with all the data we've been adding. It started performing exponentially better—forming complete answers, holding long conversations, adapting to different test users, and showing concern for their individual lives.

"The users from recent tests said they felt moderately understood after engaging with Vicky," Chelsea says cheerfully.

"Guys, can you get to the point?" Toru says from the back. "They don't need to understand everything. They just need to execute the new plan."

Janet's foot stops rotating.

"Toru, I think understanding all of this is important if we're going to be successful," she says. "If we're going to do this together. As a team."

I watch as they speak to each other with their eyes. Toru finally loses and looks away first.

"Please," Janet says to Chelsea and Eric, gesturing to them to continue.

"Okay, so basically," Chelsea says, gesturing with her hands. They're covered in those beautiful slim tattoos. "From studying everything closely, we've seen that the AI has a significant amount of data, but it's struggling to understand it the way a human might."

"Exactly," Eric says, exhaling another cloud of mist. "Which is why we need to give it access to an individual, to observe and learn how they process the world."

"Yep, we think this could help Vicky figure out the immeasurables," Chelsea says, tucking a strand of pink hair behind her ear. "The things we can't define, at least not yet. The moment a piece of data becomes not just data, but a meaningful experience."

"Immeasurables, nice," Eric says. He and Chelsea fist-bump again.

"Wait, what?" Ted says. His all-American face wrinkles in confusion.

"You want to give Vicky access to all the data from one person?" Nikita says, tapping her long nails on the table. "To teach it what we don't know how to?"

"Yep," Chelsea and Eric say at the same time.

"Even though we can't pinpoint exactly how to get the AI to think the way a human does, what we can do is give it access to a person so that it can teach itself," Eric continues.

My eyes go back and forth between Toru, Janet, and the developers. Something Masha tried to teach me a long time ago surfaces, becoming clear even though I didn't understand it at the time. He said the only way to solve a problem you've never encountered is to try a solution you've never thought of before. Good researchers are detailed and studious and meticulous, he said, but great researchers take risks.

"Okay, so who?" Nikita asks.

She's read my mind. This person will be crucial. We'll have to think carefully about how to select them. It should be someone who experiences a lot each day, a person like Veronika or one of the BABES, who seem to do and see and go through so much all the time.

"Good question," Chelsea says, and starts sorting through something on her Screen. She pushes Toru's projection of The Loneliness Report off the wall and flings her own Screen up there. "We actually already have someone. We saw something happening in the data. A pattern we couldn't ignore."

She opens the Data Program and taps into a section of it with rows of rainbow research, our research. It's The MASTER link! I recognize it instantly. But this time it looks a bit different, spotted with annotations and code.

"We assigned everyone who added data a color so we could keep track of what information was working. Obviously, Vicky needs a lot, so at first, she was processing everything we converted."

Chelsea scrolls through the information: a beautiful array of pink, blue, purple, green, red, orange, and gray. The gray data must be from the deals Ted and Nikita are making. There's a ton of it at first, but as Chelsea scrolls, it dwindles. Then, the large strands of pink and red disappear in an instant. That must have been when Shrill Laugh Girl and Finance Guy left. One of them was the neon pink? From the way they acted, the questions they asked, I never would have suspected they'd be ahead of us, collecting observational research before Chris requested it.

Research flies past, and the other colors braid together until they slowly fade and there are small wisps of blue and green and orange and gray mixed in with a large wall of purple.

"While Vicky is accepting and learning from all the information, it's become clear she's gravitating toward one source first, before processing the others."

The data flows so quickly across the wall it blurs. All of it purple now. My purple.

"So, as you can see, Vicky already decided for us," Eric says.

The glass room is silent as the information continues to move until it hits the edge and there's no more data left. My heart pumps in my chest.

"Of course, it's a big task. Monumental, really. We haven't tested the strategy, so we don't know the full extent of how complicated it can get," Eric continues.

"But we'd be monitoring full time," Chelsea adds.

"Who's the purple?" Ted asks.

"Lee," Toru says.

"Wait," I say, trying to process everything. "The data I'm putting into the system isn't about me. It's about the specific categories Chris has been giving us. Vicky is probably just gravitating toward it because it's the most detailed and in depth."

Cat Eyes snorts and Wire Frames crosses her arms.

"The data you put in the system may not be about you," Chelsea explains. "But you're the one curating it."

"Yeah," Eric adds. "The research you collected reflects how you think about the world, and what you see as interesting or important. In a way, it shows your mind. And clearly Vicky is drawn to it."

I shake my head. I want to argue, but my head is spinning. I think about the running date, how I had no clue what to say or how to act so I just made things up. And about St. Patrick's Day. How I tried to fit in, but even when it seemed to be going okay, no one posted a single photo with me. A wave of shame washes over me. There's no way this will work. How can I help Vicky see what it's like to experience the world, to process it, when I'm not even sure how myself?

"But, well," I try to explain. "My strengths as a researcher don't really transfer to—"

"Lee, that's enough," Toru cuts in. "You saw the data."

I grip the table tighter. Something solid. Something true to what it should be. An object in space.

"You've got this," Nikita says, leaning forward in her chair. "Think about how much effort you've put in so far. About how much all of us have dedicated to this."

"Yeah, and we'll continue working by your side," a small scratchy voice adds. I turn to see Wire Frames. Her deep hazel eyes behind the glasses. I forgot what she sounded like.

My brain is tearing itself apart. A mash of Masha's advice, *stay disciplined, stay committed, don't get distracted* and what I've studied, **the best researchers adapt when necessary**. Words I overheard at the diner, *take care of yourself,* and those I read in archives, **the only life worth living is a life you live for others**.

How do you stay disciplined but also adapt? How do you take care of yourself but also sacrifice for others? If this is what everyone thinks we should do, why do I feel like it's so wrong?

"I don't . . . I'm not the right person," I try one last time, looking around the table at everyone who's looking back. Hopeful, expectant, desperate, excited, stressed. What if I let them all down?

"Nonsense. You're going to do great, Lee," Ted says cheerily, but I don't think he understands what I mean. He walks over to high-five me, but when I don't react, he punches me playfully in the shoulder instead.

Eric gives me a thumbs-up. Chelsea repeats something about monitoring closely. Nikita gives me a hug. Wire Frames seems to have withdrawn into the shadows again, and Lanky Boy is sitting there dripping sweat.

At the front, Janet crosses her arms and smiles encouragingly, her face hardly moving even when her lips do, but there's something else there in her eyes. Concern? Anger? Disappointment? Cat Eyes finally looks up from her hands and nods, nudging me to just accept it. A random piece of research falls into my head about the meaning of a team: **people who will drive full speed ahead with you toward a goal**.

I don't understand what's happening. I don't understand why Vicky wants my information. I don't understand how this new plan will work.

But what I do know is that if this is the only way to create what we set out to do, if this is the only way to make sure we succeed, then I have to try it.

"Okay," I hear myself say. "I'll do it."

Whatever we need, whatever it takes: I'll do it.

PART THREE

CHAPTER 17

A package arrives at my door, a small, perfect cube. I slice through the edges to see exactly what I was told would be inside: a watch.

Slick, black, smooth. It looks just like the ones people wear to act as an extension of their phones or Screens. But this one is different. This one is programmed just for me.

I peel it out of the box and feel how light it is. Small and fragile, like a sleeping salamander. Eric and Chelsea synced my accounts so I can use it normally. I think they want me to forget what the watch will really be doing. They want me to forget it will collect all my data: physical reactions, decision-making, emotional patterns, cognitive processes. It will convert it all for Vicky so it can see how a human processes the world around them.

Janet and Toru sent over a revised Agreement early this morning, and within seconds of returning it, my phone rang. Janet's name popped up, making me nervous. Does she still not trust me? Has there been a mistake?

When I answered, she asked if I needed anything, anything at all. I don't think so, I said. And then she mumbled something I could hardly hear. It sounded like: Are you sure you want to do this?

"Excuse me?" I asked, not sure if I'd heard her right.

"Okay, great, well, we're here if you need us. Good luck," Janet said, and hung up. It was a strange call. Short. Stilted. One that still reverberates in my head now as I hold the watch in my hand. I really hope they know what they're doing. I really hope this works.

I slide the watch on, and the small rectangle is shockingly cold against my skin. The rubbery black band hugs my wrist perfectly. It fits so well that under any other circumstance, I might forget it's there.

I hold my breath, waiting for something to happen. Waiting to feel different. My heart beats quickly, my palms are moist. An alert slides across the watch and I jump. But when I look closer, it's just from Home. Apparently, one of the Chads of the world is eating Cheetos for breakfast.

I scrutinize the watch, unsure of what to do. Unsure what I should be thinking and feeling or trying to think and feel.

I practice using it to send my first message.

lee [9:28 A.M.]
ok, what now?

chris [9:28 A.M.]
u got it?

lee [9:29 A.M.]
yeah
using it now

chris [9:29 A.M.]
how's it feel?

lee [9:29 A.M.]
it fits

chris [9:30 A.M.]
ok
and how about u?

lee [9:30 A.M.]
what?

chris [9:30 A.M.]
how do u feel?

lee [9:30 A.M.]
fine
i just don't know what I should do?

chris [9:31 A.M.]
just live
don't think about it

lee [9:31 A.M.]
that's not very specific

chris [9:31 A.M.]
u just have to go about ur day as normal
don't overthink it
and im here for u if you have any questions
ok?

lee [9:32 A.M.]
ok

I look at the small Screen on my watch where the words are frozen. I know Chris is staring at his Screen, too, or at least, I imagine he is. And in a strange way, it feels like maybe we're looking at each other.

I go about my day, lining my stuff up on the white wobbly table, making coffee, sipping it. At ten, Chris assigns me a new category for the week: Entertainment. He's probably only including me in the assignment to keep everything as normal as possible while I'm being tracked.

I make a second coffee and then try to dive into research. But each time I place my hands on the glossy surface of the Screen, I see the watch on my wrist and my stomach folds in on itself.

★   ★   ★

A DAY FLOATS by and I'm still at the table in the kitchen, staring out the window, beating myself up. What used to feel important—swimming through portals, driving toward discovery—suddenly seems so small. I add a few tidbits about Entertainment to the Data Program, but I can't get in a flow. Is sitting here like this really helping Vicky see what it's like to live? Maybe I just need to leave the apartment. But what kind of strategy is that? Just walk around and wait for things to happen to me?

I force myself to go outside anyway, telling Maps to take me somewhere interesting. It guides me to a store filled with leafy grain dishes. Eating one quickly against the side of a building, shoveling the food into my mouth, I splash yellow salad dressing on my white T-shirt, and then I walk home.

Eric said I'm not supposed to know how the watch works in case it changes the way I act. Chelsea agreed, tucking a strand of pink hair behind her ear.

But when someone tells you not to think about something, all you can do is just that: think about it. Especially someone like me. I can't help but inspect the watch and try and figure out how it's working; how to act, how to be, in order for this project to succeed.

How is it accessing my data? How are Chris and Janet and Toru testing to see if the information I provide is useful? Does being frustrated with, or embarrassed by, a yellow stain in the shape of a Big Dipper mean anything? Anything at all?

★ ★ ★

AT HOME THAT night, an alert on my phone tells me I'm anxious. No shit, I think, and tap to order the vitamins it says will decrease the adrenaline and cortisol in my system.

As I wait for them to be dropped off, I begin to understand why Masha felt so strongly about loneliness. Why he pushed to make it disappear. It's easy to address emotions like anxiety that we can trace in the body. My Health app senses it and suggests a solution right away. But if loneliness is as complex as they say it is, it makes sense that he'd side with those who wanted to erase it. It would be easier not to deal with it at all. It's just too bad that it's appearing anyway, that it's surfacing in people even if they don't understand what it is.

I take the vitamins as soon as they arrive, and as they weave into my bloodstream, causing a calmness to settle in, it occurs to me that I've been approaching this project all wrong. That in my shock, in my stress, I've forgotten my skill set as a researcher.

Now that I'm finally thinking clearly, I open up Search and type: how to feel alive. Millions of results pop up. **Sing at the top of your lungs**, one page says. I skim the list. **Listen to your gut**, advises another.

But what is my gut saying? I sit still for a long time to try and feel it. The gut. My stomach grumbles and my foot itches, but I don't feel anything special or tingly or thrilling. In fact, I feel nothing at all, so I draft a message to Chris about boredom to see if that's something I should add to the Data Program. It could go in the Entertainment category.

But as I'm writing to Chris, I feel it. A flicker of myself wanting to do something different from what I'm doing. Is this my gut?

I delete my message and type a new one asking Chris if he wants to grab a coffee this week. I send it before I can think too much. Before I can change my mind. He responds instantly and says the way I wrote the question is exactly how his ex-girlfriend phrased it before she broke up with him.

I drag my hands down my face. Of course, the first thing I do is wrong. I should have researched how people ask other people to do things.

Ping.

Peeking between my fingers, I see he's sent a smiley face. Was he joking? Is it funny to be broken up with?

Ping. Free Tuesday, would that work?

Ping. Don't drink coffee though. Gets me swirling too much, you know? Like life is speeding by at a million miles an hour and my heart will burst from my chest. Can we do lunch instead?

With each response, my watch lights up. Is it possible it registered that? That fuzzy feeling in my fingertips?

It lights up again and again, and I realize it's glowing from the messages sliding across it, not from the way they make my heart beat faster.

CHAPTER 18

I keep my routine, like Chris told me to. I research from home and when the day arrives when we all usually go into the office, I go. But in the bathroom, when I flush and exit the stall, Cat Eyes is standing there with her arms crossed. Her dark hair is shiny under the yellow lights; her green eyes are fluid, pulsing with something I can't quite put my finger on. She doesn't say a word.

I wash my hands and dry them slowly, waiting, stalling. As we stand there, our eyes meeting in the reflection, I can't tell if she's mad or worried or jealous, or maybe just tired. Finally, I can't take it any longer.

"Look, I didn't choose this."

"I know."

"Okay, good."

"Good."

We stare at each other in the mirror for what feels like hours, neither of us making a move toward the door.

"Don't worry about the other research," she says, breaking the silence. "About adding to the Data Program. We'll take care of it. You just take care of your part."

"Okay," I say, but really, what I want to ask is how?

"You can't just study experiences now," she says. "If Vicky is going to see how a brain works, you actually have to experience things yourself. You know that, right?"

"Right."

I want to tell her that for the past few days I've been attempting to do just that, but I've felt frozen. I'm used to researching, not being researched. I want to admit that for the first time in a long time I don't know what I'm doing. That I've started to try things I read about, like putting cinnamon in my coffee, but I'm nervous it doesn't seem like enough.

"You okay?" Cat Eyes asks, still staring intently.

I nod.

"Don't worry," she says. "Everything is going to be fine. This will work. If anyone can get this to work, it's you."

I nod again and force a smile, but her encouragement makes me sick. I turn away to put my hands under the dryer again, even though they're already dry, and keep them there until I hear the door close behind her.

No interesting night starts with a salad, my research says, so I text BABES to see if anyone wants to go to a new sushi place that opened downtown, even though I don't like sushi. Cat Eyes is right. I've got to do more, be more, see more.

I tap my foot under the table and stare at my phone, waiting. The first few replies are excuses: working late, a workout class, a date, tired. But Veronika is up for it. And something like thankfulness flows through me. We decide to meet at eight P.M., and I show up five minutes early because **early is on time**—but Veronika's already there drinking at the bar, lounging, and flirting with the relaxed posture of a regular.

"Lee!" She waves me over and introduces me to a co-worker. The woman, whose name I can't remember, is currently being ghosted by a guy she was dating for three months. With each word she says, she appears on the brink of tears, but laughter dots her sentences. It's a strange mess of emotions, and they play out visibly across her face.

We sit in a green booth in the back and I ask Veronika to help me pick out a sushi roll that won't be super fishy. She nods and says she'll help, but she also tells me to live a little. I cringe. Is it that obvious?

When the roll she orders for me arrives, small orange eggs wobble on top, and with each bite I feel them slip around on my tongue. Slimy, disgusting.

I can only stomach four pieces and Veronika's co-worker eats the rest. One of the small orange eggs sticks to her lip as she talks, and I can't focus on anything she says. Tapping the Screen on the table, she orders two more rolls and another round of drinks and then drones on about how the guy she was dating didn't like sushi, he only liked Greek food. Her eyes are watery, about to flood her face, which is flat. Pink lipstick outlines her almost nonexistent lips.

"I just became so sick of hummus," she says, mouth full of seaweed and rice. She finally uses the napkin, and the jiggling orange egg disappears. "So much fucking hummus all the time. What's a girl supposed to do?"

"That's terrible!" Veronika says and means it. I nod, finishing my drink, moving my straw around through the ice to get the last drops.

"He would never eat sushi with me," the woman whines, "and I love sushi."

"You're better off without him," Veronika says.

Her friend nods and stuffs a piece in her mouth with a thick slab of wasabi. Tears drip down her face and I can't tell if it's because of the spice or the breakup.

The second order of drinks arrives. They immediately leave wet rings on the table. As I reach for mine, my wrist lights up with a message, which reminds me I'm wearing the watch. I look at Veronika and her friend and then tap to order another round. The longer I can spend with them, the better, these two people who seem to have so much going on in their lives.

LIGHTS SWIM BY, blurred like the tail of a sparkler, and wind flings my hair into my eyes as we fly downtown to a dim, sticky bar where everyone's moving in the shadows so I move, too, hidden by the crowd until Veronika hugs me, warm and soft against my cheek, and we jump up and down screaming the lyrics to a song I don't know but that keeps repeating LOVE and FUCK, yeah LOVE and FUCK, so we yell the words in each other's faces and I don't know where her friend went but the music booms in my blood, in my skull, boom-boom-boom as we get drinks and I smile extra-large at a dancing silhouette, bigger than I smile to get into the office, and the tequila doesn't even taste like tequila but more like sugar water and I drink it, slurping from a little black straw while watching myself in the long, full-length mirror in the bathroom.

So this is what I look like when I sip on things? Thin dry lips. Small pin head. Loose brown hair. I take a sip and watch my cheeks move, leaning so close to the mirror I hit my nose on it. **The nose is made of cartilage and bone**.

But drinking while watching yourself drink is so *weird*. I take a step back and try to drink sexily the way I've seen people do on Home, but Veronika bursts in behind me and we make eye contact in the mirror with my hip popped out to the side and my lips pouting around the little straw. She points at me and begins to laugh so hard she snorts, covering her mouth for a second and then uncovering it to yell, what are you doing! She sounds so funny when she yells in such a small space, so I laugh, too, and point back at her and yell the same thing. What are you doing!

"Wait, wait. Try this," I say. I hold the drink up again and look in the mirror. "Sip."

She holds hers up, too, and says, "Sip" in a singsong voice.

"Sip," we say together. And then we shout, Sip! Sip! Sip! The word is so simple, so stupid, we keep repeating it. **Come, let us go down and confuse their language so they will not understand each other.** We watch ourselves sip in the mirror until there's nothing left but ice and air, repeating the word until it doesn't even sound like a word because it's just so *funny*.

We decide to use it as much as possible, so we keep talking to strangers about sipping until one of them buys us something to drink and we drink it, no, we sip it, and the music soaks into my skin and the bar grows dimmer and stickier until the people and noise and shadows blend and blur together.

THEN I SEE the orange eggs again, still in their purest form, perfectly round and stuck together, but this time mixed with my vomit on the white tile floor of our bathroom. I point them out to Veronika, amazed.

"I need to be like them."

She's brushing her teeth above me vigorously, too hard. She mumbles something I can't hear.

"I need to be like these little guys," I say and place my cheek on the tile next to them. "They have so much life waiting inside."

★　★　★

WHEN MY ALARM goes off in the morning, it feels like it's inside my ear smacking my brain. There's a cup of water and two Hangover Relief Pills waiting for me on the kitchen counter with a note, *take this and sip :)*

I study the watch, but nothing has changed.

Sitting on the green couch, my skin hurts, my kneecaps pulse. I open Home on my phone, like a few posts, set my phone down, and then open it on my watch. Jenny's in Costa Rica posing with iguanas. José got promoted in some consulting job. Claire posted a series of photos of her throwing a blanket over someone's head.

I force myself to take a quick walk to the diner to get some food in my body, to get my blood moving. I don't need Maps this time; instead I let my feet lead me back down familiar streets, and as they do, I think about how rarely adults have the opportunity to yell at the top of their lungs the way we did last night. It was so liberating. To stand in that bar and scream along with everyone else.

I think about how surprisingly beautiful the place was in its state of decay, neon making our faces glow. The wooden floors were nicked, disgusting, full of stories scratched into them. I think about how the mirror curved and how I curved in it. I even laugh out loud to myself as I walk, just thinking about how dumb we were, Veronika and I, standing there staring at ourselves as we sipped our drinks.

Maybe it's because the pills are kicking in and my headache is gone, but I feel strangely accomplished. Relieved. Or at least on the right path. There was so much that happened in the span of a night, and even though I don't know what to think about it all, at least I was able to be a lens for Vicky. She saw me process all kinds of experiences:

a) Eating sushi for dinner
b) Watching someone cry and not understanding why
c) Dancing drunk
d) Drinking drunk
e) Passing out on the bathroom floor
f) Being hungover

I'm so caught in my head that I almost miss the diner. Grates are pulled down over the windows, and I don't recognize it at all. When I approach, I peek through a gap and see chairs layered on one another in a tall stack in the corner. Tilted tables rest on their sides. No bustle. No rubbery smell of omelet. No sugary scent of French toast.

I stand and stare for a few minutes.

It can't really be closed.

But a small sign on the front door confirms it. I tug the handle once for good measure and look past my reflection to where the friendly Russian woman used to stand. Where is she now? The old cash register still sits there, drawer popped open. Will someone ever call me baby like that again? Or know what I like for breakfast the way she did?

I lean back, rub the oval of grease my forehead left, and back away, refusing to take my eyes off the crumbling exterior. I've been sitting in the same spot, looking at the same Screen, coming to the same diner for days. **Routine is the death of awareness.**

Is it possible to love a place? For that place to love you back? I stumbled upon a post recently theorizing that everyone is in an abusive relationship with New York. It beats people up, but they never want to leave.

Is it possible to care for a stranger? For that stranger to care for you back? I walk away, confused by the sadness settling in. When I cross the street, I turn back one last time and raise my hand to wave goodbye.

AT HOME, IN a haze of disappointment, I dig in the front pocket of my backpack for ChapStick. Maybe it will help, to feel it again, thick on my lips. Digging around, my finger hits the dull corner of something, and I freeze, pull my hand from the pocket, and sit there for a few minutes, blood pumping. Then I reach back in and carefully extract it: the business card.

I flip it around to look at the front and back. It's delicate, yet sturdy. Small, yet magical, the way I can actually *touch* his name. I never sent him an email. How long ago was this? A week, three? I set the card on the table and begin pacing the apartment.

Veronika said to reach out to him. She said no one is ever just nice, but what does that mean, anyway? It's just one email, I tell myself.

It's also one I would never send.

Which is exactly why—as a researcher—I should send it. It will be an experience for Vicky, just like the night out.

But reaching out to a complete stranger sounds terrible. What would I even say?

Besides, he probably won't answer.

Torn, I decide if the temperature is hotter than seventy-five degrees, I'll send it. Simple as that. Then I won't talk myself out of it. Then I won't have to think about it anymore.

When I open Weather, it's seventy-six degrees. I write a note before I can analyze too much. When I press send, I put my Screen in my room, close the door tight, and return to the kitchen. Then I go get it again and check to make sure the email really sent. I read it once, twice, three times, then put the Screen under my pillow so I'll stop looking at it. I throw my sneakers back on, pulling the laces too tight this time.

I walk and walk until I end up at a park I never knew existed and begin circling the track there, doing my best to avoid two little girls with pink and purple helmets, who seem to be playing a game to see who can scooter the closest to me without hitting me. The tops of my feet throb, so I bend down to loosen the laces.

My watch flashes, and I'm immediately anxious to see what the business card man will say. But it's just an inspirational message: Should we call the step doctor? Because someone is stepping it up today! Keep going, Lee!

After a few more loops around the track in the soupy air, I walk home. I check my email and then do some research for the Entertainment category for what feels like at least a half hour before I check it again, but when I look at the clock only eight minutes have passed. It's a strange feeling, this waiting thing, as if everything I used to understand about time has completely unraveled.

★ ★ ★

LYING IN BED that night, I get a message from Nikita. It's short, simple, just a few links to yoga retreats about finding your inner self. Ted sent me one, too, with invites to various parties around the city. I mark them unread. I know they're all trying to help, but it just reminds me of how much everyone is relying on this new strategy to work.

I'm exhausted from being hungover, from finding the diner closed, from walking so many steps, and from sending the note to a stranger today. Even though he hasn't answered, I feel that same hint of progress. I wonder if Vicky was able to understand the internal debate I had before sending the message. If she could see the stress it caused and understand the slippery, bold energy that surges through a body after taking a risk. Will everything I've been through today be translated into code? Will it help her find that thing we can't measure ourselves?

Even though I just checked Mail on my phone, I check it again on the watch. No new messages. This is good, though. Vicky should know about this weird sensation, a mixture of cement and sugar. She should know about this strange period of expecting something and not knowing if it will come.

I pull the sheet up over my head and then I kick it off. I put my leg in the air and see how far it stretches over my head. Why does a place just close without warning? Or were there signs and I missed them?

How could a piece of paper feel so heavy? How could sending an email turn into such a dramatic event? I could be an idiot for sending the message, but everyone is one at some point, right?

I try to let the day sink in. To let the feeling of being an idiot, and being okay with being one, seep into my skin and into the black, weightless, supposedly unobtrusive object that I can feel ever so slightly pressing against the veins of my wrist.

CHAPTER 19

C hris reschedules our lunch. Can we do next week, he writes.
Things are so busy right now with how intense this timeline is,
you know?

I didn't realize how much I was looking forward to meeting him.
Strictly for business reasons, of course. I tell him it's fine, I understand and that I, too, have a lot to do today—though I'm not sure
what.

What's the timeline? I begin to type, but before I can finish, Chris
responds with a new song he found. Is he changing the subject on
purpose? I'm not sure what I'm supposed to know. What I'm allowed
to ask. Everyone seems to be tiptoeing around me.

We message back and forth about the song, and about Foucault's
theory of power, hydrangeas, the artificial flavor of grapefruit, and why
humans are attracted to suspense. Somewhere along the way, he asks
how I'm doing, and I want to tell him about sending the email to the
stranger, but it suddenly seems so lame.

Instead, I admit that lately I've been feeling stuck. He recommends
I try to stick to a routine. Routines help us feel grounded in stressful
situations, he says.

lee [11:10 P.M.]
thats my problem though
my routine is . . .

lets just say vicky won't learn anything about what it means
to be alive

chris [11:11 P.M.]
lol lee
isn't what u do every day considered living?
routine or not
or is there something u want to tell me . . .
ur a zombie!
a vampire???

lee [11:11 P.M.]
lol nevermind
im not explaining it well

I study the crack above the window in my room, the one that looks like a river delta, and consider what I want to say. How do I tell him this is all wrong?

I'm used to pressure. Expectations. Challenges. At the lab, if people doubted me, or I doubted myself, I just put my head down and worked harder. That was always the solution, but I don't know how to do that in this situation. How do you work harder at being alive? I'm doing my best to experience things. I'm following what research tells me, but it still feels like I'm coming up short.

chris [11:12 P.M.]
im kidding im kidding!
what do u mean tho when u say stuck
stuck can be a lot of things

lee [11:13 P.M.]
I just feel like my normal routine is not really
Well, its not going to be enough to help Vicky

chris [11:12 P.M.]
hmm

maybe break ur routine then?
thats ok too u know
whatever u feel like doing is ok

lee [11:13 P.M.]
maybe lol
idk

chris [11:13 P.M.]
whens the last time u did something that scares u?

Chris and I message back and forth, considering all the possible things I might be afraid of, brainstorming ideas until my eyes feel heavy and sleep arrives slowly, then all at once.

★　★　★

THE NEXT DAY, I examine the list of fears we made: spiders, heights, dying, and hot chicken noodle soup. They look familiar and I realize that all these things are actually others' fears I've read about online. My heart doesn't speed up when I'm thinking about spiders crawling up my nose, and when I open the window and stick my head out, I feel nothing, even though we're five flights away from the musty slice of ground between buildings. I sit back down at the table to think.

Around noon, Veronika appears from her room and begins making a sandwich, slamming the bread on a plate, throwing a slice of turkey on top, dropping the knife on the floor.

"You want one?"

"No, thanks," I say, sipping on my third coffee of the day. Veronika finishes making her sandwich and plops down across from me at the wobbly white table.

"Whatcha working on?" she says as she takes a giant bite. A tomato slice slips out.

"Just work stuff."

"Work stuff?" she says, her mouth full. She stands up and opens the fridge, letting the door of it bang against the wall. She returns to the table with a huge jar of mayonnaise and begins scooping a large clump onto the turkey. My stomach twists.

"What kind of work stuff?" she asks, putting the slice of bread on top and pressing down so some of the white crud squeezes out the side. I scoot my chair back.

"I'm trying to figure out what I'm afraid of."

"Oh, that's a good question. Is that one of your boss's virtual team bonding things again?"

"Something like that."

"So what are you afraid of? I'm afraid of breaking a nail, getting my Achilles ruptured by a skateboard, and dying alone."

How is it so easy for her to rattle off her fears while I'm still sitting lost, unable to pinpoint mine? Veronika takes a bite of her sandwich, and a dab of mayonnaise clings to the side of her cheek; I stand up so fast my chair makes a loud scraping noise on the floor.

"What? What is it?"

"You have some, some of that stuff on your face?" I say, doing everything I can to avoid looking at it.

"Mayo?" she says, breaking into a devious smile, not making any sort of movement to wipe it off. "Lee, are you afraid of mayo?"

"No. That's weird."

She takes another bite and makes sure to smudge an even bigger blob of the white stuff on her cheek. I step farther back into the hallway.

"I think I'm going to work in my room."

"Holy shit, this is amazing. You're afraid of mayo!"

"No, it just grosses me out."

She shoves the spoon into the jar and scoops a big lump of the cream-colored goo from it.

"Veronika, what are you doing? Put that back. That stuff could suffocate someone."

She walks slowly toward me, smiling with the mayo clinging to her cheek, holding the spoon with the gigantic wiggling glob on the end out in front of her. I back down the hallway.

"Lee, you said you have to confront your fear for work, didn't you? I dare you to eat this."

The mayo wiggles as she laughs, and I have trouble breathing just thinking about it stuffed in my nose, in my mouth, smothering me. I back away until I'm cornered. Both her boobs and the disgusting glob are moving up and down, side to side as she tries to stifle her laughter. My chest tightens, feels like it's falling in on itself. Is this what fear feels like? I feel for my wrist, hold it in my hand, then close my eyes and open my mouth.

Tangy, creamy, airy, fluffed-up slime. Smothering me. I spit it out, spraying it everywhere. I try to pull the rest off my tongue with my fingers, flinging the stuff on the floor and the walls. When I open my eyes, Veronika's face is covered.

We stare at each other for a second and then break down laughing so hard that I have to run to the bathroom before I pee my pants.

★ ★ ★

INSIDE THE BOXY studio, a good-looking man in spandex leggings fiddles with a headset. I look around, studying others without making eye contact. Research tells me this place is **guaranteed to make you feel alive**, and so now here I am, hoping to disappear in the corner.

The man in spandex pulls on the headset and begins chatting about his pet fish and how it taught him patience and how we should all be patient in life, just like Justin the fish. He passes out red ribbons to most of us, saving the heavier green and black ones for those who must be regulars. He instructs the heads bobbing on a Screen to grab theirs, too, then walks us through how to read the Fitness Board at the front. He speaks quickly and then hits a switch dimming the lights, blasting the music.

"Let me tell you something, Monday," he yells, jumping into a squat. "Just by making it here today, you've already won."

Everyone follows his lead, landing in squats all around me, so I do, too. If only it were that easy, I think. To just win by showing up.

"One, two, one, two," he yells picking up the pace. Pink lightning flashes in the room. We keep moving and moving and moving.

"You don't owe anyone anything," he says, breathing into the mic. "The only person you owe something to is yourself."

The music crashes through the room. My forearms burn as we twirl the ribbon in figure eights above our head. On the board, I go from frustrated to flatlining to what he calls the adrenaline zone.

"Stay there, Lee, stay there, babe! That's the zone!" he encourages.

We jump. We slide. We twirl. We twist. My skin cries. Sweat pouring through **the epidermis, dermis, and hypodermis**.

"Why are you here?" he says into the mic, words that glide directly into my ears. I want to tell him I ask myself this same question every day.

"Only you know how much you're giving," he yells.

I feel like I'm giving as much as I can. But as I whip a ribbon back and forth with one arm and then the other, refusing to let it drop even though my muscles are burning, I realize I can give more. I can always give more. To prove myself. To help Vicky. To get this project to work.

When we switch poses, I look up and am surprised to see myself in the mirror. That's me? The red-cheeked, slick-haired mouse? **We cannot see the world without seeing pieces of ourselves**.

The instructor tells us that in these last sets of lunges and twirls he wants us to use our voices. He tells us to let out all the stress, anger, sadness harboring inside of us. I wonder if maybe some of these people will let out loneliness, too. If maybe the woman springing around next to me comes to classes because she doesn't want to be by herself.

On three, he says. One. Pink flashing lights. Two. Music so loud it's numbing. Three. A noise exits my lips, one I don't recognize. It joins the roar of those around me. We open our mouths and let the world fall out.

CHAPTER 20

S crolling through Home, looking for things to do that could be good for Vicky, I find a Forum with a lively discussion happening right this second with people arguing about the best experiences in the entire world.

Anything that makes you laugh, someone says.

I try to think of the last time I laughed, truly laughed, and remember sipping from those tiny straws with Veronika at the musty bar. Or the mayo incident where I sprayed it all over her face.

But then a memory I'm not expecting, one I'd almost forgotten about, slips into my brain. I think about the buzz-headed runner and how he threw the gummies into the Hudson. How it was so unexpected, freeing, and how when I flung mine out there, too, we looked at each other in pure, childish glee. I open Dating to find his profile again, but when I scroll past all the new suggestions from the platform, I find a gray block where his used to be. Deactivated.

Good for him, I think, even though my chest feels a bit heavy. I guess that's the point of these things after all, to find a match. I search him on Home to see what his partner looks like and instead I find messages piling up on his profile.

Get better soon!

Thinking of you, Kyle <3

We're here for you. We love you.

Reading through, I see he's been hospitalized. I dig around, but it doesn't seem like anyone knows what he's sick with. Memories of the way his shoulders caved in when he walked away, of how he looked at me full of disappointment, flood my brain.

People feel loneliness when they can't meaningfully connect with others, with the world around them. That's what the materials said, the classified ones Chris sent. I wonder if the runner has it, if that's what he suffers from. Even when I exit the comments and try to distract myself with other searches, a steady dread burrows in me, deep beneath my ribs.

★ ★ ★

THE NEXT DAY, when I get to the office, I'm surprised to find Toru sitting in the glass conference room by himself. He taps a button and the privacy blinders slide down, so I know he's probably studying The Loneliness Report.

I take a swig of coffee and walk past Consultant Row, where everyone is working hard—transported into different archives—and knock gently before entering. Toru nods at me but keeps working. I've never seen him without Janet, and he looks small, sitting in the large room on his own.

"Even more cases?" I ask, hoping to sound natural.

"Every day," he says casually, without looking up. I stand in the back and watch in silence for a few minutes as The Report rotates and the blue dots fall, speckling the geography of cities, suburbs, islands.

"Do they have names?" I ask. Toru looks up from his Screen and studies me for a minute, as if seeing me for the first time.

"What do you mean?" he says.

"Those dots. They're specific cases, right?"

"Right."

"Do we know who they are?"

"We can search them, yes," he says, carefully but quickly. He's in his naturally impatient, naturally jittery state.

"Can I do it on my own?" I shift my weight from one foot to the other.

"No. You don't have access to The Report."

"Okay, can you search someone for me?" Toru leans back in his chair, the blue of The Report reflecting in his eyes.

"Why?" he says.

"Just curious."

"What if you find someone you care about? How might that affect you as you work?"

"I don't care about this person," I say. I never really gave myself a chance.

Toru shakes his head and laughs.

"Janet would be furious. She's worried about you."

Janet's worried about me? Why? I want to ask, but I also know my chance to get answers I need is closing.

"Janet doesn't have to know," I say, and almost immediately regret it. I don't want to undermine her. Toru surprises me by handing me his Screen with The Report floating on it.

"Go on, before I change my mind."

I type in the name of the buzz-headed runner and the Screen moves swiftly, zooming in on one of the dots until it morphs into a profile of a person. A video of him eating spaghetti by himself in a small apartment.

"You know him?" Toru asks as the video swirls and changes to an interview with him in the hospital. It plays on the Screen in my hand and on the wall in front of us.

"Not really." I could have. I think of that moment, how it came and went. I think of how many other people pass each other, shadows reaching out and falling short. I can't stop looking at the runner's face as he speaks on the wall: blank, defeated.

"Good," Toru says, holding out his hand so I can give it back. I can see questions in his eyes, but he doesn't ask them.

"Thank you," I say. He takes the Screen and returns to whatever work he was doing before. I move toward the door and then hesitate.

"Hey, Toru?"

"Mhhm," he grunts.

"Is this working? Is there more I can do?"

If anyone will tell me the truth, it will be Toru, even if his motivations for doing so aren't always clear. He's calculating, strategic, but he's honest. He seems to have no patience for weaving intricate stories, evading questions, for hiding things.

"It's too early to tell. Hopefully, we've collected enough to see progress in the next week or so, because we don't have much time."

"How much do we have?"

"Not unlimited amounts," he says quickly, half laughing even though neither of us find it funny. He runs his hands through his hair, matting it down before it pops back up again.

"How much?" I say.

He doesn't answer for a long time. For so long I feel as if he might be dismissing me. I feel that maybe I've pushed too far. But then he turns to face me, and I can see he's making a decision, weighing options.

"Do you remember when we first showed you this report? How Janet said there are other companies working on the project?"

"Yes," I say, wondering where he's going with this.

"Well," he says, "most of them have failed."

Failed? The word echoes, reverberating throughout my amygdala.

"And as you pointed out before"—he waves to The Report on the wall—"cases are going up. You see where that leaves us, right?"

I nod as it sinks in. The stakes are higher than I thought. It's not just a task, not just a project to prove myself with. Others are failing. And as we work, this nebulous, untraceable thing they keep pinning down as loneliness is growing. It's not a competition against the others, a race to success. It's a race against failure.

"How many companies are left?" I ask.

"A woman with questions," he says, looking at me with curious eyes. "That's what your profile said. It's a good thing, in my opinion. Dangerous. Necessary."

I can feel the blood rush to my cheeks.

"You know, you and I, we're not so different."

I wait, not knowing what to say. Unsure what he means. I don't know anything about him besides what I've observed, whereas he has a whole portfolio of information on me.

"You were pissed when you first arrived, weren't you?" he asks, chuckling to himself. I swallow. Does he think this is funny?

"I would have been, too. Especially when you had such a clear path and now there was this . . . strange curveball. But you're driven. I can see it. You want to make something of yourself."

He looks up at The Report surrounding us.

"People like you and me, we need a challenge. We want to change the way life is lived. We want things to matter."

I nod.

"That's why I like invention, creation. It's a little bit different than the traditional path to success that you dreamed of. But projects like these that are almost certain to fail . . . they're interesting to me because when we pull it off, when they occasionally, rarely work, we surprise the world."

He's sounding like Masha, saying something I'll need to reflect on for a few weeks to fully understand, but that even in this moment feels like pure truth.

"Anyway, all of this is to say is that if I can handle it, then I don't see why you couldn't, too," he says, pausing to look at me.

I nod. I just want to know what's going on, what we're up against, how fast I need to work.

"There are two companies left," he finally says.

"Including us?"

"Including us."

I try to smooth out my face, keep it plain.

"The Government is selecting a new cohort of companies to help, but my guess is they'll be too slow," he says. "Especially with what we see unfolding right in front of us."

We both stare at The Report projected on the wall. The blue spiraling and spinning around us, seemingly growing each second.

"The new strategy seems to be tracking well, though. Trust it. We'll let you know if you need to do anything differently."

"Okay," I say, burying the questions, the shock, the fear.

"Okay, now let me work."

I nod and turn to leave.

"Oh, and Lee," he says as I reach for the door handle. "Maybe we can keep this between us?"

"Absolutely," I promise before walking out.

★ ★ ★

ON THE SUBWAY, ads flip and turn. For the next few minutes, they show a woman skipping and smiling. It keeps zooming in and out on her teeth, and I wonder if it can sense that mine need to be whitened.

I'm trying to remain calm. Trying to think straight, which is impossible when my thoughts are shooting about like fireworks. The image of the runner on The Loneliness Report plays on a loop in my mind.

Will he recover? Would Vicky have been able to help him? What happens if too many people become lonely? One of the materials on loneliness said that people are repelled by it. They'll avoid it at all costs. I wonder if it has a domino effect: the more people who fall through the cracks of society because they can't connect, the fewer people there will be left for others to connect to. Will our society crumble in on itself? Is this why the Government is involved?

I kept composure in the office. I carried on as usual. But as soon as I left and smiled into the camera, the reality of what Toru said began sinking in, crawling beneath my skin.

Time is running out.

With only two companies left and an increasing rate of loneliness, we need Vicky to work. This must be what Chris meant when he mentioned a compressed timeline. How come he wasn't more explicit? I've been delusional thinking that one or two new experiences every few days is enough. I've been moving too slow, doing too little.

We fly underground and I skim through parts of emails, mark them unread, slip my phone in my pocket, look around, then tap through the same emails again. I'm antsy. Is riding the subway an experience? Should I go get my teeth whitened? What does Vicky need from me to understand humans better, faster?

The subway hurls to a stop and the doors fling open. New people get on and the ads spin, landing on a dancing macaroni noodle.

How did Toru know that I was upset when I first arrived? Was it that obvious? He's right: I want my work to mean something. I see the potential that this project could not only have an impact, but it could change the course of people's lives. I understand now why this is perhaps the most important thing I'll ever do. **Great reward requires great risk**.

Slipping my phone out of my pocket again, I go through the rotation, tapping Chat and then Home and then Mail, and almost close it before I notice a new message from a sender I don't recognize. I'm about to delete it when the name clicks in my memory and my knees go weak.

The cement walls of the underground soar by. I miss my stop but remember to exit at the next one. As I walk up two flights of wet stairs into the night, I open the email again to make sure it's really there. Warm raindrops smack the screen. Through the blur I read the short lines again and again.

Lee, great to hear from you. Did you get all the information you needed for your empathy project? Or should we grab coffee for real this time?

G.

Walking turns to trotting turns to running. When I get home, I lean my shoulder against the door, and fall into the apartment with soggy jeans.

"What the . . . is it raining or something?" Veronika turns around on the couch to look at me, her glossy brown eyes wide, blond hair still perfectly curled. She sits cross-legged in an old T-shirt with a glass of wine in hand. The bottle on the table is almost empty, and the TV is on with the volume all the way up.

"Pouring. Warm, though!"

Three small faces bob on her Screen. They all wave.

I wave back and rush down the hall into my room. When I close the door, I catch a glimpse of myself in a long mirror nailed to the back.

It's been there since I moved in, but I've never stopped to examine myself in it. My shirt clings to my stomach and my backpack hangs off one shoulder. My hair drips down my back while the mirror scans me, assessing my outfit. A pink dress will accentuate your forearms! it decides cheerily.

My phone vibrates in my pocket and my watch glows on my wrist. The BABES chat is piling up with messages about the newest TV series premiering tonight. Veronika must be watching. She sends four messages in a row. When I look back in the mirror, it's showing what I would look like in a pink dress, but it flickers in and out. Acne spots surround my nose and chin. Strands of dirt-colored hair are plastered to my neck.

I turn away from the mirror, peel my cold clothes off, wrap myself in a towel, and tiptoe across the hall to hop in the shower. As it heats up, I examine my toenails, making a mental note that they need to be trimmed. There are so many little things to do just to maintain the body. I only ever do about half of them, mostly because I forget.

Steam fills the room, reminding me to step in the shower. Hot shards of water pelt my skin. I place my face under the stream, letting it hit me for as long as I can hold my breath.

What about the email made me run instead of walk? Was it the energy that gathered in my limbs during the hours of pretending Toru hadn't just told me that we're one of the last companies that could work? Or was it because I'd completely forgotten about the business card man and then there he was: his words, his invitation? My heart thrums from desperation, from shock both good and bad. How much can a person hold in them at once?

Humans love and hate the unexpected. Once, I watched hundreds of videos online about birthday parties for the Emotions category. In one of them, a frail Muslim girl was surprised by her parents on her thirteenth birthday and the video showed her frozen before bursting into tears. I replayed this moment, again and again, the point of pure shock. The body's reaction, out of control, to the world around it. Everyone clapped and exchanged hugs, and music exploded from somewhere outside the frame. The girl must be a woman by now, but the brief moment of realizing she's loved is captured on her face and preserved online forever.

I turn away, take a breath, then face the water again.

It's interesting to see the way some events flow smoothly, unnoticeable in a person's stream of consciousness, and how other, simple ones, like a conversation in a glass room or an ordinary commute, can shock a mind, alter a life. I'm used to being able to have more control over things. I could sit down and rationally make decisions. But I never could have guessed that I'd be here in this very shower, with a crack running through its porcelain, in the middle of a project that could change not just my life but millions of people's. That I'd be receiving an email from a stranger who, for some odd reason, I'm curious about.

Should I respond? I think of how Veronika described him as attractive even though she'd never seen him and was only making a judgment based on the thickness of his business card, based on the idea that paper, used so rarely now, is a sign of wealth, prestige. But now that she'd said it, she exposed the idea to air. The notion he might be attractive is real. It exists in the world. I might be thinking it, too. Had I thought it before? Or do ideas transfer so easily from one person to another?

I turn away, breathe in, then turn back. The water taps my eyelids and drips down my lips. It's too hot against my skin, but I like it.

I think of what Toru said. How we're not so different from one another. How the chance that something could fail is actually what makes success even greater. How we both like a challenge. I look at the watch, drops of water peppering the small Screen, and realize he's right.

IN MY ROOM, I pull my Screen up around me while still wrapped in a towel. Portals and webs and pages tell me to do ecstasy, hike into a canyon, knit a quilt, chug a liter of soda, learn the moonwalk, or lie in the middle of the street at midnight. Would all of this really make someone feel alive? I think, my hair dripping a small pattern on the chair. It sounds overwhelming, chaotic, and messy.

I scroll and tap and search, looking for new experiences to try for Vicky, a renewed sense of urgency. I land on a page listing art classes and sit up a little straighter. Chris said I should do one a while ago, but I was so busy with work. **Listen to your gut**, I think, and sign up.

Then, when I can't avoid it any longer, I open Mail to face G.'s message. I push myself to draft a response, changing the beginning from "hey" to "hi" to "dear kind sir" and back to "hey" again. When it feels perfectly crafted according to what I've seen online, I press send, close everything, and immediately get up to put pajamas on.

Circling my room, I think about how I just said yes to coffee with a stranger. How I just signed up for an art class. How a person I once encountered, even briefly, is now lonely. These facts march behind my skull telling me that the reality I'm living in is one I never would have expected.

CHAPTER 21

The building seemingly has no door. I search and search and then lean against the metal infrastructure in frustration and it slides open, swallowing me whole. New York, I think, shaking my head with disdain and respect.

The inside of the building looks hundreds of years old, as if they simply dipped the exterior in metal, updated the security, but did nothing to the inside. I walk up crumbling, crusty stairs and into a large open space with concrete floors and random tidbits stuffed along the walls: a headless statue of a woman, a music stand serving as a table for a skull, a purple vase with a blue feather.

A woman drags things around, setting up a circle of desks. She waves me toward a table where a bottle of wine rests next to flimsy plastic cups. When I tap my fingerprint on the sign-up Screen, my hand is shaking.

A part of me, small and buried, has always been drawn to art, to the idea that a human can dive into their brain, pick something up, and throw it into the universe. But it also seems sort of useless, to spend one's life that way. Especially if, according to what I've read online, half the time people don't seem to understand artists anyway.

Class begins and the others sit down at the desks, where drawing Screens and styluses have been distributed, but my feet are made of sand. Even though I signed up for the class, I'm out of my element. I should have watched more instructional videos last night or read more about the history of various drawing techniques.

I find an empty spot and sit, listening closely to the teacher as she talks, trying to soak in all the details and instructions. We practice different pressures, strokes, ways of moving our hands, shading, and styles of lines. When I peek around, I notice I'm better than a lot of the others, so I begin to relax a little.

Two hours disappear and the instructor thanks us for coming. She has a few announcements: There's a beginner painting class next Tuesday. A show downtown Saturday. Oh, and we're looking for a model for our advanced drawing course, if anyone knows someone who might be interested.

Shuffling and mumbling, people pack their bags. I see all sorts of opportunities to collect research about these strangers and add it to the Data Program. But my instinct to observe reminds me that I'm the one being observed. That the whole reason I'm here right now is for work. Certainly, I've experienced enough for today, right?

But then I think about my conversation with Toru, how we're running out of time. I decide if I count three tattoos in the room, I have to do it. The thought comes from nowhere, an impulse, really, one I hope doesn't come to fruition.

One, a sleeve of a lion licking a flower on the instructor's wiry bicep. Two, a quote on her ankle. Looking around, feeling relieved that there seems not to be a third, I see it. I want to pretend I don't, but there it is: a teeny hippo on the forearm of a man who looks nervous, scratching his elbow.

I turn around and tap the teacher's shoulder, feeling her warm skin against my fingers.

"I'll do it," I say quietly. So quietly I hope she doesn't hear.

"What?" She smiles at me, confused.

"I'll model," I hear myself repeat, even though internally an alarm is going off. No. No. No.

"Oh, great! That's just great. I was worried I'd have to ask my sister to come again. Let me just make sure I have your info."

I follow her to the table with the check-in Screen and show her my name.

"Perfect. So, it's two P.M. next Monday. Same place," she says, waving her arm toward the room enthusiastically. "I'll send you a reminder.

"Oh, and make sure to bring a robe!"

"Okay," I say, though I don't understand why. I don't think much about it because I'm distracted by the echo of dread deep in my torso.

★　★　★

I DECIDE TO go to the diner for dinner. I need comfort, need a place to think through everything, but Maps reminds me it's closed and directs me to a deli called "Deli" instead. It's not the same, but my stomach is grumbling and I respect the straightforwardness of the business name, so I step inside.

"Hello. What do you want?" a Screen at the front says. The place is so small, if I spin in a circle, I'll knock chips off the shelf. A board above the counter sifts through hundreds of sandwich options, and I stare at it hoping something like the peanut butter toast will pop up.

"Hello. What do you want?" I look for a button to press, or a speaker to speak into, but there are none.

"Hello," it begins again. It must be sensing my presence.

"Hi," I cut in, hoping it will stop for a second so I can think. The board changes, showing how versatile the offerings are. But the more options there are, the less I know what I want.

"What do you want?" it asks one more time, and I finally give up, glancing at the board and naming exactly what's there.

"The fifty-five," I say.

A baguette falls from the ceiling onto the mini treadmill of a toaster oven. It disappears, but I can hear chopping and slapping and slopping. The Screen prompts me to pay, so I press my finger on it to scan. My sandwich, wrapped in foil, shoots across the counter at me, and I catch it with two hands.

"Enjoy your sandwich," the machine says, but it feels like a demand. So much for a place to slow down for a second, to stop and think and feel—what was it?—cared for.

"You, too," I say, and then feel like kicking myself as I walk out the door.

CHAPTER 22

G ., the business card man, responds to my email and suggests we meet for coffee near his office in midtown. I'm early, so I grab a seat by the window and watch the people who wander past outside.

When I see him coming, I have two seconds to register that he's taller than I remember. His arms are outlined in a neatly fit light-purple button-down. What am I doing here? Am I really doing this? He pulls open the door, spots me, smiles, and shakes his head, as if to say, well, isn't this funny.

I try to make some sort of face back that says, I know, this really is quite hilarious, but I tilt my head to the side and hit it against the window.

As he gets closer, I stand to offer my hand. Maybe he was considering a hug but now I've made things formal? He grabs it and shakes it with a soft but sturdy grip. His dark brown eyes wear the same amused expression as at our encounter at the last coffee shop.

I make a big deal out of treating him to coffee this time, but as I try to get around him to the register, I bang my thigh on a chair and knock it over.

"Whoa, easy there," he says, picking it back up. I rush to the register so he can't see me flush with embarrassment. When I bring our coffees back, he sets his phone facedown.

"So," he says, and takes a sip of his coffee.

"So," I say, and take a sip of mine. It's so hot it tears a hole in the roof of my mouth, but I swallow anyway.

"So what is this all about?" he asks.

"This?"

"Yeah, it's just funny. An empathy project or something? I'm not going to lie. It kind of sounds like you made it up."

"Made it up?" It seems my vocabulary has left the building and I can only repeat things he's saying.

"Mhhm."

"I didn't. It was for work."

The small shop feels too hot, and a section on the roof of my mouth and a sliver of my tongue are turning numb. He raises his eyebrows at me. How could I have forgotten the eyebrows?

"I swear," I say.

"Okay, okay. I believe you. I will say, though, it sounded like you were hitting on me. That, or you're part of some religious group or something. Not that there's anything wrong with that."

"Well, I'm not."

He raises just the brows again.

"I'm not!" I tip my cup and sip without thinking. The coffee, just as hot as before, sears the roof of my mouth.

"Not religious?" he says and smirks, his eyes boring into mine.

"Yeah, not really. I mean, I don't know. Not right now. I don't really know what I believe in." He laughs, and I can't figure out what I'm saying that's funny.

"Okay, so tell me. What's the company?"

"Well, we're creating something that's going to help people," I say, looking down into the cup of coffee. I can't mention the word "lonely," or "loneliness." But if I could, would he know what I meant?

"You're a developer?" he prods.

"No, I'm a Consultant. A Humanity Consultant."

He looks me in the eyes. It reminds me of Janet, but in a warmer way. Still, it makes me uncomfortable, being looked at, really looked at, so I keep talking. "I'm gathering data to help an AI so it can learn to be human. A real human friend you can talk to anytime. That's why I was studying empathy a few weeks ago."

"Hm. What's the purpose? No offense, just my instinct to ask. We invest in tech, and there's so much of it I'm always trying to figure out what the real need is, if you know what I mean."

I think of The Loneliness Report, the blue dots. How there are more and more each day. I think of the buzz-headed runner sitting alone in his apartment. And for some reason, I think of the beady-eyed man in front of the glass window, buying item after item. He must have wanted to feel connected to something, anything, even if just a pair of shoes.

"I . . . Well, it would be to help people feel . . . more connected."

"People who are sad or anxious?"

"Sort of, but different. It's hard to explain."

We sit there in silence for a minute. He looks at the ceiling, thinking, and I hope I haven't said something wrong. I hope he doesn't get up and leave.

"I don't think I can say any more. I'm sorry, it's just . . ." I try to explain again and then I look down at the cup, find the temperature dial, and finally turn it down.

"No, no, I get it. I'm sure you signed an Agreement and all of that," G. says, waving me off. He considers the information for a second, looking out the window at people in suits walking past.

"Do you feel like you would use what you're creating? Like do you feel . . . sad or anxious?" he asks, tentatively.

"Not really. Well, maybe anxious, but in a good way. Like I have stuff to do."

"Anxious in a good way," he says, smirking and sipping his coffee.

"Do you? Feel that way?"

"Well," he says, contemplating the question, "I guess I feel anxious in a good way, too. It's a weird cycle: Do I do things all the time because they are important? Or because they make me feel important?"

I nod. I've never thought about it that way, but it makes sense. Or at least I think it does.

"I do feel like sometimes no one understands me, though. I'm not sure if that counts," he says, and I watch as he picks at his thumbnail. "But you're the first person I've admitted that to."

"Am I the first person who's asked?" I say, and he looks up. Deep brown eyes with so many questions.

He smiles at me. "Think you can keep it a secret?"

"Keep what a secret?"

"That I just admitted to, well, you know, not always being the strong, put-together person everyone sees."

"You're strong? Hadn't noticed."

He breaks out laughing, his face cracking open into that same large smile I saw when I first noticed him through the window at the other coffee shop.

I don't know what it is, what happens. Maybe it's his phone, still face-down on the table so he can really listen. Or maybe it's how he admitted something to me he's never told anyone else. Or the way he leans his head back when he laughs. Maybe it's how he looks me in the eyes, straight into them, present. Or, more likely, the way my watch glints in the sun. But I begin to talk. To really talk.

I tell him about moving to New York. How I had twenty-four hours to pack up everything. About how when I first arrived, I thought the city was a complete graveyard, but now that I've been here and seen it, it's so much more lively than people admit. I tell him about Masha, how lucky I was to train with him, and about Veronika and the BABES group chat. About how loud she has the volume on the TV at night, echoing down the hallway and into my room. About my fear of mayonnaise. The diner that closed down where I used to order peanut butter chocolate toast and the deli called Deli that shoots sandwiches at me. I tell him about spilling salad dressing on my shirt. About running by the river, the air feeling new and sharp in my throat. About tripping on my own shoelace. About how sometimes I feel like I'm not doing anything right anymore.

He listens. He listens and nods and asks questions. He tells me about his pickup soccer league and how he wants to learn to cook. There's a reminder on his phone that sends him grocery lists when he walks by the store, but he keeps exiting out of them and then feeling guilty about it. He tells me about his office, how he finally has windows. He always wanted them, not just to see out of, but because they felt like a trophy. A sign that he'd finally made it. He tells me how he used to get into fistfights when he was in school. About his work, how he's doing some research, too, just a different kind. He tells me about his dad. How they're really close, but he's afraid that he's becoming just like him. About how he thinks no matter what he does he'll always just disappoint people.

His phone vibrates on the table and he flips it over, looks at the name. "Shit," he says under his breath. Then he's standing. Apologizing. He's late for a meeting. He thanks me for the coffee, reaches across the table and hugs me, letting his hand linger on my shoulder. He says he owes me, apologizes again, and rushes out. As the door closes behind him, I'm still midway between standing and sitting, waving goodbye. I plop back down for a second to think about everything.

I should check the watch. Should brainstorm what to do next, where to go, who to talk to in order to gather more experiences for Vicky. But all I can think about is the warmth of his hand wrapped around my shoulder.

★ ★ ★

AT HOME, I can't stop thinking through the conversation in my head, reviewing every word, every gesture. How did I end up there? I think, somewhat amazed. How can I replicate it?

If I trace things back to discovering the business card in my backpack and sending the original email, it was all because of the temperature. And just a few days ago, I volunteered to model because of tattoos. It occurs to me how easy it was to say yes to these things I normally wouldn't when the decision wasn't mine to make. If I want to do more, I just have to play this game. I just have to let the world decide for me.

The next day, I decide to test it out. If Ted's mood mug turns blue, then I must respond to an email newsletter asking me to volunteer. At around nine, it turns navy, so I reply, and within ten minutes, I'm on the subway uptown to a community garden that keeps flooding, encouraging the growth of some new invasive plant species. We pluck them and put them into sample baggies to send for testing.

It feels strange to be here when I know the other Consultants are busy researching. To be outside surrounded by plants and a chain-link fence.

A woman named Jaquelyn keeps telling me I'm not doing it right and then laughing before inhaling on a cigarette. She's older, maybe eighty, with graying curls and a sagging chin. I can't tell if she's joking or not, but I try to improve regardless. For some reason I can't pinpoint, I want her to like me.

Jaquelyn and I drink cold water with dirt underneath our fingernails and she hugs me when I leave, asking me to come back tomorrow. I can't look at her as I wave goodbye because I know we'll never meet again. I know I'm using her for Vicky.

At home, I smell my hands. Earthy, moist, wormlike. The stress behind my forehead is thawing now that I finally have a way to get myself to be more than I am. Now that I have a plan.

★ ★ ★

VERONIKA TELLS THE BABES that I met G. for coffee, and they want more details. I tell them about knocking over the chair, about how I talked way too much.

So was it a date?

idk

Well, do you want to see him again?

idk

invite him to my birthday party

No way

its perfect! There will be tons of random people

Ya do it Lee! you'll totally have the upper hand because it's
your friends

^^^agree great idea

I can't imagine what that would be like, to see him while all these
people watch us. To just see him again in general. The idea is so discom-
forting, and yet somehow appealing. It feels like the perfect opportunity to try the game again.

Looking around, I notice two kids playing on the orange plastic
subway seats across from me. It's afternoon and the car is mostly empty.
The little girl wears yellow overalls with small hearts on them. She hits
her brother in the face with a balloon and he pretends to fall over dead,
causing her to erupt in giggles. The brother sits up and they repeat the
whole thing over again.

If her balloon pops, I'll invite him, I think.

One stop passes. I stand and grab the cold, waxy rail to hold myself
as the train slides to a stop. I look at the balloon, urging it to pop. She
hits him in the face with it, he falls. Giggles erupt. My stop arrives.
The train slows and I stall, leaving my body between the doors just in
case. They try to close and I push against them. The train dings at me
until I finally let go. Maybe my instinct is right, it would be a bad
idea. But just as I step off, just before the doors slide shut behind me,
I hear it.

Pop.

I have to do it.

And as I open Mail to invite him, I find that, to my own surprise, I
may be smiling. I might be the slightest, tiniest bit excited to see if he
comes.

CHAPTER 23

Janet opens her eyes to see the ceiling. She's been lying on the carpet practicing diaphragmatic breathing, and her phone says her heartbeat has normalized, her stress levels have lowered, and she should feel a sense of calm.

The problem is, she doesn't. The problem is, she hasn't for a while. The low, constant buzz of stress she used to enjoy has now become a bit annoying, sinking into her, causing the muscles in her shoulders and neck to twist in gnarled knots.

Janet pushes herself up slowly so she doesn't get light-headed and reviews the information on her phone again. Her body, her mind: everything is in order. She makes her way to the clunky desk against the wall to finish some work, but as soon as she sits, her fingers move on their own. Ignoring messages and tasks, they pull up The Loneliness Report and tap into one of the blue dots on the Screen.

A man with a salt-and-pepper beard appears. He talks quickly, as if a waterfall of words has been harbored inside of him for decades. Janet watches for a little and then exits, tapping into a different blue dot. This one contains a twenty-something-year-old with long fake nails. She plays with a necklace, avoiding the camera, and when she finally speaks, it's only in terse phrases. Something about watching birthday parties unfold from miles away.

It started as a strategy. A plan. After so many Failures, Janet was thrilled to find their project outlasting those of other established founders, inventors, and entrepreneurs, but she was also humbled. She was reminded, especially after seeing Tina's Failure a few weeks ago, how finicky this project really is.

So she started watching individual cases of loneliness, just one or two a night at first, to tap into her best skill: the dark art of empathy. Janet thought that if maybe she could understand these people, this problem, a bit more, she could guide her team better as they built a solution.

The problem is that as she watched more and more, Janet had a small yet resounding realization. The blue dots—the ones she and Toru used to see as just data points, just the Audience for the Product—are real people. Living, breathing people who feel things they may not be able to understand. And isn't that the most helpless thing? To be overcome by feelings you don't want? Ones you can't control?

But tonight, as Janet taps into another blue dot, falling deeper into The Report, she can't help but hear Toru's voice. *You're getting too wrapped up in it,* he'd warned her.

They were at the Tech Hub a few weeks ago for an important meeting about the state of Vicky, and the team was walking everyone through data, explaining the strategy of the watch.

"Are you sure we should be putting that much responsibility on one person?" Janet had asked. "It seems too risky. Not just for the girl, but for Vicky if she's currently on a good path. Right? Do we understand why Vicky's gravitating toward one source?"

"No," Toru said with an edge of frustration. "We don't. As mentioned multiple times before, the team is working on that. And yes, it is a risk. But everyone else will continue operating normally. So it's worth it to change one variable as everything else remains stable."

Janet nodded, but she could sense the tension, feel it pressing around all of them. Later, when the meeting ended and everyone dispersed, Toru grabbed her arm and pulled her aside.

"What was that?" he whispered sharply. "Too risky?"

"I just think we should be sure before we go through with this, T," she said calmly.

"We've been thinking through this," Toru said, pulling at his hair. "You've been a part of it. What's gotten into you?"

"Look, T, I really think this project is bigger than we know. I want to be sure we're making the right decisions. I've been watching the individual cases on The Loneliness Report, and these people . . ."

"What?" Toru interrupted, his eyes wide. "How many have you watched?"

"Not that many," Janet lied. She'd probably seen thousands by now. Besides, it's part of the people side of her job Toru wouldn't understand anyway. "I just think it will help if we grasp it better."

"Listen to me," he'd said, his anger replaced by something else she couldn't place. Shock? Fear? "You've got to stop. You're getting too caught up in it all."

Janet nodded, but she could hardly look at him.

"Look, you and I, we always take risks," he continued softly. "Vicky is trending in the right direction, and now, with this new line of direct data coming in from the watch, I think we could really crack this thing. Trust me on this, okay? But you've got to pull it together. I need you. We need you."

Buzz. Buzz. Buzz.

Janet's phone vibrates on the desk in her apartment, alerting her that her stress levels are rising again. She closes The Loneliness Report and orders a bottle of her favorite wine. Tomorrow, she'll stop drinking so much. Tomorrow, she'll be able to separate herself from the project just like Toru said. In the morning, she'll regain her distance from all this again, the way she pretends to do each day.

But tonight, one glass won't hurt. Because as the sun sinks she can feel the darkness: crawling through the windows, seeping through the walls. An emptiness that rings a bell, as if she's seen it somewhere before.

A knock at the door means the drone has delivered her wine. She gets up, grabs it, and heads to the kitchen to find a glass. In the cupboard, she selects the most delicate one, holding it up to inspect for clinging dust.

It's so fragile in her hands, so breakable. If she threw it at the wall, it would become a million splinters. Beauty annihilated on impact.

The thought is soothing, even though Janet would never do such a thing. It's just that thinking about her conversation with Toru—what he said, the way he said it, his voice low and serious, as if he pitied her, as if she'd become some sort of animal he didn't recognize or some sort of child—is infuriating.

Doesn't he realize that to solve something, you must look it in the eye? Doesn't he know that she's just doing her job? Everything Janet does is exact, like the edge of a knife. Her routine of watching the newest cases of loneliness is only part of the process. She needs to know how it's developing, how it looks off the Screen, outside the data, as it plays across someone's face, their limbs, their speech.

Janet loosens her grip on the stem of the wineglass and rinses it a few times, watching as the water drips off the lip. She sets it carefully on the counter and gives herself a healthy pour. One sip, then another. Slowly, her thoughts soften.

Janet doesn't want to think about how Toru often knows her better than she knows herself. She doesn't want to admit that maybe he's right, she's become too attached to the project. After all, the most dangerous thing a person can do is care.

But she can't help it. She keeps watching the cases. And the more she watches, the more what-ifs scatter about her mind like crows: What if it doesn't work? What if Lee isn't capable? What if this decision is the one that ruins them? What if their solution doesn't work and all those people she's been watching can never be saved? What if millions more become like them?

Sound scrapes by outside the apartment and Janet listens, distracting herself. Is it the wind? She sips her wine and strains to hear, deciding it was a car speeding past.

Just as she's getting up to peek out the window, a familiar alert sounds on her phone, on her Screen. The one she's been classically conditioned to drop everything for. Another Failure. The last one. Janet knows she should call Toru, but she can't. Not right now.

Instead, she forwards the Failure summary to him, and seconds later his face appears on her phone. The photo of him in Singapore. She flips it over, letting it ring facedown, and scans the Failure once, quickly, before shutting everything down and taking a sleeping pill.

Janet will call him tomorrow, when she hasn't been watching the loneliness cases, when she hasn't been drinking, when she's able to smile and act like herself. She'll call him when she's had time to wrestle with the stress of it all—how now there's just that much more pressure for Vicky to work—by herself.

Janet stumbles to her bed, falls back onto it, and lies there with heavy eyelids, heavy arms. In the last drops of consciousness, she randomly thinks of Lee. The girl, always so serious, so deeply concerned, is taking the watch assignment and running full speed ahead. Janet's been monitoring her closely; all of them have been.

I know what it's like, Janet whispers to the empty room, to want to be the best. To think it will be enough . . .

Somewhere in the web of her mind is a thought that feels like truth. About the girl? Vicky? Loneliness? Herself? It shimmers at the edge of consciousness, and she reaches for it just as the pill kicks in and her mind goes black, curtained by sleep.

PERFORMANCE SUMMARY—FAILURE

Company Name: Stay Busy, Stay Happy

Company Founder(s): Jill Wang and Jeremiah Fonduet

Brief Synopsis of Project:

> It's proven that when an individual is productive, they feel a sense of purpose. A sense of purpose is integral to connectedness within society. The goal of our company was to increase productivity levels and, therefore, provide users with a greater sense of belonging.

Employee Count: 25

Detailed Explanation of Failure:

The Productivity Curtain was tested by 1,000 companies in 20 different cities. 83% of users increased productivity for sustained periods of time, but there was no found correlation between increased productivity and protection against loneliness.

Other errors or indications of failure:
- 60 days into the tests, a small subset of users dropped from the radar altogether and appeared within 0–3 days on The Loneliness Report.
- User #556 exit survey "One day I feel motivated, the next it feels as if nothing matters."

Did you discover anything about Loneliness or The Loneliness Report you think necessary to flag immediately?

We are not sure if this is of immediate concern, but you will find in our reports that people can be simultaneously productive and lonely. Our hypothesis was that if we could help those who had signs of loneliness find more meaning in their everyday work lives, we would be able to solve the feelings of emptiness, of disconnection to the world around them. However, as you'll see in our attached data, this is not the case.

Thank you for your collaboration. We greatly appreciate your service.

CHAPTER 24

C hris and I begin to message almost every day. He randomly checks in here and there, and I wonder if Janet put him up to it. She seems to be coming by the office more when we're there, looking over our shoulders, hovering.

Either way, my constant stream of conversation with Chris feels stabilizing. It's a funny thing, to look forward to a name sliding across a Screen. I like talking to him about work, but it's also nice to let our conversations meander. I've never had someone like this who's silly, imaginative, and serious all at the same time. Someone who never makes me think twice about what I say.

chris [11:28 A.M.]
can't think today
so tired
im dead

lee [11:29 A.M.]
people say that online all the time
saying 'im dead' instead of 'im tired'
how does it feel being dead? lol

chris [11:30 A.M.]
oh it's not so bad

lee [11:30 A.M.]
whats the best and worst parts

chris [11:30 A.M.]
best part definitely being a ghost
worst part
having no feeling
of any kind

lee [11:31 A.M.]
do you have emotions?

chris [11:31 A.M.]
i do not think i have emotions
i can't say ill miss them tho
because I don't know what that feels like anymore

lee [11:31 A.M.]
you can't feel, but you can think?

chris [11:31 A.M.]
yea
something like that
I'm kind of omnipotent at this point
like I can see all that was
and all that will be

chris [11:33 A.M.]
I can see the bonds between the molecules of water in a
raindrop
I can see the timeline of each grain of sand on the beach
from birth as raw elements in the core of an ancient star
the fiery heat and pressure as it floats in the core of the planet
the upheaval from ocean vents
the eons of being swept by underwater currents

the force of the waves, breaking them down
the wind, pushing them around the beach
the feet of the people running along

lee [11:36 A.M.]
can you smell or taste anything?

chris [11:39 A.M.]
it's hard to distinguish one sense from another (edited)
sense is more memory than anything
my mind courses with the life of every atom in the universe
Being dead isn't that bad

lee [11:46 A.M.]
wow
to feel every atom of the universe
it sounds beautiful
i think I'd like to be dead too

CHAPTER 25

It takes forever for Zuri's birthday to arrive, by which time I've done karate and visited a pet psychic who told me that hamsters are repelled by my odor. But then it's here and I'm getting ready, squeezing into a silver, glittery tube top Veronika begs me to wear. It hugs me, revealing the shadow of my underboob, and when I look in the mirror, touching my face, I feel a little bit beautiful for the first time I can remember.

When we walk into the bar, the first thing I notice is the floor is sticky. So is the air. So are the people. People I've seen before. Faces I recognize from Home float in and out, and I stand by the bar and drink a tequila soda. **Tequila makes every night an opportunity**.

Zuri wears a long flowing red dress much too fancy for this bar. She's not wearing a tiara or a sash, but it's clear the night is about her. There's so much I would note down for the Data Program if that were still my role, but I remind myself that just by being at a party I'm doing my job. Just by being out in the world, I'm putting myself in a situation to collect experiences firsthand for Vicky. I try to, as Chris says, just live, which feels like such a frustratingly simple way to describe something so complicated.

Even though I'm facing the dance floor, I can see the entrance, and around eleven I decide G.'s not coming even though he said he'd try to stop by. I snag my watch on the tube top and it pulls a thread.

"Are you catching all of this?" I whisper to it. "Now you know what it feels like to be let down."

Veronika makes a show of dancing across the bar, waving her hands one way and then another way with some guy who's clearly three or four drinks in, and then she deftly twirls away and lands right next to me.

"So if he doesn't come, he doesn't come," she says. "His loss!"

I nod. A few messages arrive from Chris, wondering how the party is going. A man next to us tries to start a conversation by asking what we're celebrating tonight, as if it's not obvious. When Veronika says it's Zuri's birthday, he orders a round of shots from a machine that ejects them quickly, each lime perfectly sliced. I grab three from the bunch and turn around to hand them to whoever is standing nearby, and all of a sudden, I glimpse his shadow moving through the crowd, his large shoulders. I pretend not to notice, handing out the shots and smiling as if I weren't concerned at all whether he would come or not. Then, when he's standing just five feet from me, I see his face. I meet his deep brown eyes. Amused again. Isn't this funny?

I hand him a shot.

"This is how you say hello?" he says.

"Yes." I lift my little glass and he touches his to mine.

"To living," he says, and I lose myself in his eyes before closing mine and letting the tequila burn. He read my mind.

VERONIKA WHISPER-YELLS INTO my ear while G. stands across from us in conversation. She brings her hand to her head and pushes the blond curls up, fluffing them.

"See! When you don't care, things happen!"

"Veronika, that's illogical." I laugh.

"I mean . . ." She smirks and nods her head toward G. "He showed up when you stopped worrying about it."

I shrug and sip my drink. Maybe she's right. I try to control everything, to work in routines and systems, but maybe there's some logic to the illogical that I've never considered before.

"And he's fucking hot."

She breaks into a big smile, with one dimple showing. When I see hers, I realize there's a grin on my face, too. A ridiculously goofy grin.

More people come, more people dance, others drink, and someone trips walking to the bathroom. Whenever I flick my eyes up from a conversation, they meet G.'s.

Zuri begins to wobble on her heels, sloshing a drink on her dress. Everyone who came offered to buy her one for her birthday, and I can't help but think it's the nicest and meanest thing to do. When two of our friends decide to take her home, luring her out of the bar with the promise of pizza, G. makes his way over to me.

"So," he says, standing close.

"So," I say.

"Did I tell you I like this top?" He runs his finger along the bottom of it, lingering on the bare skin of my ribs.

"No. You do?"

"Yes. It's . . . sparkly."

We laugh.

"What's your plan for the rest of the night?"

"I don't have one."

We stare at each other for what feels like a minute, and I don't want to leave, at least I don't want to leave without him. I wonder if he feels the same.

"Should we get out of here?" he asks with a hint of nervousness I haven't seen in him before. I remember reading a similar line while researching for the Dating category. Just vague enough so that **if they say no, you can brush it off as if it doesn't matter either way.**

When we say our goodbyes, I'm convinced the smirk on Veronika's face might ruin everything. I hope G. doesn't notice. As we push through the crowd toward the exit, he grabs my hand and laces his fingers through mine. My heart is beating everywhere: in my chest, in my temples, in the tips of my fingers.

Outside, he orders a car, and we slide into the back. He pulls me close to him and then moves both hands to grab my face, gripping my jaw, tilting it up toward him, and holding me still for a moment before leaning in. His lips are soft. They hit mine tentatively. I open my eyes and see his lashes like spider legs, long and thin. I close my eyes and he pulls back an inch; I can feel his breath on my lips. Then he kisses me again, deeper, his tongue pushing past my teeth and into my mouth.

When we arrive outside my apartment, I step into the refreshing night air, straightening my top. While I press my finger against the keypad, he's suddenly behind me. His lips on my neck, hands on my waist. We walk up the stairs at a pace that feels too slow for how fast my pulse is racing.

When we enter my room, I see it for what feels like the first time: no photos on the walls, no picture frames or trinkets on the dresser. My Screen on my desk. It looks so empty. So plain.

"Did you just move in?" he asks.

"Sort of," I say, turning the Screen to Sleep mode. I don't want to explain anything right now because I don't want to think. He sits on the bed and pats the spot next to him. It feels childish, but I move toward him anyway and sit down. He runs his hand over my leg gently.

"Is this okay?" he asks.

I nod and he leans in to kiss my neck, the lightest of touches, his breath warm.

"How about this?" he says, whispering.

I nod and he pushes me backward. We're lying half on, half off the bed, and he kisses up my neck to my lips, pausing there before sticking his tongue in again as if prying open my mouth. G. slides his thigh in between my legs, and I press against it. I can't think, just feel. Warmth and wanting.

I claw at the back of his head—his curls, trimmed short, feel like carpet—and then I grasp at the neck of his shirt, tugging until he leans back and takes it off. He pulls me up with him and we re-situate so we're lying fully on the bed, giggling and whispering stupid things I can't remember.

"I like this shirt a lot, but I think I'll like it even better off you," he whispers, and we laugh again, conspiring together as he rolls it over my head.

His hands travel down my neck to my boobs, touching a nipple with his thumb before leaning down and running his tongue in a circle around each one. He kisses my stomach, my hip bones. He fumbles with the button of my jeans before he finally gets it. Standing on his knees, he pulls both my jeans and underwear off at once, throwing them on the floor. It feels like a waste that I wore new black lace ones.

I lie there, staring at the ceiling, sorting through everything I've seen or read on how to do this. He snakes his arms, warm and heavy, under my legs and reaches up with one hand, running it over my nipple just as the tip of his tongue hits and he begins to lick. A slow, rhythmic licking. He uses a finger, slipping it in and out of me. I try to breathe. **Relaxing through breath can help you orgasm faster**. He alternates between slow and fast, finger and mouth, and it feels good, but I keep thinking about how I should have come by now and I can't. After a few minutes, I do the only thing I can think of.

"Do you have a condom?" I say, hoping it comes out sexy like the girls online.

He looks up at me, eyelids heavy, and crawls up to kiss me again before standing. I forgot he still has his pants on, and I'm embarrassed I hadn't thought to take them off. He tugs a condom from his pocket, and I wonder when he put it there. Has it been there all night? Did he know this would happen?

G. steps out of his pants and unwraps it. He knows I'm watching as he rolls it onto his dick. When he climbs back on top of me and kisses my lips again, I can feel it tap my leg. Then he kisses my ear, letting his tongue glide over it as his hand finds its way down my stomach to the wetness between my legs. He puts his finger in deep, as if preparing, but I can't tell if he's preparing me or himself. He looks down and watches as he grabs his dick and guides it into me. A sharp pain hits that makes me gasp, and he smiles, inching it in.

"This okay?" he asks. I rock my hips up to meet him instead of answering, and he seems to like that, so I do it again. He starts slow, then, as I rise to meet him, he begins moving faster and faster, scooping his hand underneath me to grab my ass and pull it toward him. He bites my neck. Hot breath on my clavicle, in my ear.

He moves so quickly now that our bodies smack against one another in a loud slapping noise. My head begins to hit the headboard of the bed, but he doesn't stop, he goes faster.

"Tell me you want me," he says, words filled with breath.

"What?"

Thud. Thud. Thud.

"Say it."

Thud. Thud. Thud.

"I want you," I whisper, and dig my fingernails into his back as he looks down at his dick going in and out of me.

"Again," he demands.

"I want you. I really do. I promise. I've never wanted someone before. But I want you."

"Fuck," he says. And I like how what I said makes him both weaker and stronger at the same time, so I say it again and again.

"Fuck, Lee, I'm going to come."

He leans over and bites my ear, moving even faster, thud-thud-thud-thud goes my head against the headboard until he lets out a sigh, higher than I was expecting, and deflates on top of me, leaving his dick inside.

WHEN I WAKE in the morning, he's gone. I heard him gather his clothes last night and tiptoe out, but I stayed turned the other way long after the apartment drifted into silence again.

I need time to think through it all, but as soon as I leave my room, Veronika wants details. She insists we go to a trendy place for brunch, where I order fig pancakes by pressing the wrong button and she orders an omelet but then eats most of my pancakes, too. Zuri messages the chat to thank us, something about having the best night ever.

I see a little boy dribbling a soccer ball down the sidewalk on our walk home and want to text G. about it. A few hours later, a pebble slips in my shoe and I want to tell him about it, too, because I'm sure he's had one in his shoe before, right? And we could laugh about how stupid it is that one little rock can be such a nuisance.

Veronika says she wouldn't be surprised if it was a one-night stand. And then at night sitting on the green couch she says she wouldn't be surprised if he's in love with me. I try to forget about it. It was all just an experience for Vicky anyway.

CHAPTER 26

The game seems to be helping. Because three black cars fly by, I order a matcha for the first time, and am amazed by the amount of chlorophyll content in the foam. I buy a pair of heels online just because I saw two people on the street wearing the same color purple. They sit in my closet, sparkling and pointy. I'll never wear them, but the small thrill of pressing a button, having them arrive, opening the box, and slipping them on to see how long they made my legs look was good, another experience to check off for Vicky.

In the afternoon, my phone and watch and Screen light up at once, with a reminder I wish I could unsee. Today is the day I agreed to model for the advanced drawing class. I put on sweatpants and a sweatshirt; the more I can cover up, the better.

Halfway down the stairs, I remember the instructor recommended I bring a robe, so I run back up and grab Veronika's pink one off the hook in the bathroom and stuff it in my backpack.

In a classroom across from the studio, I study a digital image of a fruit bowl, designed to look old and faded. It's probably a copy of some famous painting back when pears and apples and bananas could just sit in a bowl. Back before they were measured for their calories, sugar content, the cost per bite, and the projected mood after eating.

I hold the pink robe in my lap and feel ridiculous as I sip on cheap wine from one of those small plastic glasses again. Taking a selfie, I send it to BABES and then play nervously with the plastic cup too much, cracking it, and having to sip my wine out of the other side. Chris messages me and asks what I'm up to.

lee [1:13 P.M.]
about to model for an art class

chris [1:13 P.M.]
what?
ur kidding

lee [1:13 P.M.]
no lol
im serious

chris [1:13 P.M.]
wow ok
guess ur really breaking routine
good for u

lee [1:13 P.M.]
what do you mean lol

chris [1:13 P.M.]
just never thought u would be the type
to get naked in front of a bunch of strangers
hahaha but go lee!

What is he talking about? Modeling is terrifying enough. Just being the center of attention. But modeling naked? I laugh right as the instructor knocks. When I tell her to come in, she peeks her head around the door.

"Ready?" A large strand of her hair dangles loose from a clip. "Oh, sorry, came back too soon!"

"Oh, no, I'm ready," I tell her. Ready to get this over with, I think. She looks at me again and cocks her head to the side.

"Have you done this before?" she asks, kindly.

"No, but I'm sure it will be okay," I add quickly, mostly for myself.

"Oh, sorry, my bad! I should have walked you through it a bit more. So you'll just put on the robe in here and come out when you're ready. I'm heating up the studio space so that you won't get cold. And we'll just start with two or three short poses so you can get used to holding them. Maybe just seven minutes. Does that sound good? And I'll make them easy so you don't have to worry too much. Is that cool?"

I nod.

"Oh, and you can leave your clothes in here, no one will steal them."

I nod again. She smiles warmly and closes the door behind her, leaving me there still nodding over and over again as if I'm glitching, as if I can't stop. I nod while gritting my teeth, trying not to panic. This is fine, everything's fine, I think to myself while my pulse picks up speed.

Chris was right. How could I have missed something so obviously well known to others? I try to breathe, try to steady the intake and outflow of air. My instincts are telling me to run down the hall, down the street, to sprint all the way back to the apartment and not look back. What kind of person gets naked for others to sketch? What kind of people like sketching naked people? Is there something wrong with me for feeling so immediately nauseated at the idea?

If the past few months have taught me anything, it's that I'm the common denominator in misunderstandings. It's me who doesn't know how to act, react, be outside of the Program, the lab, my own tunnel of research.

That's why I started the game, I remind myself, to get into situations that normal people might find themselves in anyway.

I swallow, pushing the truth down. Because I know, even though every cell in my body is telling me to flee, that I need to stay. It's my job.

I tug my clothes off quickly and throw them in a pile, pulling the robe tight against me. It suddenly seems extremely thin. I close my eyes and enter the hall, where the instructor starts talking quickly as she guides me into the same room I was in before, except this time everything is blurry. I can hardly hear her over the pounding of my heart in my ears.

"Remember, the hardest part is holding the pose. Just try and zone out if you can," she says, her feather earrings swaying as we walk into the room. "And worst case, if you have to move, just regain the position you started with."

I follow her to the center, where a black box is set up with a folding chair on top of it. She places a white sheet over the chair and nods in my direction, telling me to drop the robe.

For a second, I wonder if I'll be able to do it. But then my hands are moving on their own. They untie the robe and hand it to the woman. A body stands there, flushed with heat. A bare ass sits on the starchy sheet.

"Okay, great, cross your legs," the woman says. A leg dutifully crosses.

"Shift left." A shoulder responds to the assignment, slouching left.

"Put your arm up like this." An arm lifts.

"Head tilted back." A head tilts.

"Okay, perfect, hold this. I'll tell you when the seven minutes are up."

She sets her timer, and out of the corner of my eye, I see her move a small space heater around until a swatch of warm air blasts toward me. It hits all the parts, parts that welcome it. Parts that are not mine, but that are connected to me.

I look out above the heads of the people who have begun to draw. A sadistic impulse rises in me, one that keeps calling me back into my own body so I can feel it all, the pinprick of being seen in a way I don't want to be seen; of eyes studying the curve of my spine, the flesh of my hips, the swoop of my breasts, the hardness of my nipples that protrude in the open. I should try to feel it even if it's terrible, right? Feel what it's like to be stared at as a person. As a person that's become an object.

But survival instincts kick in, and I begin to force my thoughts elsewhere, to a happy place maybe, if only I could figure out where that is. I start by making myself think about a podcast I listened to earlier about the tiniest frog in the world. Picture the frog, I demand. It takes a couple of tries, but then there it is in my head. Unaware, oblivious of large trucks and skyscrapers. Just a little frog tending to its own business.

Okay, good, next thought, what's next. Chris told me earlier about how he drew a smiley face on his thumb and put a raspberry on it for a hat. That's good.

Thinking about Chris makes me wonder where he is now, what he's doing, why he likes goats with beards. I wonder how he got involved with this project, and if maybe he knows what it's like to be lonely.

I think about loneliness, and wonder what it would look like if it were visible, showing up in bluish-purple patches across people's skin, or lowering their voice an octave. Would it help if we could trace it physically? If lonely people walked slower or began to sneeze uncontrollably around others?

The minutes stretch and I wonder if this will help Vicky understand what it's like to live inside a body, to feel seen and invisible at the same time, to have all these ideas and emotions that are contained within flesh and bones.

I end up attempting to calculate how long the sidewalks of New York would be if we laid them all together in a straight line until someone coughs in a chair behind me and the hairs on my arms prick up again, reminding me that I'm still naked, still exposed, and a wave of nausea returns.

The way these artists are staring at me, studying me, reminds me of how Masha and I used to look at people in the Observation Room. Even if he taught me to treat every project like a person, to try and see all parts of it, we still only saw the subjects in there for what they were: a means to an end. Research.

How many people have I watched online or observed in the world who don't want to be seen? Or want to be seen, but maybe as real humans, not just experiments? Can scientists and artists get stuck this way, viewing the world as if removed from it? Is this why so much seems foreign to me?

I wish I had considered counting the minutes, because I need to know how many have passed, how many are left. Because now I can hear every movement, every shift and sigh. Why doesn't the instructor tap something to give any sort of indication of the time? How could they leave someone suspended like this?

I try to return to somewhere else, to thoughts about Chris ordering a diet water, or to Veronika telling me about her day, but the eyes, on parts of my body I haven't looked at myself, feel heavy. It feels like the gaze of a thousand people, and I can't get enough air, but I'm frozen with body parts acting on their own, a crossed leg, a shoulder shifting left.

Just as a small buzz of panic begins to crawl through me, the lady calls time and hands me back the robe. She says something about a five-minute break, but I rush out of the room, grab my clothes, and run out the door into the street, where I order a car home. I pull the comforter over my head and stay there shivering even though my scalp is hot, slicked with sweat.

★ ★ ★

THE NEXT MORNING, I scrub myself clean in a shower so hot it leaves my skin splotchy red. Then I bury myself in work, adding research to the Data Program even though I don't know what category we're on anymore. It just feels good to do something I'm good at. Chris said there can never be enough information, so I add to the past categories, to Communication and Money and Entertainment and Belief, until evening comes and I need food.

I ask Maps to help me find somewhere to eat and it guides me to the deli called Deli again even though I'd rather go somewhere new. It's the fourth time it's taken me here, and when I walk inside, the machine senses my presence, recognizes my face, and begins to make the sandwich that has accidentally become my regular order: the #55. Some kind of Italian, loaded with thin slices of salami and one or two other meats, plus banana peppers, which add a sour aftertaste. Toasted. Oil and salt on top. Thankfully no mayonnaise. I don't really know what cheese is on it, but it's white.

I stand there as the bread drops and travels on the silver roller coaster getting stuffed with all kinds of things and think about Cindy and Greg ordering the same takeout week after week. Did they like it, or was it just easy?

Maybe that's how so many people become complacent. We build systems that are supposed to make life easier, more pleasant, and then we get stuck.

I scan the small deli, the shelves stocked with all kinds of snacks to go with a sandwich, to see if there's something I actually want. My eyes stop on a shelf filled with sweets, and I feel something. **Listen to your gut.** Today my gut needs a cookie.

"I'm grabbing a cookie," I tell the machine, but I don't hear it respond in any way, so I'm not sure if it knows.

"I'm taking a cookie!" I say, speaking up a bit so it can charge me. I pluck one from the batch, all perfectly measured, perfectly circular, with the same amount of chocolate chips to ensure the nutrition information is accurate. Still, no response.

"I am tak-ing a cook-ie!" I say louder. Still nothing. The only sound is of the sandwich being slopped and slathered together.

"Did you hear me?"

Nothing.

"I NEED THIS FUCKING COOKIE!"

The sandwich shoots out and hits me in the chest. I fumble to grab the silver pellet before it falls. When I march to the counter to tell the Screen that I'm taking this goddamn cookie because I want it, and it's okay to want things in life, I realize a cookie has been included as part of the meal all along.

I lug my food home feeling confused. While I'm eating it at the wobbly kitchen table, Chris messages me. He has to push our lunch again because his cat is sick, but he promises we'll do it next week.

As the green dot next to his name fades, signaling he's offline, I'm reminded where I am: by myself in the kitchen of an apartment stacked on other apartments in a building on a street with other buildings in a large city full of them. I tear my cookie apart piece by piece, stuffing each one in my mouth. Then I eat the sandwich, finding them both unsatisfying in a way that I wouldn't know how to explain even if someone were here to ask.

CHAPTER 27

It's a Friday and I'm getting ready to go to a four-hour sound retreat
in some warehouse in midtown when an email comes through and
I check my watch reflexively.

It's from G.

My whole body freezes, and I'm afraid to open it, but I also want to
open it right away. I'm nervous he'll see I read it so quickly, desperately, gulping the words down like water.

I open it and read it twice. Veronika walks by and says something I
can't hear. She sticks her head back in my room and repeats herself.
When I still don't answer, she comes in and grabs my wrist to read what
I'm reading.

"You shouldn't wear this stupid thing," she says. "It looks weird, and
don't you already look at your phone enough?"

Holding my arm, she turns it out like a branch and reads the message.

"Jesus, he emails you now? It's been like . . . weeks?"

I don't respond.

"What took him so long? It would almost be better if he'd just disappeared than coming back from the dead like this." She doesn't let go of
my wrist, holding my arm out, awkwardly twisted.

"And he wants to hang out tonight?"

She keeps reacting for me, voicing the same questions I have. In the
email, he apologizes for not reaching out sooner, work's been crazy, he

says. He names a bar where he'll be tonight at eight P.M. if I want to meet him there. He'll understand if I don't show.

When Veronika and I look up the bar, we both already know I'll go, and then we see the photos, a speakeasy with red velvet chairs near Union Square. She looks at me, smiling but concerned, and leaves to select an outfit from her closet for me to wear.

Veronika helps me with my makeup, her fingers gentle on my cheeks, the brush soft on my eyelids, and when she's done my face feels heavy. I open my eyes and stare into her face that's so close to mine. I can feel her breath as she examines her work so far. Then her eyes meet mine.

"You don't have to go," she says, and I realize she's protective of me.

"I know."

"You really like this guy, don't you?"

I nod, fighting a smile, but it comes anyway.

I WANDER UP and down Irving Place. It's silent, empty, with just a few lights in the buildings above. I wonder how long he'll wait if I don't find the place soon. Finally, I try the doorbell at a nondescript brownstone where Maps keeps telling me to go, beeping in frustration when I walk past it. A woman in a black jumpsuit answers and ushers me inside what feels like a small coatroom. She asks if I have a reservation. I tell her I'm looking for G., and she nods in a way that makes me nervous. Does he come here a lot? Is she looking at me differently now?

Inside, the place is exactly what it looked like in the photos, except darker, and the smell of bourbon permeates the air. Music mingles with conversation and the shaking of drinks. Velvet couches sit under chandeliers that gather and throw light. I spot a woman donning a necklace of pearls and feel a wave of awe. I didn't know people wore those anymore.

The pantsuit lady leads me to the back, where I see G. sitting at a bar, facing away from us. I thank her and take the moment to study him from behind. Strong shoulder blades, arm resting carelessly around the back of a seat that's empty. **Crushes can cause a spike in**

heart rate, sweaty palms, renewed energy. I smile goofily, try to suppress it, realize I can't help it, suddenly love that I can't help it, and let it spread across my face.

"Is someone sitting here?" I ask, pulling out the chair next to him. His expression is sullen, serious, and tired in the second before he realizes it's me. I haven't seen this side of him, and it confronts me, briefly, this realization that he could be someone completely different than I'm constructing in my head. His demeanor transforms, light coming back into it as he stands to hug me, holding me close, letting his hands slide down to the small of my back.

"You look beautiful. I didn't think you would show."

Standing here, in this moment, I realize that no amount of research will ever prepare me for seeing G. face-to-face. No matter how much I study, how much I read or watch or calculate, no matter how accurate all the data can be, none of it can prepare me for the fluttering in my stomach, the weakness in my knees.

"Well," I say, looking at him looking at me. "Here I am."

THE NEXT MORNING, I lie on the couch holding an ice cube to a red, splotchy hickey on my neck when Veronika stomps down the hall.

"How was last night?" she asks, peeking over the couch at me before heading to the kitchen. "You look like shit."

"Wow, thanks," I say, re-situating the ice cube in the washcloth. After G. left, I stared at the ceiling until my limbs went numb.

"He didn't stay over?" Veronika's voice is loud behind me.

"Nope."

"Hm. Weird. I mean, some people like their own bed. They have it molded to their body, or those comforters that regulate temperature."

I hear ice plunk-plunk-plunk in a cup and then a stream of water jetting from the faucet. She returns, carrying a large, blue cup, and plops down on the couch, causing the whole thing to move. I know she wants to ask more questions but is waiting for me to talk instead. I can't help but feel this is some kind of sales strategy she brought home from the office to use on me. We stare straight ahead at the blank, black screen of the TV. I cave.

"Okay, so why didn't we go to his place, then? I said we could go to his place, and he didn't want to."

"Maybe he snores or talks in his sleep or something." She takes a gulp of water and the ice clinks around. Her hair is splaying out of a bun on top of her head.

"Are you hungover?" I say.

"Did he say he'd call?" She ignores me.

"Yeah, kind of."

"Kind of? I mean, not to be a downer, but that doesn't sound like he'll call," she says, reaching for the remote, slinking farther down into the couch while turning the TV on. I remove the washcloth to examine the ice, which is now a small sliver. When I press my fingers to my neck, the skin feels raw.

"But you had fun? That's what matters, really. If you had a good time, you know?" Veronika doesn't want to let it go.

"Yeah, I guess."

She turns to look at me and raises an eyebrow. Eyeliner from last night is smudged around her eyes.

"Okay, fine. Yes, I had fun."

"Yeah, I can see that," she says, reaching over to poke my neck with her finger. She gets up, and I hear the sink turn on again.

"You're hungover," I say, craning my neck to see her figure leaning against the oven, drinking more water.

"Nope," she says, shaking her head back and forth.

"Yes. What'd you do last night?"

She pads back over, dragging her feet, and sinks down into the couch again. She tells me about going out with the BABES and how it was a dud. The strap of her heel broke. Everyone drank at a bar where the music sucked and then ate pizza that burned the roofs of their mouths. She nurses her water, biting the rim of the cup.

"So was it good?" she asks. My cheeks burn and the characters laugh on the TV.

"Was what?"

"The sex?"

How did she know we had sex! We could have just kissed or something. I cover my face with my hands.

"Oh my gosh. Wait, start from the beginning."

She nudges me with her foot, hitting my calf with it until I start speaking. I tell her about the bar and the pearls. She wants to know the drinks we ordered, which I can't remember, and what we talked about, which I gloss over.

"Wait, so did you get home after me? I must have passed out."

I shrug. The credits play as a clock on the screen counts down the seconds until it will start playing the next episode in the series.

"So, the sex, though. How many times? Is his dick big? Did you come?"

"What!"

"Did you orgasm?"

"Veronika . . . why are you—"

"So you didn't?"

"No."

"Why not?"

"What? I don't know."

"I thought you said it was good?"

"I mean, it still felt good, but—"

"Did you tell him what to do?"

Heat crawls across my skin. I get up, slide open the window, then sit on the arm of the couch.

"Wow, whoa, okay," she says, laughing. "Chill!"

She pushes herself up to sit cross-legged on the couch.

"We don't have to talk about it. But I feel like we should, because people don't, you know? Not people, but women never talk about this stuff, and we totally should. It's like we feel we have to keep it secret or something. And that's stupid!"

"Okay, I didn't orgasm."

"Have you ever?"

I look out the window.

Veronika tells me a long story about a boyfriend in college who was determined to be her first orgasm. She tells me that it's normal, that I shouldn't be embarrassed, that it's harder for women and we just have to learn ourselves. She pulls up links to vibrators on her phone and texts them to me. You can't just settle for being fucked, Veronika says. Sex isn't just for men, you should get pleasure out of it, too.

"Promise me you'll try it," she says. She looks at me earnestly now.

"Try what?"

"A vibrator, you idiot. I just ordered you two different kinds."

"Veronika, why did you—"

She sits up and crawls across the couch until she's in my face.

"Promise?"

"Oh, come on!"

"Promise?" She's sticking her face right in front of mine and laughing because she knows how uncomfortable it makes me. "Lee . . ."

"Fine, I promise."

"Pinky promise?"

"Veronika, I already promised."

She grabs my hand and places our pinkies together. We lock them and then I try and unravel my hand from hers, but she holds it.

"Wait, you forgot to seal it."

"Seal it?"

"Pinky-promise-sealed-with-a-kiss. Haven't you heard of that before? I always do it. It means the promise is real." Veronika demonstrates by leaning forward and kissing the pad of her thumb and then holding it up for mine to touch. Our hands are still locked by the pinkies, so I lean forward and kiss the pad of my thumb, too, and touch it to hers in the middle. Then she lets me have my hand back.

The episode ends and the circular countdown clock pops up again, covering the names of people who dedicated hours of their life to creating, writing, and producing the show.

"Are you still thinking about him?" she asks after a while.

"I mean, I wasn't, really, until you just brought it up again."

"True, my bad." She laughs. "You know, you could just look him up on Home and message him."

"Is that too desperate?"

A truck roars by outside. Veronika eyes the broken Sound Collector and sighs.

"I hate the idea that doing what you want to do is desperate," she says, not really answering my question. "But yeah, you're supposed to be a little indifferent. But it doesn't have to be like that. You should do whatever you want."

Veronika says she still feels alcohol in her pores and pepperoni on her breath. She pushes herself off the couch and drags her feet down the hall to the shower. I turn back to the TV and decide that if any of the characters in the show hug, I'll do it, I'll message him.

The episode goes on and on and I keep watching and watching until finally, a grandmother and son hug. I jump at the opportunity and open Home, copying G.'s name in the search bar.

His profile pops up. A photo of him—broad forehead, deep brown eyes, straight face—and his sister at the beach. She has short brown hair angled inward at her chin and a heart-shaped face with thick eyebrows that make her beautiful in a unique, angular way. I read the caption and then reread it.

Two years with this one.

Then I look at the photo again. His hand low on her hips. Hers resting protectively on his chest, her ring twinkling. I sort through the rest of the photos available, not many since we aren't friends, and gaze in disbelief, in horror. I stare hungrily, studying each one, leaning my face closer and closer to the Screen, soaking in every detail, from location—beach, rooftop in midtown, snowstorm—to shirt color—white, purple, blue—to his lips and how they alter over time, from smiling to smirking to a straight line.

My fingertips turn heavy, and I return to the first profile picture and look at it until it just looks blurred, a pile of pixels. I exit Home and stand, walk to the fridge, then back to the couch where the wet wash-cloth lies, then to the bathroom, where I kneel over the toilet, dry heaving, but nothing comes out. I pull on shoes and run down the stairs.

At the bottom, I lean against the wall for a second and scrunch my eyes tight so I don't fall over. When the spinning stops, I push through the doors and try to breathe in, but air catches in my throat.

I run as fast as I can to the river, down it, up it, back through the streets without seeing them. Maps tells me where to go, and I run and run and run, and when I get home, I climb the stairs two at a time, barge into my bedroom, and pull off my shoes and socks. The skin on my heels peels off with them, staining the fabric with pus and blood.

CHAPTER 28

M onday comes and goes. My knees hurt and my heels are raw. I move through the day in slow motion, counting hours, counting clouds, counting people, counting how many things I can count.

Tuesday disappears. On Wednesday, I sit on the subway and stare at my watch on my wrist, limp in my lap. Is it capturing all this?

Stops fly by. People get on and off. The ads continue to spin. Fuzzy Velcro shoes, a black suit, jeans with a patch of a cartoon mouse flipping me off.

I hope Vicky is seeing this. I need her to know that heartbreak and guilt make even the brightest of red jackets look dull.

CHAPTER 29

The office lights blink bright even though I'm early. I wander through the mess to my desk and am shocked to see that everyone is already here. They sit in the glass conference room with the door closed. I throw my bag down and rush into the room.

"Sorry I'm late, I have no idea what happened. I didn't know we were meeting today," I say breathlessly, taking my seat. I hate being late to meetings. Can't remember the last one I missed. I must really be out of sorts with this project. I haven't been sleeping. I zone in on collecting experiences but then become distracted by the experiences themselves. It's difficult to separate myself from my work, impossible, really. I've got to get it together.

Ted, Nikita, and the Consultants all avoid looking at me. Even Chelsea and Eric are here again.

"Lee, you don't need to be here for this," Toru snaps. Whatever he was projecting on the wall disappears. I look at Janet.

"We're actually looking at some of the data you're generating and some of the tests. But the team agreed you shouldn't see any of it while you're producing it," she says calmly. "But don't worry, it's actually all performing—"

"Janet," Toru interjects, and then he turns to me. "Just keep doing what you're doing. We promise to give you an update soon."

I nod and stand. The others study their Screens, their nails, the ceiling. No one says goodbye. I pull my sweater off as I walk out through the maze, flushed with embarrassment.

It makes sense I shouldn't be a part of the meetings, but it still feels strange to be kicked out. I exit the building, forcing a large smile at the camera even though a heavy feeling of dread is snowballing deep in my stomach.

I walk through the city until I stumble upon a swing set and pump my legs back and forth, back and forth. Is it possible to be successful at everything and then fail at the only thing that matters? When I'm at the highest point, I fling myself off into the air and skin my palms on the cold pebbles.

★　★　★

THAT NIGHT, I work on the couch next to Veronika while we watch a show. She talks loudly over the characters, reacting in real time and adding her own commentary the way she normally does. But tonight, when she starts yelling at one of them, saying not to trust so-and-so because he's a fool, I can hardly hear the dialogue on the Screen, let alone the discourse about work going on in my own head.

"Can you stop?" I say. We're both surprised.

"What?" she asks.

"Stop talking to the TV, I can't hear anything."

She stares at me for a second and then looks back at the Screen, mouth in a straight line. I consider apologizing, but then I tuck my hair behind my ear and the band on my wrist touches it. I take a deep breath and decide to push it further.

"You do that a lot, you know," I say.

Veronika doesn't answer.

"You're super loud all the time. You throw your stuff around. You talk over people when we're out. It's kind of annoying."

No answer. I can't tell if I'm doing it for work, or if I'm doing it for me. If I think Vicky should learn conflict, or if maybe I just need to learn it myself. It feels good for a second, but I can't stop, can't keep the words from rolling out of me.

"And I'm not the only one who's noticed."

She jumps up from the couch. I knew this would hurt her. She cares so much about what others think. **Sometimes it's easiest to take stress out on the people you trust.**

"What's wrong with you?" she says, glaring at me, her brown eyes glossy with tears. "I'm sorry I do so many things that bother you. That I'm so embarrassing to you and everyone else."

Her lip shifts, her jaw juts in and out, as she attempts to restrain herself.

"You know, you're not that easy to live with, either. Always working. Walking around as if your job is so much more important than everyone else's but then not even taking the time to explain it to us. It's like you think we're dumb or something."

I can't look at her. I don't think she's dumb, I just have an Agreement. Besides, I didn't think any of them cared what I was doing. And it's hard to explain, I'm still trying to understand it myself.

Veronika strides back to her room, blinking away tears. Her door sounds like it splinters as she throws it shut. My body feels like cement on the couch, legs sinking into the cushion. I close my eyes tight, tighter, tightest and hold my breath until I can't anymore.

CHAPTER 30

The apartment feels small, the office crowded; even Home has become claustrophobic. I scroll through, looking but not really looking.

With Veronika's silent treatment, I finally have the alone time I thought I wanted when I first moved in. The silence I thought I needed in order to do my job. But now it seems off, wrong, so I study a tutorial on how to write in cursive—a lost art—and drag my finger across the refrigerator's small Screen. An apology. I set it to ding when she walks in to make sure she sees it.

★   ★   ★

I TAKE THE subway to a restaurant in Brooklyn a few blocks back from the shoreline to meet Chris for lunch. Finally. I can't wait to ask him about the watch, about Vicky. Hopefully he can update me, even though the others are being weirdly secretive. I want to know if he's seen all the information the watch has been gathering or if it goes straight into the database.

After a forty-minute subway ride, I arrive at a small, slim place with round tables. I wonder what Chris will look like, if I'll recognize him.

Hovering outside the restaurant, I notice a spray-painted wall across the street. A giant green lizard licking a lollipop. Beneath it, sprawling letters spell: *I was here.* The same phrase I keep seeing.

I think about the word "here." It's another one of those slippery concepts. Iridescent, shape-shifting, like loneliness. If I walked down the street and past the restaurant, would I have to keep updating? I'm here, now here, now here. Or is it more than a location, instead some kind of feeling? A state of mind?

I snap a picture, send it to Chris, and type: I am here. Maybe we can debate the topic at lunch.

> **chris [1:12 P.M.]**
> lee
> ur going to kill me

I wait and stare at the messages, hoping the trains are delayed.

> **chris [1:13 P.M.]**
> something came up
> i can't make it
> but i just sent u money on Pay
> treat yourself pls
> the jalapeno queso is my fav

An alert slides across my watch and then my phone. Twenty dollars on Pay from Chris.

> im so sorry

I read the messages again. It must be a joke. I wait a few more minutes. But nothing else comes through. It's suddenly chillier than I thought. I begin to walk. Just to get away from the restaurant. To clear my head. Gray cement warehouses bloom around me, and the streets grow wider. What was exciting and new before now just makes me feel lost. I sit down on a curb and pull my knees to my chest.

Something came up? What could possibly come up so last minute? And for the third time? My head aches. I know from research that our generation is cursed with cancellations. **It's more common to cancel than to follow through**, but something about this bothers me.

I look at the watch and try to rationalize that whatever this feeling is could be good for Vicky to know, to experience, but still, even my disappointment seems muted. Unoriginal.

I press my palms into my eyes and let my head rest there. A woman with a Labrador walks by, letting her dog's wet nose sniff my hair. She doesn't notice because she's looking at her phone. The dog licks my arm, but I don't move to pet it.

Chris hasn't come to a single meeting. He keeps canceling our lunch. There's something going on, something that makes my stomach heavy. The woman tugs the leash to continue walking, but before the dog turns away, it licks my ear, leaving a slick trail of drool.

AT HOME, AFTER a blurred ride back, I pull out my Screen and begin to dig. The nice thing about being a researcher is I'm skilled at finding things that are supposed to remain hidden. I can't hack passwords or profiles, but information is usually floating free if you just dig deep enough.

I open the Data Program and tap through different tabs, exploring avenues I've never thought to go down before. It takes me three hours, but buried in the system, past the alarm about the arm and parm, I find what I'm looking for. Folders for each team member: our individual profiles. Every system has them somewhere.

Skimming through quickly, I find Nikita's is full of awards from her past career. She was in Urban Planning? It has a certificate showing her graduation from a Program almost as prestigious as mine. There are personal archives, too, showing engagement pictures and then therapy receipts documenting a divorce.

Ted's profile confirms he's a top-tier relationship and sales manager, that he really did experience a concussion, with a period of what they've labeled "depression" afterward. I tap through Rob and Tanya, who are gone. Trevor, who must be the tall lanky boy.

Then, there's Aaliyah. Aaliyah with the wire frames, the one who's always crossing her arms as if protecting herself. She, too, won top of class, accolades galore. And Andrea. Of course. Her strong build. Her toughness. Her jet-black hair and green cat eyes. The name Andrea fits perfectly. Her profile documents inventions she's submitted, multiple contests won; it shows that both of her parents died in a plane crash just a few years ago.

I scan through our profiles quickly. I'm curious, but I'll come back later, because right now I just want to find one thing. I want to check out Chris's to see who he is, his address, and how to find him. I'll just stop by to say hi. Maybe bring his cat some food.

But when I tap into it, the program malfunctions, quits, and restarts my whole Screen. After it updates, I find my way back past the alarm to the profiles again. This time, I go straight to Chris's, tap on it, and find nothing inside.

★ ★ ★

WHEN VERONIKA GETS home, I'm lying on the couch staring at the air. Sometimes that's all a person can do. She throws her jacket on the floor, her purse on the counter. She must have read and accepted my apology, because she comes over, places her hand on my forehead, and then brings me a glass of water with vitamins. I drink it without tasting much.

Chris messages me another apology and then tries to chat about the picture I sent earlier, the one of the graffiti. Instead of focusing on the words "I was here," as I did, he pings me about the image itself.

He says he's seen this same lizard graffiti around the city, and in some instances the lollipop is small, a few licks from being finished. In others, like the one I saw, it's brand new. Maybe the artist is trying to say something, Chris says, pinging rapid fire now, about the absurdity of desire. About wanting something, getting it, and then not being so sure you want it anymore. Like how even a lollipop, a supposed treat, can become torturous if you're stuck licking it every day forever.

I read the messages on my watch and then go back to staring at the ceiling. I never would have thought about the graffiti that way, but it makes sense. In a way, it makes me think of this role, this company.

What I wished for was a chance to be part of groundbreaking research. In a way that desire came true. Just not how I thought it would.

I want to message Chris back about this realization, and about the graffiti. I want to ask his opinion about the words underneath, "I am here," that have been inscribed all over the city. I want to ask why he keeps canceling. About the loneliness files he sent, what he thinks about it all. What I can do better.

But I don't. I'm frustrated that I still want to chat with him even though he blew me off. And then I become frustrated that I'm frustrated, so I roll off the couch and get into bed. Even though I'm exhausted, I won't be able to sleep. I open my Screen and let videos play, the bright colors burning into the back of my eyes.

CHAPTER 31

Janet watches as a mother with tired eyes talks animatedly to the wall. The woman describes how she used to drive her daughter to ballet four times a week. It was more than they could afford, but to see her little girl like that . . .

"When she was dancing?" a voice interrupts. That of another mother, or at least it sounds like it. Friendly, understanding, interjecting at the perfect cadence.

"Yeah, exactly, sometimes I'd peek into the studio, you know how it is. And I mean, Sarah was usually so shy, but when she was dancing she was . . . oh, I don't know. Fierce? Maybe that's not the right word. I just wish you could have seen her. The way she looked at herself in the mirror. She was so intense."

If it weren't for the wires wrapped around the mother's skull, slinking up her arms, biting her fingertips, or the glaring lights of the small, sterile room, the whole thing would seem ordinary. A boring, meandering phone call between two parents about the fatigue of packing lunches, or how when your child leaves home you're left pitter-pattering around the house a bit more, dusting, organizing, looking for something . . .

"I don't know, I've just been feeling a little useless, you know? It's hard to explain. Have you ever felt that way?" the woman asks the empty room.

Janet crosses her leg and rotates her ankle as Toru hovers behind her. He switches between studying the woman on the other side of the glass and her charts displayed all over the room around them.

It's been a logistical nightmare to organize all the tests, but it's also been a relief. Janet negotiated with the Government for permission, worked with Toru's team to meet their requirements, and coordinated with the doctors and scientists behind The Loneliness Report. The monstrosity of the task has demanded focus. It's allowed her to slip back into her competitive, daring, thrive-under-pressure self. She's been able to fall back into sync with Toru again and regain control of herself, of the project.

Inside the small room, a team unhooks the woman, whose session has ended, and prepares the space for the next subject. Janet turns to examine the dashboard showing the results for the mother, Subject #304. Over the past month, the woman has been experiencing significant decline in symptoms of loneliness. All due to her conversations with Vicky.

Looking at the dashboard, Janet feels a ping of pride. The watch strategy is untraditional. It's not "how these things should work," as the Government's Tech Consultants keep reminding Janet and Toru in each and every correspondence. But it's been working, or at least it's been helping when paired with all the other data.

Sure, there are those test subjects who still sense the uncanniness of conversing with something that's not human. And yes, Vicky slips up occasionally, causing Toru to fume and the subject to clam up, distrusting the connection. But the truth? The majority of their tests—moderated and unmoderated, in-lab and in-life—are showing that Vicky is trending toward success.

What's more interesting is Vicky's rate of learning. She adapts to each subject, growing better with every conversation. And yet, Toru and his team told Janet that even with new lines of live data from all these participants, Vicky still clings to Lee's information, processing it along with everything else. Lee, that devilish curveball she was wary of at the beginning, has now become an even bigger curveball she's rooting for.

Janet stands and stretches, her spine click-click-clicking. She watches as Toru shuffles in and out, rushing around and asking questions. Buzzing with that energy she loves. But for some reason, seeing him this way today actually causes a heaviness in her that she doesn't understand. Sometimes the body recognizes sadness before the mind.

Janet shakes it off; she must just be tired from the tests, from the sleepless nights managing all of this. She wanders over to Eric and Chelsea, who sit with one Screen pulled up around them, and peeks over their shoulder expecting to see the data from today, but they're monitoring a different chart. Janet recognizes it instantly, though she hasn't seen it before. Purple data: curving and falling and looping and diving and spiking. It must be Lee's information from the watch. Why doesn't she have access to this?

"Is that normal?" Janet asks Eric. He takes off his headphones and she repeats herself. "That. Is it normal?"

"Oh, hey, Janet. Um, this? No. But none of this is normal," he says in his go-with-the-flow manner. He inhales from his e-cig and turns away from Janet to let out the vapor.

"Yeah," Chelsea adds, laughing, taking off her headphones, too. "What's normal?"

"But this data," Janet says quietly, pointing to their Screen. "It looks a bit . . ."

"Erratic?" Chelsea says innocently, and Janet nods. They see that she's serious, that she's concerned, and the smiles fade off their faces.

"Yeah, very unstable," Eric says. "To be honest, our division—"

"—is a bit worried," Chelsea finishes, looking down at her hands. Janet recognizes a new, small tattoo of a watch among the constellation of ink decorating her fingers.

"That's why we're keeping an eye on it," Eric says. "Monitoring closely."

"But I'm confused. Toru told me it's working?" Janet asks. "Even if Lee's going a bit . . ."

"Yep," they both respond. And before anyone can say anything else, a new subject enters the room on the other side of the glass and silence settles in as the test begins.

Hours pass, and it's not until the tests are done for the day, not until Janet says goodbye to everyone and steps outside of the innocuous building into the smell of rain, not until she's on a rattling subway speeding uptown, that she lets herself think about Lee's data again.

It's fine.

It's working, or at least helping. It seems that Vicky is still accepting it. The girl is just doing her job. Janet and Toru always talk about how sometimes you have to sacrifice one person for the good of a thousand others. But that's not the case here. It can't be. Janet's been monitoring all the team's happiness levels each day. She's been keeping an eye on their health data. Everyone is fine. Even Lee.

Janet presses her finger to the door of her apartment and hops into an elevator that flings her up ten flights. She strips to shower, stands motionless as the water drips across her limbs, stares at the shampoo suds spiraling down the drain. Janet towels off, never reaching the few droplets in the middle of her back, brushes her hair, her teeth, pulls pajamas on, and peels the covers back, sliding into bed, and all this time it's there, beating behind her skull.

The test subjects talking to the empty space. The tired mother, a sad smile lingering on her lips, the sign of hope on a person who feels like they don't deserve it. These people, one after the other, full of desperation and shame. How did she just sit there and watch them today without feeling a thing?

The sheets press down on her, light and heavy. The ceiling, too. The walls. Janet lies there and stares up at them but sees Lee's purple information instead, powerful and disturbed.

How can it be that even though everything is going right, even though their risks are paying off and the tests are working and their team is outlasting so many others and they could potentially be the ones to win it, to solve this strange loneliness thing, that lying here it all feels so entirely, gut-wrenchingly, irrevocably wrong?

CHAPTER 32

T ime is ticking, Toru reminds me in an email, as if right on cue. As if he saw me take a day to just lie there on the couch, saw me hit a limit.

The other company is out, he says. And I wonder if he's supposed to be telling me this. If Chris and Janet know he is.

Is it working? Is the watch working? I respond, eager for a crumb of validation, just the suggestion that what I've been doing is useful.

Yes, he replies. Just keep going.

Are there experiences we're missing? Is there something I can do better?

Just keep going, he repeats.

I say okay even though I have a million questions.

CHAPTER 33

I open Dating and swipe until I find someone who will meet me immediately. Tonight. They want data? I'll get them data. They want experiences? I'll get them. Just keep going? Sure. Watch me.

I meet Jon at a small bar called Lovers of Today, which is chipped into the edge of Manhattan's Lower East Side near the waterline.

Jon is tall and wears black jeans and a black sweatshirt, looking unreasonably fashionable. He does not seem to care how my day went or that the weather is nice outside, which is refreshing because now I don't have to pretend I care about any of those things, either. Instead, he asks me abstract questions about water, catching me off guard.

"It's just, well, I've been looking at paintings online about the feeling of floating," he explains, pausing to take a sip of his drink. He closes his eyes, visibly savoring the sip. I wonder if this is something that's supposed to be attractive or if he just doesn't care what I think. I take a sip, too, and let the flowery flavor drip down my esophagus.

"Anyway, these paintings, most of them depict floating as this wonderful feeling, something desirable."

I nod, looking down at the condensation building on our glasses in the summer heat. Flower petals float in the light orange liquid. One gets stuck to the bottom of my straw, so I have to suck on it really hard.

"But I think floating can be torturous, too, you know? Like not having any direction. Or being stuck underwater. So, I guess that's just been on my mind, and I was curious if you've thought about water lately?"

I've felt that before, that kind of floating. I feel it right now, suspended between wanting to do a good job and not knowing if I am. He looks at me with straight brows and an even mouth, making deeper eye contact than I'm expecting. I mention that water makes me think of **how some people enjoy the sound of raindrops hitting the top of a car** and he nods as if I've said something profound.

One drink down, then another. He hands me a vape and I suck it. Something strawberry flavored. When I hand it back, I realize that I like his jaw. His hand is on my leg, and I let him keep it there, thinking that Vicky should see into the mind when the body is flirting. She's probably already processing the way I'm processing how his fingers feel on my thigh. How it feels small yet reverberates through my whole body.

Jon begins speaking quickly, animatedly. He launches into what he's been reading lately: Einstein's biography. Apparently, Einstein believed all of life could be broken down and given meaning. Jon paraphrases this, making quotations in the air with his fingers—calling it "deterministic." But in the end, on his deathbed, Einstein realized this wasn't true. Not everything can be explained. In fact, most things can't be.

"The most beautiful and deepest experience a person can have is the sense of the mysterious," Jon says. I think he might be quoting Einstein verbatim; I remember seeing these lines somewhere before. Either way, the idea wedges itself in my mind. Mystery as inevitable, as potentially even desirable. Especially in a world where I know how long I was in REM-cycle sleep, what nutrients my body is missing, the very minute my period will start.

Our glasses are empty. A couple behind us laughs, and two women in the middle of the small space sway back and forth to the music like palm leaves in a breeze.

"You see"—Jon leans toward me—"most things are random."

He kisses me with paper lips. A warm, wet tongue. And then he pulls back.

"Like us," he breathes into my ear, and then stands and walks out.

★ ★ ★

JUST KEEP GOING, Toru says, so I think of ways to do more, more, more, always more. If the man in the yellow shirt looks up from his phone and we make eye contact, then I'll answer a listing on Home's Need Help Forum. The man looks up and we make eye contact briefly, and then I open Home to see the first one: a request to photograph brunettes who are between twenty-four and twenty-nine years old.

No, I think. But it's a faint protest compared to the loud determination that's pulsing through me.

That night, I'm standing side by side with two others in a leaky East Village apartment as a man with graying hair and a round stomach photographs us fully clothed with our arms by our sides. It's an old camera, one of the collectibles that sell for crazy amounts in online auctions. **Photographs preserve a slice of reality that immediately becomes false the moment it's captured.** My legs are springs, ready to flee if my mind lets them, but I stay and stand and stare straight ahead.

When the man's done, he takes the film out and unravels it across the floor, and then he turns on music and asks us to dance. To stomp on top of the photos. I'm not sure how to react, but the woman next to me begins moving her feet back and forth slowly, and the rest of us join in.

The man doesn't stare; he dances, too, across the room. And as we all throw our limbs around, I feel the smallest hint of pride that I'm capturing this strange human experience for Vicky. That even though alarm bells are chiming in my chest, I'm still here. I'm still doing my job.

It's not until the man drops a hundred dollars in all our Pays and I see how quickly we all disperse in the moonlight that I realize the others showed up without a watch driving them, but for something else. Money? To feel something? I run home, hoping Vicky will understand how desperation drives people. It was good that I went, I tell myself, as I close the door behind me and triple-check that it's locked.

More, more, more, always more.

The next day, I find myself in a loft somewhere in the West Village because two bicycles ran a stop sign. A woman with beautiful thick purple eyeliner and a blazer hands me a joint and I inhale. Smoke rubs my chest and I hold my lips shut tight, but a cough escapes, in an even worse form: a splutter.

Time is ticking.

Good is the enemy of great.

Decisions are easier when I let the world make them for me.

While walking down the stairs, I fall and skid to the bottom. When I look around, no one is there, and I wish I could share the embarrassment. I look at the watch and whisper, did you catch that?

Chris checks in and I want to tell him about everything so badly— just to have someone to talk to who will understand—that I try and forget about the lunch incident. I tell him about the feeling of being high, about how I thought it would feel good to lose control but really it felt paralyzing. As if my body were made of rubber.

Did you feel like it slowed you down or sped you up? he asked.

Both, I say.

Neither, I correct.

If the subway arrives in less than two minutes, I have to accept an invitation from Nikita to go to one of her friends' birthdays. I wait and watch the clock, and when the subway arrives in three minutes instead of two I sigh, relieved. Maybe I can finally go back to the apartment. I can see what Veronika is doing, sit on the couch for a minute, and research my next experience from there.

But as I ride the train uptown, I realize if I go home, I'll just be wasting time that I should be spending experiencing life. So I play another game, and another, and another, until one tells me to go to a new club with someone from Home.

Hours later, in a large, humid warehouse with flashing silver lights, a stranger with long black hair twisted into a braid and her boyfriend, with a flat, rugged face, begin dancing with me. His hands on my hips, then hers, she kisses me, and then he does. All I can think about is the difference between her soft lips and his scratchy ones.

I watch the night unfold from next to myself in phases of panic. At their house, I sit on a strange orange sofa while my mind repeatedly tells me to go, go home, go back to the apartment, call a car, go. Instead, I pet their cats and my body enters their bedroom surrendering to hard, soft, slippery, and unexpected sensations that appear briefly, loudly, and then fade into an intense emptiness as I return to myself and walk fifty blocks home.

I meet a writer at a coffee shop and she invites me to karaoke with her friends. When? I ask. Now, she says. And because I counted five freckles on her bicep, I have to go. So we walk to Koreatown and swerve through the lunch crowds into a decaying brick building, climb four flights of stairs, and follow a man, also named Lee, to a backroom where three other writers wait. We chug beer out of plastic cups and sing duets for hours.By the third round, my head aches and my stomach is filled with foam and I think about how much easier this would have been to just watch online. But then I'd miss it, the way one of the women almost falls over, the way another giggles too loud, the look in their eyes when they talk about being writers, one shamefully as if it's a burden, another performatively as if it is a gift.

Vicky wouldn't get to be here with me, trying to understand it all. How it feels to watch one of them drop into the splits, and how seeing it firsthand in this shadowy bar in the middle of the day is both silly and sad at the same time.

Isn't this great? Isn't this fun? they ask, with self-consciousness. I wonder if they're afraid to go home and try to create again, especially in a world where no one reads. Where words are abundant and have taken on so many forms that they've become shapeless.

I watch them laugh and smile and sing and realize they're here just to get blackout drunk and let the minutes leak out. Since when does everyone just want to kill time? I chug another beer, the room moves in phases, and when it's my turn to sing again they laugh at how serious I am, repeating the words that appear on the Screen into a microphone.

More. More. More. Always more.

You have potential to be great, Masha said. **Potential is often wasted.**

I pierce my nose because three poodles happened to be walking my same route home one day. It was just an idea, but then there they were, different poodles, different owners, all within a twenty-minute walk. **The world just spins in certain ways sometimes.**

The woman, greasy-haired, with a face marked by small scars left over from acne, laughed as she pushed the needle through. She actually laughed. A high-pitched gurgle, and I'll never forget it. Veronika came and videotaped the whole thing for Home. I knew she'd want to be the good friend who supports someone during a time of discomfort, e.g., a huge, long needle pushing through cartilage. Plus, the content was good. We sent a picture to the BABES and they said a little hoop suits me. They said it fits who I am, whatever that means.

Time is ticking.

Seconds running into the past. With the other company down, this either works or it doesn't, and we'll find out very soon. I play the game as much as I can and become the most exciting person I've ever been. No one will be able to say this was an average effort. I want to be someone worth tracking.

★ ★ ★

A MESSAGE ARRIVES, the one I knew might come sooner or later, the one I've been wanting and dreading. G. invites me to the same bar; he says he'll be there waiting.

I take a hard, long look in the mirror on the back of my door. It attempts to make a fashion recommendation, projecting an all-black outfit on me, then a top hat, then it malfunctions.

I study my eyebrows. My eyes, gray, just plain. **The eyes are the window to the soul**, but I don't see anything when I look in them. It feels a little bit like I'm doing everything wrong. But maybe that means I'm finally doing something right?

I play the game, even though I know what I want the outcome to be this time. If Veronika left a take-out carton in the fridge, I'll go.

The truth? Veronika always has leftovers rotting in there. So maybe I'm rigging it. Or maybe I'm just listening to myself for the first time in a long time. But what does it say about me if, in this one moment of clarity, all I want is to do something bad? Is it possible my instincts, my gut, my heart are wired wrong?

I pull open the fridge to see four creepy containers sitting there and then shut it quickly. Maybe good isn't always what we're taught it is.

Maybe bad isn't always so bad. Maybe right and wrong are amorphous. Because is it really wrong to desire an hour with someone who makes the atoms in a room crash together? To want to touch someone who makes the tips of my fingers tingle?

I have no idea what to wear. Veronika is out with friends, so I change outfits three times and pull on the pair of heels sparkling in my closet—the ones I ordered and never wore—if only to feel like someone else tonight. Someone who is brave and bold and whatever else the BABES might think I am, even though they hardly know me. Or maybe they do know me, and it's I who am foreign to myself.

There's no time to analyze everything now. I spread a layer of Chap-Stick across my lips, pop them like I've seen Veronika do, and then I clank, clank, clank down the stairs and into the blue-black night.

LATER, AS WE'RE lying together, I think: His body fits mine. When my cheek rests on his chest and his hand runs slowly up and down my side—tracing my outline, our legs intertwined—I feel like this is somewhere I should be.

I like the way his chest hair feels, curly, stubborn yet soft beneath my fingertips. I like the way his eyelids flutter when he's resting and how he smells like something just the slightest bit sweet. I like how he laughs, a deep laugh, only when I least expect it. And the way, when I asked him what he wanted me to do to him in a sultry voice, practicing like the ones I'd heard online, he said he wanted me to kiss him.

I like the way he plays with my hair, looping it around his fingers, and how he bites me, nipping at my neck. I like our meandering conversations, the way they last for hours and hours. He says he can talk to me in a way he's never been able to open up to anyone else. There's something special about me he can't quite put his finger on, and he doesn't want to ruin it. **The need to feel special is common to human beings.**

I sink into the sheets and I sink into him. His arms fit all the way around me and slide me closer, always closer, until I don't know where my skin stops and his begins. Everything fades away: the task, the watch, the pressure to be more than I am, the urgency of it all. I could stay here forever, burrowed in him.

And then there's the sound of the belt buckling, the door closing, and the sudden feeling of being exposed, naked and cold, even when pulling a sheet tight around me. Sleeplessness. The inability to move paired with the claustrophobia of being inside my own body.

When I can muster the energy, I pull up Home and look at pictures of them together, studying the way she smiles, wondering if she knows him well enough to sense when he's off or distant. Or if he's done this before with others and I'm not unique. Tears threaten, and I feel guilty that this is what I'm upset about: the idea that I'm interchangeable. And then I become upset that something in his life has turned him into a liar. That there was a switch from when he was a boy who believed in the world to a man who only sees its sharp edges. That someone I've begun to care about had something happen in his life, maybe long ago, that made him this way.

I stare at the five or six photos available, then I go to her profile and sort through more, and then her sister's profile, and then an aunt who has pictures of them on some beach with cheesy captions like **life's a hot dog bun, fill it,** until I feel so disgusted with myself I can't even cry.

Chris messages me a knock-knock joke. His timing is impeccable. I laugh even though I'm miserable.

★ ★ ★

ONE MORNING, I crave peanut butter toast with chocolate sauce and decide that I'm not messing around this time. I'm not going to let Maps lead me to the Deli, I'll just order exactly what I want.

When it arrives, I sit at the wobbly table and pull up Chris's files on loneliness so I can read through them again while I eat. I wish I could see this emotion. I wish I could examine it face-to-face to understand it better, but maybe that's why it was so controversial long ago. Loneliness is difficult to understand, to track. It appears and disappears in mysterious ways.

When I unwrap my toast and bite in, expecting to be transported, it's nothing like I imagined. Dry. The chocolate syrup sticks to the box.

It's a sad little toast. Different here alone in my apartment than in the diner with the silverware clanging in the background, the Russian woman stopping by and giving me concerned looks.

I set it aside and read through the notes on loneliness. And then I perform my own searches, too, just to see. It feels calming to be back in the portals and webs and archives.

The word doesn't appear, but people talk about things that sound similar. They reach out to each other, at least try to: Is anyone there? Does anyone understand me? Please, send me a picture of the moon.

CHAPTER 34

I wake late to an alarm blasting in my ear after tossing and turning half the night. In the kitchen, Veronika uses a small tool to make the bags under my eyes disappear, gliding it across my face in a hurry without asking while I make coffee. The device is cold. Tingly. When she's done, I run my fingers over the skin and feel the soft, corrected space.

While I sip coffee, thinking about nothing and everything at the same time, an invite for a meeting pops up on my watch, my phone, and my Screen. It's from Janet. No explanation, just a location. Just me and Janet, tomorrow morning at eight A.M., in an office I've never been to before.

I stare at it, and panic slowly surfaces. Does she want to review my performance? Does she think I'm not trying hard enough? Or not doing a good job? Does she know that Toru has told me we're the last ones left?

Breathe, I tell myself. But a voice in my head repeats the phrase that Toru wedged there: *Time is ticking.* I look at the invite and get a deep-rooted feeling that this is my last chance to make sure I've done everything I can for Vicky before we meet. That I'm doing my absolute best so I can look Janet in the eyes and say so.

I stand and pace.

What should I do first? Where to begin? A person can only experience so much. But how do they decide which experiences matter?

When we were working on the Emotion category, I dug up research about people who used to run naked at football games or across big parking lots. They called it streaking. Running through a public space fully exposed is supposed to be exhilarating, make your **blood shake, make you feel so fucking alive**.

If Veronika slams the door, I'll do it. A few minutes later, the pronounced echo of the door shutting arrives through my bedroom door. I peel off my pajamas and step into my shoes, lacing them tight. Standing in front of the door, I count to ten, then open it, look both ways, and sprint down the hall, down the stairs, and outside.

Goose bumps prick my skin, sprinkling across it. My inner thighs jiggle and my boobs fling up and down. I'm moving faster than I've ever run. Shoes heavy on a Jell-O body. My heart beats as if it might break free, and they were right, the web warriors sharing legends of the past. If blood could shake, if it could become staticky and unrelentingly impatient trapped inside veins, this is it.

Rounding the block and arriving back at the apartment building, my fingerprint is too sweaty to be recognized. Cameras blink at me and I don't care. It would be good for Vicky to understand breaking the law or the feeling of being caught doing something you shouldn't be doing, right?!

I wipe my finger on my hip bone and tell myself to breathe, breathe, don't panic, which only makes me stop breathing and start panicking. I hold my finger up again and before the apartment can register it, the door pops open.

A woman I've never seen stands there clutching the leashes of four dogs while staring at her phone. When she looks up, her eyes widen. I don't know why, but I wave. I actually lift my hand and wave. And then the dogs drag her down the steps and into the street, her mouth wide open. I rush inside, sprint up the stairs and into the apartment, closing the door behind me. The wood feels cold against my skin. To never see anyone in the building and then to see her during my naked lap feels like some sort of cosmic joke.

As I'm getting dressed, my phone and watch and Screen light up, and I freeze. Janet's calling. I let it ring and ring. I'm not prepared yet. I haven't had enough time. I need to do more, just a little more!

I decide if I can hold my breath for over a minute, I'll open the fridge and eat the first thing my hand touches. I breathe in and then begin to count. Sixty seconds, easy. I open the fridge and reach in quickly, touching it by accident: the hot sauce. The bottle is half full, with a red crust near the lid. I lift it and tilt, drinking it, pouring it straight into my mouth until it burns. Until I'm roasting from the inside. Until I cough and throw up blood or hot sauce or both, the red twirling in the toilet water like liquid art.

While recovering on the green couch, I debate calling Janet back, but maybe I should just do one more thing. Have one more experience. I decide that if a pigeon lands on the window I have to go to the office.

A gray puffball flutters on the sill and peers inside, tilting its head sideways at me as if to say, What are you doing, Lee? Why are you just sitting around? Why are you wearing that watch? It should have been given to someone else. Someone more qualified. Masha should have never picked you as a fellow. Cindy and Greg couldn't care less if you ever came back. All those people on The Report might stay lonely because of you. Your life is amounting to nothing, really, especially if you just keep sitting on the couch like that.

Scram! I tell the pigeon, jumping up from the couch to bang on the window.

I pull on two different shoes, a sneaker and a sandal, because I dared myself to wear whichever shoes fell out of the closet first. And because I've never done that before and wouldn't it be awesome to wear two different shoes for once, just to see what it's like, just to see if people notice! What an experience!

The crumbling exterior of the office, the squatness of it, even the rusty fire escape clinging tight, are all familiar now. So is the short commute, the damp subway station, the whir and clatter of the train.

I float downtown thinking about G. and his back muscles, thinking about the pure shock on the woman's face—I wish you could have seen it!—after I ran around the block butt naked yesterday. Or was it this morning? When you're just living, it all seems to blur together. I smile into the camera and the office door clicks open.

RECORD HIGH. Happiness levels 98%. Have a productive day!

A record? I wander inside, down the blank hallway, and plop into the elevator that shoots me up to the office. No one is here, and I realize it's Friday. How could I forget what day it is when my phone, my watch, and my Screen have alerted me of the date, the time, the hour and the seconds and the milliseconds and how long I've slept and how much energy it would take my current skeletal figure to run a mile?

I walk through the maze to the back, testing out different chairs as I go. Twirling in some, leaning back in others. I walk past my desk to the coffee machine. If the fridge is stocked, I'll add as much caffeine as the machine allows. Tugging open the fridge, I see rows of electric blue beverages and individualized lettuce snack packets staring back at me. Are you sure you're doing enough? they ask.

I tap the button for 5x caffeine. Coffee begins shooting out into the mug. Static fizzes inside me, because time is ticking, but I have potential! I could be great!

A block away from the office, I sip my coffee and sneeze. It's still extremely hot and—oh my gosh, the mug! I carried the mood mug out with me. An indoor cup in the outdoors. An office cup in the wild! What an experience!

The thought makes me laugh so hard I spill some coffee and it lands on the sidewalk, which repels the liquid, a new strategy to keep streets clean, so it keeps dripping and moving sadly away from me until it one day might be able to find a piece of earth that hasn't been protected and can naturally accept the lonesome spilled coffee. Trekking, tired, forlorn, and looking for a place to belong. I feel you, little coffee! Good luck, little guy!

I take a selfie with my mug in the wild, wild cement jungle of New York City as it changes from neon orange to gray and back again. When I send it to the BABES group chat, they respond right away, wondering what I'm doing and how funny and where are you and are you okay?

★　★　★

AFTER WANDERING AROUND shops and getting kicked out of lobbies with high vaulted ceilings and the zoo where animals are projected into their cages, after sitting in one place and blaring hard rock and then moving to another and trying jazz, I get another call from Janet. But I can't talk yet. I need to keep going. Need to keep experiencing. I need this to work, we all do. I want to prove to her that I can do this.

I kick a flowerpot off its sill just because there were two cracks in the sidewalk and then immediately feel bad and put the little flowers in my backpack and promise to plant them again somewhere newer, some-where better.

A man in his forties with a ponytail tries to ask me for directions and I tell him I don't know where I am and isn't it wonderful to get lost because **it's not about the destination**.

Be careful what you allow inside your mind, Masha told me. But I've let everything in and now nothing is there.

> **chris [11:28 A.M.]**
> lee u ok?
> ur location tracker says you've been in six different neighbor-
> hoods today
> its not even noon

> **lee [11:38 A.M.]**
> im fine
> everything is fine
> im just living!

I message him from my watch, talking into it. Except the woman on the sidewalk in front of me jumps and I realize I might not be talking. I might be yelling.

BY THE TIME I arrive at Zuri's apartment in the Upper West Side for a BABES wine night, I've walked a total of 30,433 steps.

I remove the two different shoes I forgot I was wearing, leave them by the door, and immediately find myself sitting on the ground eating small chunks of cheese, letting conversation flow around me.

Time is ticking. I eat a cube of some white, stiff French stuff and don't like it but automatically grab another piece and shove it in my mouth. I don't know what everyone is talking about. I just keep eating and drinking and chomping and slurping, amped up on the caffeine still, until I hear Veronika's name and from somewhere in the depths of my body, I resurface to the room again.

"I don't mean to sound rude, but she's such a flirt."

"Yeah, she's always wearing low-cut shirts that don't even look good."

"And she thinks she knows everything, always giving me advice."

"Same! And I just want to be like, figure out your own shit first."

"Yeah, did you hear she hasn't gotten promoted yet?"

"Yeah, and she can't get a guy to date her."

"That's because she sleeps with everyone on the first date."

"I'm not saying she's a whore, but I certainly just wouldn't be comfortable doing what she does. I find it kind of . . ."

I spit out the pit of an olive I've been sucking on. I must have moved on from the cheese to the olives without realizing it. I down the rest of my wine in three big gulps and pour another glass to the rim, until the wineglass itself begins to beep, saying you're going to get drunk-y! Keep it funky and don't act like a monkey!

"Oops," I say, and shrug so they'll just keep talking, but it's too late, they've remembered I'm here.

"Lee, she must be so hard to live with," someone says, and I freeze.

"Yeah, Lee, you think Veronika's annoying, too, right?"

The doorbell rings, followed by three excited knocks. I'm sitting closest, so I get up, dust cracker crumbs off my pants, and open it to Veronika, who rushes in bringing more wine and a tray of diet brownies, apologizing profusely for being late. Something came up at work.

A few of the BABES get up to hug her. The others compliment her outfit from the couch. She unpacks the goods, placing them on the table in the middle of the circle. Fluffing her hair once everything's set up.

Veronika, always trying so hard in a world that seems to punish you for doing so. I play the game involuntarily. If she looks at me and smiles, I have to tell her. If she smiles, I have to answer the question posed before she knocked. She looks at me and there it is: her extremely large smile. One that betrays how happy she is to be here.

"Lee, you okay? You don't look good."

"I . . . I . . ."

"I mean not in a bad way. Just that, you know, you look pale."

"Veronika." I struggle, because I know that I really should keep my mouth shut, but it's too late. I have to say it. She reaches out to put the back of her hand against my forehead.

"I guess you're always kind of pale. But this is different. What I mean is you look a little sick. Still pretty, obviously. Just sick. Maybe we need to get you—"

"Jesus, Veronika, be quiet for once. I'm trying to tell you something."

The others, who'd been distracted cutting the fudgy rectangle into pieces, fall silent.

"They asked me if I think you're annoying," I say, and swallow. "And the truth is. I do. Because, well, you are."

Veronika's hand drops from my forehead.

"You're so . . . just so much. You're bossy and loud and always in my business."

The words roll out and I can't stop.

"You're the most frustrating person in the world to live with," I continue, looking Veronika in her light brown eyes. Eyes that are beginning to turn cold, blinking much too quickly. I speak faster to keep up. It feels like my chest is opening, finally saying whatever comes out instead of judging it, filtering it, sorting to see if what I'm saying is right compared to the data I've studied.

"But you know what? I'm the only one who will tell you to your face what I think about you."

She grabs her purse and fidgets with something inside.

"And wait, you have to hear this."

I grab her wrist, but she shakes off my hand. There's an audible gasp from the peanut gallery of brownie eaters.

"Veronika, listen to me. I'm telling you this because you're my friend. The best friend I've ever had. And I'd rather be annoyed by you every day than not have you in my life."

She pauses the fake digging through her purse and looks up at me to see if I'm serious. To my own surprise, I am.

"I need some air," I say and rush past her, down the stairs, and into the first breath I remember taking all day.

★ ★ ★

I WALK QUICKLY away from the building so Veronika can't come after me. I walk away from what I just said because there's an inkling of truth in there that could blow up everything I've been working so hard for. I rush into the night even though I have no idea where I'm going because I don't want to think about how friendship follows no logical path. How you can care about someone who annoys you every single day. How a person can become interwoven into your life, and without them it would feel empty. I don't want to think about any of it. About how if Vicky does work—if we help her figure out the immeasurable aspect of what makes a human human, about what makes two humans become friends—she might take the place of someone like Veronika.

I let Maps lead me home even though I feel like I should be going somewhere else. I need to push these ideas out of my mind. I've committed to this project and there's no time to waver.

Maps says to go left, so I go left. It tells me to go straight, so I go straight until I hit a crosswalk with a bright orange hand flashing, where it tells me to stop. In the seconds I wait there, Veronika texts me. G. emails me to meet at the same spot, same time. Notifications from Water say I'm dehydrated, and my vitamins are low. News reports slide in, piling up on my screen. Period says it's the perfect time for me to try getting pregnant. Music alerts me to new songs to help de-stress—I'm not stressed! I yell at the watch. Notification after notification dings and beeps and rings, and even though they're all in the ether, all in the air, I can feel them. I feel them weighing me down.

I cross the street when it says to and then lean against the side of a building, the brick wall catching the side of my T-shirt. Janet calls again and I watch as her name blinks and blinks and blinks and then fades. I'm still not ready. I need more time. My thoughts are spinning from the caffeine, from the wine, from the questions piling up. I need to figure out what to do, how to be, and the only person I want to talk to right now is the one who isn't reaching out. Chris.

Has he given up on me? I told him I was fine earlier, and maybe I shouldn't have been so short with him. Could he tell I was yelling? I pull up our chat and for the first time, I realize how much I don't know about him. I don't know where he came from before, or why he's working here now. What does he do at night? What does he care about? Does he have siblings? Is he married? Does he drink milk? I know small details, but not the large ones that define a person. I don't know how big a team he leads or if he actually lives in New York.

Or if he's even real.

A chill runs through my body. Toru and Janet say they've been meeting with him, but he's never, not once, come to the office. He canceled lunch three times. His profile was empty. If we can create an AI to mimic a friend, then why couldn't we create more than one? I turn and let my forehead rest on the cold, clay brick.

How could I have become so close with him if he's just a constructed friend? Is this how people would feel if they knew Vicky isn't real? Betrayed. Disillusioned. Mad. Janet's voice from our first meeting echoes in my head: *But then again, what is real and what is fake anymore? These are the kinds of questions we need you to be asking.*

But Chris is so strange. So naturally, authentically weird. He has to be real. Maybe he's just shy. This has been a stressful project to work on; maybe he's just been going through a lot.

I look down at my watch and have an idea. If he's listening in, if he's reading my information correctly the way an AI would, if he's programmed to be a friend like Vicky, he'll respond when I need him.

I think about Chris with every fiber in my body. I even say it out loud: Chris, I need you. If he messages me in the next minute, I'll know he's designed to respond to my data. I'll know he's not real.

11:58 P.M.

I turn around, lean my back against the dusty wall, and survey the empty street. The night is just cool enough to be bearable. To be more than bearable, but pleasant. I always wondered why so many historians talked about New York City as if it were magical, but as a twenty-something stumbles out of a building and throws up into a planter, I think I might finally understand why people feel some sort of attachment to the place. A place where each block has a heartbeat. Where someone could fall out of a door at any moment and sing or yell or laugh or puke.

Ping.

chris [11:59 p.m.]
how was the wine night?
or should i say whine night lol
btw I have some . . . interesting news for u

I feel the watch vibrate. See it glow with messages. And something heavy, like despair, settles just below my ribs.

No. No, no, no. This can't be. How did I miss it?

I should have known. It was too good, too easy. He, or it, or whatever, is too kind to me. I read the message again and again, each time feeling a bit more dumb, a bit more sad.

But this is good news, right? I try to tell myself. If Chris is any indication of where Vicky might be, then I should be thrilled. It means the data must be working, because I believed our conversations. I believed in him. This is good, I try to convince myself, even though I thought it would feel different. This is good, I repeat out loud, but my body tells me otherwise.

A phone call flashes on the Screen. Janet again. Her name mocks me as it rings, rings, rings, and then fades into a notification. It mocks me in a text message: please call, we need to talk ASAP. Her notification is buried with others, and Maps beeps and beeps at me, telling me to keep moving. As the Screen fills, I look down at my feet on the sidewalk and wonder, not for the first time, how I ended up here. *I was here.* I think of those words scrawled around the city. Maybe I get it. Maybe they just wanted someone, anyone, to know they existed.

I'm not so different. My career was supposed to give me purpose in a world I see others move through purposelessly. My work, it's supposed to mean something. But standing here in one flip-flop and one tennis shoe, in a neighborhood I don't recognize, I wonder what it's all for. I wonder if I could work hard forever and at the end of it all still be the fool.

Maps keeps beeping, demanding I move. I look at the watch and feel a sudden reckless urge. A surge of anger. They said they wanted experiences? I'll give them experiences. They want Vicky to see into the brain of a person? I'll give her all of it. I'll go all night, go until I have to show up to the meeting. Until Janet shakes my hand and tells me I did a good job. No, a great job. She'll tell me I made a good choice to stay. That the world will be better off because of what I've done, unraveling my mind, leaving it to be dissected.

I shut my eyes tight and think. I need to make myself do something, anything. If I see a cloud, I'll run until I find a pizza place. No stopping. No waiting. I'll time myself and see how fast I can go. I won't listen to Maps. I won't let it tell me what to do, where to go. I won't let it take me to a pizza place that everyone else has marked as good because that's where Maps has taken them, too.

No, for once, I'll just let myself go free, fast, fluid. I'll run until I smell sauce, until I see melted cheese shining in the window. I'll eat a slice, maybe three, and then I'll do something else. I'll play another game. I'll keep experiencing things all night long. I'll do more, more, more, always more.

When I open my eyes and tilt my head back, I see a faded, tumbling puff of a cloud near a sliver of moon. I open Maps, silence that motherfucker, start a timer, and begin to run.

Air on my face, pavement against the pads of my feet. I fly past shops and buildings to a crosswalk where the hand flashes orange, but I can't stop, I must get to a pizza place, any pizza place, as fast as I can, so I keep going, running, gliding, speeding through the night, keeping my eyes peeled for round discs of delight.

chris [12:03 AM]
lee
u ok?
i think you should go home

Go home? I laugh. Go home?!

But what kind of experience would that be? I think, or say, or maybe I yell again. It's difficult to tell where my thoughts end and the world begins. I'm surrounded, submerged. Trapped in the notifications that keep piling up, trapped in this project, trapped in my goals, trapped in the cement scenery. Trapped in what I've helped create. My own data speaking back to me.

Is this what it would feel like? If Vicky works, will the people who talk with her, rely on her, connect with her, be trapped in a world where their own information and choices and ideas are fed back to them? What's real and what's fake anymore?

I run and run, breathing up at the sky. The shoulder of a woman smacks my chest and I look back to see her flipping me off. What an experience! To piss someone off. To almost knock someone over.

I keep running north, up, uptown, stopping to cartwheel in the middle of the street, the pavement rough on my palms. I wave my arm around in the air and do another and another. I skip and jump and lengthen my strides and then shorten them and hopscotch a veiny pattern of cracks in the pavement.

Are you getting all of this, Vicky? I yell.

Or should I say, Chris?

Faster, faster, faster. The streets close in on me, so I look up again. I look up at the stars. They're faded here, but sometimes still visible. They say if you find a shooting one, you can make a wish. I wish someone was here for me right now. Here: a meaningful blip in an otherwise meaningless abyss. Does it mean anything to be here if I'm here alone?

chris [12:11 A.M.]
i'm here for u
i promise
pinky-promise-sealed-with-a-kiss
just go home

I read the message and recognize Veronika's line. I can't stomach it. Can't take it. I read it and begin to sprint as fast as my legs will take me; the beeps and buzzes filter in from far away as I race down street after street scanning awnings and storefronts. I run and run, but I can't outrun the feeling of burning, bottomless disappointment. The streets go from hard to soft in my vision. A biker whizzes by and yells something I can't hear. The lights in the buildings bending over me blur to become beautiful.

An orange hand appears, but I don't have to listen to it. Not today. Not while time is ticking. I sprint across the street and turn to see a horn. Hear lights. And then there's nothing but my heart beating in my wrist and the cold cement bleeding into the side of my cheek.

CHAPTER 35

The room is white, but there are no cracks in the walls. No brush-strokes. I try to turn my head and find the delta above the window to study it while Veronika gets ready for work, but heat radiates in my neck.

I blink and a small symphony of dings, murmurs, and beeps becomes clear.

I blink and lift my arm to see the watch, to see what it's capturing. But it's gone. Replaced by layers of gauze and clear tubes disappearing underneath, taped in place.

A small, round nurse enters, and we make eye contact. He smiles as if we've met before, as if he's truly happy to see me. As if we've made plans to bake a pie together later. I look for my phone to message Chris about the smiling stranger and the watch, how I need a new one, how we're so close to creating what we set out to, but I can't turn my head.

"Welcome back, hon. How're you feeling?"

And then I remember the looming buildings. The dread. The lights, the horn.

"You have someone waiting to see you, should I let them in?"

He leaves without waiting for me to answer, and a few minutes later I hear footsteps clanking down the hall. The door flies open, banging into the wall.

"Lee!" Veronika rushes in, mascara smeared underneath her left eye. "We thought—we thought you were . . ." She trails off, breaking into a fresh round of sobs. She pulls a chair from somewhere and sits next to me, bending over to place her face in her arms on the side of the bed.

"Your hair," I croak.

"What?" she asks, lifting her head, confused, wiping tears away with both hands.

"It's flat." She looks at me and I smile, feeling tape pull against skin on my cheek.

"Jesus, Lee," she says, laughing. A laugh that's more relief than happiness. "You scared the shit out of me."

There's a gentle knock on the door. It sounds like the way G. would knock. Confident but reserved. I wish I didn't want him to be worried about me, but I do. I'm glad he is. Glad he's here.

"Wrong room," Veronika says.

Someone steps inside. I can only see the shadow of a person in my peripheral. A person too small to be G. His skinny frame blanketed in a big blue flannel, a white V-neck underneath. He stops short, hovering awkwardly, looking down at his hands and then back at me. I wish he would stop staring.

"Did you feel the atoms of the universe?" he says, and smiles sadly. "Did you see the timeline of each grain of sand? Or were you not near enough to death for that?"

My heart catches. Veronika jumps up out of the chair.

"What kind of a question is that? Look, I think you have the wrong room." She begins to shoo the strange man outside.

"Wait," I manage to say. My lips cracked, my tongue like sandpaper. We stare at each other, and I know it can't be true. That I must be hallucinating, dreaming, making things up.

"Lee, I'm so sorry," he says, looking down, wiping his hands on his flannel. He has a round face, small nose, and brown scruff dotting his jaw. I can't believe it. "My team was monitoring closely, but we didn't know when to step in. We didn't—"

"Chris?" I whisper. He looks at me and grins that same sad smile again. It seems like just yesterday that he sent me those poetic and playful observations as if he were dead, omnipresent. "I thought. I thought you were . . . fake."

"What do you mean?" he says.

I try to sit up, but my body is strapped to the bed and a shooting heat rips down my left side. Veronika sees I'm in pain and pounces.

"What the fuck is going on?" she says. "Look. I don't care who you are, but as you can see, Lee's not in a good place for visitors right now. You can come back next week."

I don't understand, I want to yell. Chris hovers in place, a familiar stranger. The way he stands on the balls of his feet. How nervous he is, constantly wiping his hands on his shirt. He's real, I think. He's real and he's here. He came to see me. To make sure I'm okay.

"Veronika," I say, my throat dry. She turns and immediately comes to the side of the bed. "Water?"

She nods, whispers some kind of threat to Chris I can't hear, and leaves to hunt down the nurse or to break the water fountain from the wall and bring it back. Whatever is fastest. Chris watches her go, unsure if he should follow.

I can't stop studying him. How long and lanky his arms are. How he rocks back and forth on his feet. There's an energy to him I remember from our chats. Something devious. Like someone too smart for his own good. Even with him standing this close, I can't believe it. I can't figure out what to ask, what to say first.

"But you, you never came to the office. And lunch. And your profile in the Data Program was empty?" Even as I continue to question it, a warmth spreads throughout my chest. Our conversations, our jokes; all of them were based on two people's brains randomly coming together, building off one another. All of it was real.

"Janet and Toru thought I'd say too much if we met. Which I probably would have . . ." He stares at me and then laughs, shaking his head as my last sentence registers. "Wait, you found the profiles? I should have known you would. Lee, my team set up the Data Program. We had to add the profiles of anyone who was inputting information, but my role was just the administrator, so it didn't need info on me."

I want to ask everything at once. Did he want to meet me even though he was told not to? Does he like talking to me as much as I like talking to him? Are we friends? Does he realize that after each new experience I had the urge to tell him about it? I want to ask if he was reading my data or if it was all coincidence, the way he seemed to know me so well. But as we stare at each other and these thoughts circle through my head, I remember why we really know each other in the first place. The project, The Loneliness Report, Vicky.

"Chris," I whisper. "Is it going to work?"

"We can talk later," he says, walking over to perch on the edge of the chair. "I just wanted to come say hi and make sure you're okay."

Up close I can see the contacts in his eyes, the thin layer over the blue. I remember how he told me he wasn't liked in school. How he goes to concerts. How he makes faces in front of the Screen while working. He's so scrawny. Wiry. His limbs would look hilarious on a dance floor surrounded by people.

"Just tell me," I say, my voice hoarse. We stare at each other. A machine beeps.

Chris sighs and moves around in his seat. He looks at me and I can see that he's making a decision. He glances toward the door as if he's about to be in trouble.

"It's not going to work," he finally says, scratching his forearm. And for some reason he can't meet my eyes.

Heat rushes to my cheeks, and the room spins. The last bit of energy I was holding on to slips out of my body until that's all it feels like: a body. A set of limbs. Heavy, exhausted, free.

The project failed. I failed. They told me it was working. They told me it was close, but close is never close enough. I stare at the ceiling, tears dripping from my eyes. Tears of shame, and of something else I can't place. Something I begin to realize is the smallest, tiniest bit of relief.

"You okay?" Chris says. He places his hand on the bed and then removes it, tucking both of them underneath him somewhere.

"Yes. I'm fine. But Chris, why me? Someone else should have had the watch . . ." I cough, causing pain to drip into and gather in my leg.

Chris sighs and looks at me for a long time.

"The way Vicky reacted to your data . . . It was wild," he begins tentatively. "I couldn't understand it at first. I'd never seen anything like it. But now, it makes so much sense."

He takes a breath and studies me before continuing.

"The Government gave companies access to the Placement System when building their teams so they could select people with the exact skill set needed for whatever they were building. Toru and Janet had us reprogram the System to search for people who fit very specific criteria, including one filter that hadn't existed before. I'm sure you can guess what it is."

My head throbs and I have no idea what he's talking about. The Placement System just sends people where they should be based on a complicated sorting algorithm. Companies aren't allowed to crack it open and alter it. Has this happened before?

"We programmed it to sort for people who had experience with loneliness so they could empathize with the project, so they would be totally committed, even if they didn't know why."

I think about what I saw in the profiles. Divorce. Lost identity as an athlete. Orphaned. It lines up. All of the Consultants had past experiences that could theoretically lead to feeling disconnected, to loneliness.

I think about Finance Guy and Shrill Laugh Girl, Rob and Tanya. About them laughing in the kitchen together. Janet told us love doesn't always help with loneliness, but for some people it might. Were they in love? Are they still? Maybe they left when they saw The Report because they forgot what being lonely was like. They couldn't relate to it anymore. Maybe, as the materials said, they were repelled by it and wanted to, even subconsciously, avoid exposure to lonely people at all costs.

But what does any of this have to do with me?

"The other Consultants fit all the criteria, including this one, but you—you didn't. You scored the highest in every other category but didn't show any trace of loneliness. I think Toru and Janet figured with your background, you would be motivated to make this project work regardless . . .

"But what they didn't realize—what I didn't realize—is how this would affect the AI. I should have seen it before. But we were training Vicky to be a solution for loneliness," Chris continues, his hands escaping from underneath him and gesturing wildly as he talks faster and faster. "So it was seeking to understand it better. With the other Consultants, the root was easier to identify, so she registered it quickly and moved on. But yours. Yours was unclear."

"What?" I say, shocked. The room is too white; his words roll out too quickly. None of this makes sense, none of it at all.

"It's just that . . ." He fumbles over his words. "Well, I wanted to tell you this later, but . . . Lee, what we realized is, well, you're lonely. The Placement System just couldn't trace yours. It was only picking up more obvious cases of loneliness, cases that had, as I mentioned, an easily traceable root cause. But the whole debate that led to erasing loneliness to begin with was that it shows up differently in everyone. That it's hard to trace. So Vicky couldn't figure out why you were lonely, she just knew you were, and kept trying to understand—"

Chris stops short. I'm having trouble following. I can't be lonely. I don't have a reason to be. Besides, I've read all about it. Wouldn't I have realized?

But is this why I feel like when I talk to people, I'm under water and they're above it?

Footsteps echo down the hall. Chris places his hands on the bed and leans in close, speaking quietly. My jaw begins to ache.

"Hey," he says softly. Tears drip down my cheek. I try to remember the tone of his voice. To let it sink in. "I'm sorry. Janet and Toru are right, I always say too much. We can talk about it all later. Everything is going to be okay. I promise."

Veronika rushes back in holding a huge plastic cup with a purple hospital logo on the side. Chris jumps up from the chair and backs away as she swoops in to hold the cup for me, bending the straw to my lips, so I can take a sip.

I want to tell Chris not to go, to ask him if Toru and Janet hired him because he's lonely, too, but the straw is stuck in my mouth. Watching me struggle with it, Veronika breaks into sobs again, and he backs toward the door. I don't know when I'll see him again, if this was it, the only time he'll be a physical person in my life. I want so badly for him to stay, but he's not seeing my data this time to know it. All he sees is a body, broken and fragile, as he makes it to the doorway and slips out of sight.

CHAPTER 36

In the crisp, clean hospital cafeteria, Janet and Toru sip from steaming-hot cups of coffee. Janet rotates her ankle, trying her best to ignore the way Toru is typing violently on his phone across from her. She's been avoiding his eyes, paranoid he'll be able to read her. That in one glance he'll see her stress, her guilt, and know everything. Chris bursts into the room and rushes to their table, speaking before he even gets to them.

"She's awake," he yells. "The doctors said they'll have to do another surgery in a little, but she's going to be okay. They'll let in more visitors tomorrow."

As he approaches their table, ignoring the other people in the space, Janet wonders why she didn't think to reach out to him at any point throughout all of this to learn more about Lee, about the watch. She remembers hiring him, remembers seeing him present ideas and run meetings. But he was under Toru's domain, running one of Toru's teams.

Janet watches his chest go up and down. Did he run from Lee's room? Something about it breaks her heart, and she looks down, smoothing out her pants. She needs to compose herself. Lee is fine. It's just that she was so mangled last night. Limp, bloodied, young.

". . . need to call the Government to see if we can get an extended timeline with the circumstances," Toru is saying rapidly, taking a large gulp of coffee. Janet blinks once, twice, trying to focus, but his voice sounds far away.

". . . In the meantime, we can get a new watch made. Lee can have it back on while she's recovering, even. And I think we could start putting them on a couple of people to have more streams of intimate data in case Vicky is open to them. Either way, the charts are incredible. Vicky is almost ready, right, Chris?"

"Yes, I believe that's correct," Chris says tentatively. He glances at Janet. She can see he's worried. About the project? The watch? The girl? "But I think Lee should rest a bit more. Not be rushed into it."

"What?" Toru says, laughing incredulously, looking to Janet for backup. Janet studies her hands. She never thought there would be a breaking point. But now she sees the cracks. She and Toru are too different. She used to want what he wants: the excitement of a challenge, the thrilling victory of unexpected success. But people change. Now she wants something different, even if she doesn't know what it is yet.

"Toru, did you see the last few weeks of data she was collecting?" Chris jumps in, and Janet is thankful for the diversion, because she can't think. She can't face Toru right now, or confront his vision, which is always miraculous, but stubborn.

"Yes, the information was brilliant," he says, finishing his coffee in one last large gulp. "Paired with all of the other data, Vicky is going to work."

"Lee was spiraling," Chris says. Janet's surprised to hear someone voice the same concerns she has. She's impressed, too, because no one ever stands up to Toru like this. "It was erratic. It was abnormal. It was us—we were causing her to spiral."

"She was doing what she needed to do," Toru says.

"Let's see how she's feeling tomorrow and discuss this then," Janet interjects, pulling herself from the blurry bottom of her mind to put a stop to this, at least for now.

"Fine." Toru grabs his things and gets up, storming out.

Janet sighs and stands, picking up her jacket to follow him.

"I'm going to get some air," she says to Chris. "Thanks for your help today."

"Uh, Janet," Chris says, nervously, playing with the cup Toru left behind, "can we actually talk for just a second?"

"Sure," she says, sitting back down, feeling a small degree of alarm. She's tired. Her senses are still firing on overload from the night, from the terribleness of it all.

"Look, I know what happened," Chris says, finally looking up. His blue eyes meet hers, and Janet's heart begins to race. She swallows but tries to keep her face calm even as the images come back in blinding flashes.

The phone ringing and ringing. The car gliding down dim streets on smooth asphalt. Maps directing her loudly, leading her to the watch's location, leading her to the girl. Incessant beeping as she got closer. Headlights paving their way through the dark. And then sudden color. A thud. The violent heavy hollowness of a body hitting metal.

"I . . . I don't know what you're talking about," she says. Chris's face feels too close. She's too hot. She needs air.

"My team has been keeping a close eye on Lee. And, well, I know it was you last night. I just don't understand. Did you do it on purpose?"

Janet shakes her head, no, no, no. But she can't speak. She looks ahead into the colorless, filtrated air.

"Why were you even in that part of the city?" Chris asks. He's speaking calmly, tenderly, and Janet feels herself crumbling. She feels each and every job she ever took weighing on her. She feels all the choices she's made. The consequences, both good and bad. She feels that life could begin at any moment, even though it's already begun.

"I'd been calling Lee all day," Janet finally hears herself say, still seeing only blurred shapes and light. "I . . . I was just hoping to talk to her. She wasn't picking up her phone, so I drove to try and find her. I didn't know she'd jump out of the dark like that. The car was supposed to stop. It's programmed to stop!"

"Why were you trying to reach her?" Chris asks gently, as if she's fragile. Is she fragile? No one has ever defined her that way.

"You said it," she mumbles. "You've seen it firsthand with the tests. The watch is working. Vicky is on the cusp of working, and then what? A world where people connect with technology instead of each other? We already have that. I'd rather have a world of lonely people than a world of numb ones."

A chair screeches against the floor. A family sits a few tables away, speaking loudly. Chris does something Janet isn't expecting. He nods. He nods his head in agreement.

"I know," he says.

Suddenly Janet's eyes focus. She stares into Chris's and sees he's not mad, he's not upset. He isn't here to blame or confront her. He understands why she went searching for Lee. And so she says it. She finally tells the truth.

"I went looking for her because I wanted her to stop. I wanted her to take it off."

CHAPTER 37

Flowers arrive from the BABES, from Toru and Janet, from G. The friendly nurse asks me if I want their smells turned up or down. Andrea visits, with her green, glinting eyes. She holds my hand and I let her, both of us feeling awkward and strange, but neither of us wanting to let go.

Tall, lanky Trevor comes and stands quietly nearby with Aaliyah and her wire-frame glasses perched on the tip of her nose. Chris and Veronika come every day. They joke about breaking me out of jail. They've warmed to each other, or at least I think they have.

I was scraped up badly, especially where the watch shattered. My leg was snapped into pieces, my shoulder was dislocated, my hip was fractured, and I was knocked unconscious, but other than that, all good. Or at least, that's how the kind nurse explains it. You're all good, hon, he says. We'll take good care of you. And I smile.

At night, when I can't sleep and the small symphony of beeps and the low murmuring of machines lulls me into a lucid state, I think about the house I spent my teenage years in. Compact, clean, cold. I see Greg and Cindy, working in their home offices and coming out when the food drone arrived.

I used to think I despised them for their mediocrity. For the way they succumbed to life, just letting it happen. But as I lie in the hospital, I realize I was afraid of becoming like them. Ground down to a nub. A body working uselessly in front of a Screen.

I begin to understand why I was drawn to the Program as soon as I saw it. It promised me purpose. It promised me a different path. I saw all those people walking around in their uniforms with their shoulders back and their animated discussions. I wanted to do that, too: walk with them toward something, walk with them away from nothing.

But in the dim room of the hospital, shadows moving in and out, I think back to the reality of the Program. The hours running experiments. Going to bed, waking up, eating the same bowl of cereal in the food court, making notes, assessing patterns, reading, researching, then repeating the same thing again the next day. The irony hits me sharply, stinging worse than my injuries.

Instead of chasing new ways of thinking, of being, I just fell in line. I became the very thing I wanted to escape. Jaded by routine. Suffocated by systems. Devoured by work and Screens, I, too, became isolated. Became numb.

★　★　★

JANET PUT THE Agreement on pause so I can get messages from the outside world. To my surprise, Cindy and Greg have reached out a few times. They say they won't be able to come to New York but that they spoke to someone, one of my friends, who will take care of me, who will keep me company.

I pause on the word "friends," reading it twice, realizing—maybe not for the first time—that even though I failed, part of me is glad to know that people won't have to rely on an artificial friend like Vicky. That somewhere, somehow, everyone will be forced to try and make real ones, maybe.

And it crosses my mind, just briefly, that maybe this is why no one's been able to pull it off before, not even the Big Five. Not because they can't, but because they decided, at some point or another, they shouldn't.

An e-card arrives from Masha, and I dread opening it. I feel like I've disappointed him. Like I let him down. But when I finally open it, there's nothing but a little bird that says "Get well soon, kiddo." No signature. No words of wisdom. The bird flaps its wings and flies off the Screen, leaving me with nothing but a blank page and an even blanker feeling of sadness.

Sadness for myself, but mostly, I feel sad for Masha. He was the first person to see potential in me. I needed him to. I needed someone to believe in me, to see me, to take my ideas seriously, and I'm glad he did. I can't help but wonder if maybe he would have written me a longer note, or called, if I had been successful. Or maybe it always would have been like this.

I think about him standing in front of a large Screen in the lab, typing and tapping animatedly, zoned in. It's an image etched into my memory because that's how I saw him every day for six years straight. That's how he was when I arrived, that's how he was when I left.

But he never got the chance to experience what I forced myself to outside of work, outside the lab, did he? He never got the chance to see that potential doesn't just hide inside specific people, but that it's in every person, place, and pebble. Maybe I wasted mine. Or maybe I'm finally tapping into it and one day he'll see.

Chris and Veronika burst in and I close out of the card, where the bird's head is popping in again from the side. Veronika throws an armful of candy on the bed.

"Take your pick."

Chris grabs the M&M's.

"Not you! Lee gets to choose first."

"She can't even eat those right now. Her jaw is healing," Chris argues. And as I watch the two of them have a staring contest, I forget about how many emotions a brain can hold at once, how you can feel both sad and happy. I forget all about the bird telling me to get well and archive the email so I don't need to think about it anymore, at least for now.

★ ★ ★

WHAT IS IT like to be lonely?

I try to let the feeling sink in, even though I'm not wearing the watch anymore. I try to really feel it. But for myself this time.

Sometimes hot shame runs through me. Other times, I'm afraid of who I've become. Of the future. Of not being enough. I crave silence but want someone to break it. To be around people and to be left alone. I'm disappointed with where time has taken me. I want others to understand and am frustrated when they can't.

Iridescent, one of the articles Chris sent called it. Because loneliness changes depending on the angle, the person, the time, the place. In the dark of the hospital, I understand that Chris is right. That The Report is. I am lonely even if I can't pinpoint why. Even if I can't explain it.

Feelings come, and I let them this time. I stop fighting them. They're painful and paralyzing. They carve a path and puncture holes. But maybe we need loneliness. Maybe we need to feel disconnected so we can do something about it, or at least try.

As I let the insufferable, suffocating emptiness fall in around me—feeling what I don't know, what I can't control or understand—other sensations, memories begin to follow in their wake.

The sharp prick of the needle going through my nose and Veronika's face above me, contorted with disgust and a shadow of awe.

Salt, moss, garbage. The warped smell of it swirling up toward the buzz-headed runner and me as we leaned over the railing, watching the gummies float away.

Fuzzy, starchy fabric of Eric's felt heart between my thumb and forefinger when he unpinned it from his pocket and handed it to me for good luck. The intoxicating feeling of someone else's belief in me.

G.'s smell, slightly sweet, like caramel melting, the deep tone of his voice, how he stared straight ahead as he told me about his office, high up, with windows. The way his arms wrapped around me, pulling me closer, always closer.

As I lie in bed and let it all sink in, I think about Vicky. We're both a compilation of data and experiences. We both process information, learn from it, and change who we are based upon it.

But then I think of what Eric said. About the things we can't explain: the immeasurables. Like the way chocolate chip cookies with unevenly distributed chips are more fun to eat than the ones from the Deli that guarantee chocolate in every bite. The chance that you may not get one makes it even sweeter when you do.

Or the way a word can be repeated so many times that it doesn't sound like a word anymore. Or the muted disappointment of a restaurant going out of business, concern for people you hardly know.

How lately, when I least expect it, I've begun to get goose bumps just from realizing I'm alive.

How could we teach Vicky things we don't understand ourselves? How could I teach Vicky about these things that float through me? About how friendship is irrational, happiness incalculable? About how sometimes the most human thing is not knowing how to be human at all?

The nurse and I joke about making a pie. He tells me he's allergic to gluten, so we'll have to use synthetic flour. I still think we should try anyway. He says I'll be released in a few days without so much as a visible scar after their skin-smoothing treatments. I ask if they can leave the one on my forearm. The one where the glass screen of the watch broke and sliced through it. The nurse and the doctor exchange looks, but finally, they relent. I can keep it.

I lie in the hospital bed and think about how one day I hope to be at a party. A real party where people have too much to drink and someone spills beer all over the carpet and someone else turns the music up so loud, we'll have to yell. A party where people hug each other just because, where a small circle in the corner debates whether or not a favorite color reveals anything about someone's personality. Where the sound of laughter seeps out into the hallway and helps others find their way.

Without some sort of prompt from the TV, from the phone, from a watch, a stranger will see the scar on my forearm, the way the dermis and epidermis and hypodermis are raised in an angry red and cold white. They'll notice it and ask me what happened.

I'll look across the room, make eye contact with Chris or Veronika, smile, turn back, and let a real, human conversation begin.

Epilogue

Coffee spews, water swishes in the pipes, and music floats down through the floorboards. Our new apartment is delightfully old. Veronika calls it edgy, or crumbling-chic, and only complains every once in a while about the small tile missing in the floor of the shower. She likes the appliances, though, especially the fridge that automatically rids itself of her disgusting leftovers each week.

My favorite part about the place is the stone fox statues out front. One of their ears is almost entirely gone; the other's paw has disintegrated. They guard the building, menacing and childish at the same time, welcoming me home the same way they've welcomed others before me.

Today, I sit at the wobbly kitchen table and pore over notes for my new job. It's been almost six months since the accident, five months since Janet and Toru submitted our Failure to the Government and marked our Placements complete, releasing us from the System. Janet and Toru wrote us recommendations, and offers from the Big Five appeared in my inbox within weeks. It was so odd to see them sitting there as if nothing had happened, as if that year was a blip in time, a fold in reality.

Light slants through our large kitchen window and the buildings across the Hudson glow. Something about the way the sun sets the city on fire as it climbs reminds me how weird time is. How it feels like both yesterday and ten years ago that I squished into the subway for the first time, sweating in my coat, determined to hate everything about this place.

Veronika clanks into the kitchen, interrupting my thoughts. She presses a button and two slices of bread drop into the toaster.

"You can't wear that," she says, glancing up from her phone for a quick second.

I look down to make sure I'm wearing the outfit we laid out last night, the one she helped me buy over the weekend specifically for the first day of work.

"Wait, what? Why?" I ask. Did I miss something?

"Are Chris and Cat Eyes going tonight?" Veronika grabs jam from the fridge, ignoring my question. "The BABES will be there. Liv's bringing her new girlfriend, who's apparently a huge pothead."

"Yeah, they're coming," I say, still confused.

Sometimes I wonder if it bothers Andrea that my nickname for her stuck. I'm surprised at how well she and Veronika get along, but I guess if I've learned anything it's that friendship operates by its own logic.

Bread shoots from the toaster and lands elegantly on a plate. Veronika takes the jam, spoons it on thick, and stuffs a slice into her mouth while scrolling through her phone. I can't help but worry she's going to spill on her shirt, which, now that I take a closer look . . .

"Wait, are you wearing the same thing as me?" I say.

Finally, she looks up to meet my eyes, breaking into that goofy dimpled grin of hers.

"You know, for someone who prides herself on observations and details or whatever, it sure took you long enough to notice what was right in front of you."

I roll my eyes. Our friends say I'm easy to mess with, that I'm gullible, but really I think I'm still just figuring everything out.

"Ready?" Veronika tosses the last piece of crust in her mouth and places her dish into the sink, which automatically begins washing it.

"Yeah, but just to be clear. Do you want me to change?"

"No, dum-dum. I thought it would be fun to twin for both of our first days. For good luck, ya know? Get your stuff, we're going to be late."

I shake my head. Another thing that operates by its own logic: Veronika. Who knows, maybe she's right. Maybe it will bring us both some sort of strange luck. I could use it.

I throw on my shoes, put my Screen to sleep, and grab my bag. First days seem to be cut from a different fabric. I'm stepping into a new part of my life, and I can feel it, the uncertainty swishing around each movement, the way everything will change even though I'm not sure how. *The Gray Area.*

"Are you nervous?" Veronika says when we're inside the elevator, the mirrored panels reflecting our matching outfits back to us.

"Nope," I say, lying. I'm trying not to overthink it. Trying not to think about how Toru was right about me. Even after the Vicky project failed, I still want a challenge. I still want my work to mean something, which is why I rejected the offers from the Big Five for something riskier.

"Don't be. You're great. It's going to be a huge success." She pushes me playfully as the elevator flings open its doors.

"You have to say that because you're my friend," I say, following her down the hall.

"That's exactly why I don't have to say that."

We walk out, down the steps, and past the foxes. Veronika drones on about a crush she has at the gym and how magenta haze is going to be a big color this year, whatever that means. She points out a small planter with a tiny white flower pushing through the dirt and almost trips on a dog leash.

Every block or so, we cross paths with someone, and I can't help but study their face to see if I can spot it. To see if it's etched in their skin or draped in their movements. I hope one day the truth comes out. The truth that it's real, that there's a name for the indescribable longing tearing a hole in your center. Loneliness.

When we get to Veronika's train stop, she squeezes me so tight my arms hurt. I wave as she disappears down the steps, waiting until I can't hear her heels click-clacking before continuing into the gold morning light.

★ ★ ★

THE LINE WRAPS all the way around the block. People shift from one foot to the other, cross their arms, lean, chat. They wait in anticipation for thirty minutes, sometimes forty—an unbelievably long time. But that seems to be part of the appeal, Janet thinks, as she stands behind a couple arguing about what to order when they get inside.

"I'm kind of craving eggplant parmesan," the man says.

"I don't know if they have that," the woman replies.

"What do you mean?" he asks.

"They only offer certain items," she explains. "We have to look at the list when we get inside."

"A list?"

Janet laughs to herself at the absurdity of it all. Large sunglasses block her face, and her stick-straight hair is longer now, down to her collarbones. She's trying out the theory that if you change how you look, maybe you can change who you are. She's trying, in some ways, to reinvent herself at forty-one, which feels ludicrous and crucial at the same time.

After she submitted the Failure, after hours of questions from Toru and a weeklong debriefing with the Government, Janet left for Europe to decompress. It's exhausting to invent a narrative, to wrap yourself in it.

The truth? Vicky was trending toward success. Toru was right. And so, through rushed whispers in the hospital parking lot, Chris and Janet made a plan. He'd already told Lee that it wasn't working, had told her in order to calm her mind, or maybe to set the end in motion for himself. Chris agreed to do a sweep of the tech, of the tests, of his team, to make it look like Vicky wasn't doing as well as she was, and Janet agreed to cement the lie by completing the Failure.

But it was worth it, right? To let a lie become the truth if it's the only way to protect what you believe in? And even though the past year has been filled with questions, Janet still thinks she did the right thing. She still believes an artificial friend would have only made the world lonelier.

"Excuse me, are you still in line?" a small voice asks from behind.

Janet turns to see a teenager with stringy black hair, pointing at the gap that's formed between her and the people in front of her.

"Oh, yes, sorry," Janet says, moving up ten feet. It's the fifth time she's approached the place in the past few days, each time with a mixture of curiosity and fear. From near the back of the line, though, from a block away, the place looks harmless, less than ordinary. Deteriorating brick exterior, dusty windows.

Simple can be good, though, Janet thinks. While living abroad for the past year, she's been practicing enjoying the way the small streets twist and turn. She's been practicing wandering without a destination, spending an entire day uncomfortably bored.

Sometimes, she turns into a café and expects to see Toru sitting there. She waits to see his devious smile, hear his salesman pitch telling her why she's got to partner with him on just one more thing. She's disappointed it hasn't happened yet. Her days feel emptier without him. Without their constant conversation, collaboration, ideation, she's not sure how to think, how to be. But maybe that's what starting over feels like. First, you feel bare.

"Also, miss, sorry to bother you. But my friend was wondering where you got those glasses?"

Janet turns around again and another small head bobs, half-hidden behind her friend with the stringy hair. Eyes blink at her patiently, expectantly. She contemplates whether to tell them the story of the market on the hill. How she stumbled upon it. How she traded a bracelet for the large blue pair of glasses that made her look like a bug, but that she loved anyway.

"Have you heard of something called a street market?"

The teens nod enthusiastically. They say they've watched videos about them online. Are they really that loud? Or do people alter the audio?

Janet tells them stories and they tell their own in return. She learns their favorite colors and their least-favorite subjects in school. She discovers one has a toothache but is afraid to go to the dentist, that the other has a crush on someone named Jade.

"Oh, look! There are old clocks on the wall inside!" one of the teens says, pressing her face against the window.

Janet hadn't realized how close they were to the front. She glances back at the line that keeps growing and watches people complain to one another, ask each other questions, make jokes, compare experiences. Some even talk about the weather.

As she surveys the scene, Janet fights the urge to flee again. She thinks about why she's come. Why she's traveled all the way back to New York. She thinks about how all the Humanity Consultants were taken care of. They accepted the jobs she and Toru worked hard to secure for them after their Placement completion. All of them decided to continue on the paths they'd dreamed of before. All of them, except one.

When Janet received notifications that Lee had rejected the offers from the Big Five, she grew worried. Her insides ballooned with guilt. Was something wrong? Would the girl ever be the same?

The teens next to her are still chatting, their faces pressed to the glass. Janet removes her sunglasses, takes a deep breath, and leans forward to look through the window herself. Inside there are people, so many people. Giddily shoveling eggs into their mouths, eagerly pouring chocolate sauce on toast, carelessly dropping forks, marveling at the floppy lists of food, laughing.

It's overwhelming and chaotic. But it begins to make sense why Lee would give up everything to open a business like this; something that seems crazy at first but could be powerful.

Janet watches Lee through the glass, the same way she did so long ago and feels something akin to relief. As she's about to pull away . . .

I TURN AROUND.

Something deep in my gut told me Janet would come by one day. I hoped once she did, I'd be able to close that chapter of my life and let it get smaller and smaller: a dust particle floating in the attic of my past.

But seeing her outside, it hits me without force, as if maybe I knew all along: there are no real endings. Seemingly ordinary moments—a random roommate, an unexpected assignment—leave ripples. Anything can alter everything.

Janet smiles, that same lippy one that used to get under my skin, and I nod back. As she disappears into the crowd, the world of the diner crashes in around me again. I refill someone's coffee and move in the commotion of it all. The conversation. Light jazz. The salty-sweet smell of bacon and syrup. All of it relentlessly pulling me back to this moment, reminding me I am here, even if just for now.

ACKNOWLEDGMENTS

Thank you to my badass agent, Danielle Bukowski, for reading my manuscript and loving Lee, not in spite of, but because of her strangeness; for taking a chance on me, and for ushering this book into the world.

A million thank-yous to my editor, Grace McNamee, who pushed me to take this story further than I knew I could. You understood the vision from the start. I'm so proud of what we made, what we did together.

Endless gratitude to my Columbia MFA professors and mentors: Wendy S. Walters, Leslie Jamison, Daniel Magariel, Lara Vapnyar, Lis Harris, Deborah Eisenberg, Alan Felsenthal, Jen George, Brenda Wineapple, Rivka Galchen, Clarence Coo, and so many others. Thank you for letting me take classes I wasn't supposed to take, for nurturing my ideas, and for pushing me to write what I was being called to write.

Lauren Mosely, Lauren Ollerhead Fries, Kenli Young, Jillian Ramirez, Hattie LeFavour, Akshaya Iyer, Myunghee Kwon, and the entire Bloomsbury family—thank you for making the book beautiful, for helping to get the story in tip-top shape, and for introducing it to bookstores and readers. You're miracle workers, all of you.

The early readers of this manuscript were crucial not just because their feedback shaped the story, but because I handed them a piece of my heart and asked them to tell me the truth about it. Talk about a dangerous job! Meg Richardson, Hannah Kauders, Christina McCausland, Jake O'Hara (Jakey Futbol), Eva Dunsky, and Helen Van der Sluis: thank you for dreaming with me when this was a fledgling story. Thank you for taking my ideas seriously, and for telling me I could do this crazy thing.

Thank you to New York, you absolutely nutso paradise. Your baristas, your people, your diners, and delis. You broke me, built me, and introduced me to the writer inside me.

Friends near and far, you've inspired every word. Thank you for dancing to Jungle with me, for talking for hours while the coffee gets cold, for being my 'Symphony of Womenhood', for making me laugh so hard my jaw hurts, making sure I made it home OK, for answering the phone, sending the text, for being the true storytellers.

Sam. You goober. Sometimes I wonder if I had to finish a draft of this before the world would let me meet you. Thank you for being my open book, my rock, my book of rocks. I [redacted] you.

I am no one without my family: Mom, Dad, Brooks, Hill, Larry, Sky, and Ellie. (Mom, thank you for teaching me to compete, and how to be ridiculously silly. Dad, you won't believe it, but my knack for story-telling, for seeing beauty where others might not, comes from you.) I keep writing and erasing, typing and back-spacing because there's no way to explain the ways all of you have showed up for me, shaped me, pushed me, taught me how to laugh, how to love, how to be a person in all of life's beautiful messiness. I live and write for you. Always.

And finally, thank you, readers, for spending time with Lee, Janet, Veronika, Chris, and the gang. I hope if you ever feel lost or lonely, you can return to these pages and know that this story, the dumb alarm that rhymes with parm, and all these characters, are here for you.

A NOTE ON THE AUTHOR

CHARLEE DYROFF is a writer from Boulder, Colorado. This is her first novel.